What others say about Hank Quense's fiction:

<u>Zaftan Entrepreneurs</u>:
". . . is an extremely funny and highly entertaining science fantasy novel by Hank Quense. This book has everything: humor, adventure, magic, war, aliens, fantasy creatures and humans. Spiced up with a hilarious political satire and a healthy dose of romance, it's a delightful fast-paced and engaging read, that will leave you craving for more. I can promise you that it's nothing like you've ever read before!"
Ji-Ye: Goodreads

"Sam is a wonderful character, funny and clever. Slash 9 is an equally compelling character (or computer) whose love and lust for Sam is hilarious. Equally funny is Dot 38. I really enjoyed the banter between all the characters. The fact that Zaftan females have three wombs and can go berserk was humorous in itself. Hank Quense has a vivid, wild imagination and obviously I had a lot of fun with these characters. This is a good read for Science fiction fans!"
Tamera L. for Readers Favorite

<u>Zaftan Miscreants</u>:
"Reminded me a lot of the Hitchhikers trilogy, in that we have a similar whacky `evil' alien race. The humor is also a little like Adam's, rather satirical in a over-the top fashion.This is a work of fiction. Names, characters, places

and incidents are the product of the author's imagination or are used fictitiously".
Wulfstan "wulfstan"

"The story line itself was not just one cut and dried road, it had a lot of little twists and side-stories and I don't want to give away too much but a lot of the goings-ons could really be paralleled to things happening here and now. Life, love, government, deception, lies, hope, despair, it's all in there wrapped up with some of the best satirical humor I've ever read. Just like a good spaghetti sauce IT'S IN THERE."
Angela Hupp

TALES FROM GUNDARLAND

By

Hank Quense

First Publication

ISBN 9780985006334

Published in the United States of America
Published by Hank Quense
Http://strangeworldsonline.com

ACKNOWLEDGEMENTS

All these stories were critiqued by an international group known as the Critters. They helped shape these stories. The stories were also read by another group of plucky writers who formed a group several years ago. This group has an international flavor with members living in the Canary Islands, Greece, Britain and Ireland.

All these folks deserve my thanks, but special thanks go to Jan Clark, and Doc Finch who not only critiqued the stories but also rooted out those pesky typos that I can never find.

The cover artwork was done by Gary V. Tenuta. He can be contacted through his website:
http://www.bookcoversandvideos.webs.com/

OTHER WORKS BY THE AUTHOR
Zaftan Entrepreneurs
Zaftan Miscreants
Build a Better Story
Mini-Collection
The Strange Worlds of Hank Quense
Humorous Yarns and Other Stuff
10 Great Fantasy Short Stories

<u>COMING SOON</u>:
Wotan's Dilemma
Falstaff's Big Gamble
10 Great Scifi Short Stories

TABLE OF CONTENTS

GUNDARLAND:
AN INTRODUCTION

The planet was named Gundar after the omniscient god who accidentally created the universe with an explosive sneeze caused by snorting a larger-than-average dose of His favorite recreational powder. The nodules of spittle flew through space and eventually solidified into suns, planets, comets and other celestial bodies.

Scientific authorities called this event the Big Achoo. Medical authorities argued that infectious diseases were the result of this unsanitary beginning. Religious authorities countered that such talk was blasphemous and that the medical authorities should accept infectious diseases as Gundar's holy will. Ordinary folk thought the authorities had too much free time on their hands and ought to get jobs.

Gundarland is the largest land mass on the planet. Populated by diverse races such as dwarfs, humans, elves, half-pints, yuks and a few lesser races, these disparate races live cheek-by-jowl in many cases and get along with no more than the usual interracial hostility.

At one time, the yuks roamed all over the island subjecting everyone to their boorish behavior and crude manners. The other races mostly put up with them, but it was a brave hostess who invited a yuk to a dinner party. They ate with their fingers because they always pilfered the cutlery as soon

as they sat down at the table. Eventually, the yuks were driv-
en into the southwest corner of the island, a land of marshes
and mountain deemed worthless by land developers.

Religion has always played a big part in many people's
lives. The biggest festival occurred in the spring when Snot-
ism celebrated the birth of the universe. Know as the Sacred
Snot-Fest, the ritual culminated in everyone simultaneously
inhaling crushed pepper to generate a giant sneeze. Doctors
loved the festival; many of them made more money in the
month following the Snot-Fest than they did for the rest of
the year. Oddly enough, the priests all wore masks during
the ceremony.

By ancient tradition, many warriors took a double major
when they studied the arts of war. The double major came in
handy during the occasional outbreaks of peace. Thus, in the
early days, knight-accountants, warrior-chefs and sol-
dier-lawyers roamed the countryside seeking combat and/or
clients.

The population has always been intrigued by magic. As
a consequence, wizards were held in high regard, even the
incompetent ones. Wizard schools offered double majors as
well as the combat schools. At first, the secondary courses
were perfunctory, but then the dukes began installing wizards in positions of power on the theory that if a wizard
couldn't figure out a solution to a problem, they could always
magic the problem out of existence. The practice of appointing wizards continued long after that theory proved to be
catastrophically wrong. The wizard schools once again took
notice and kept increasing the importance of the secondary
courses until wizardry became the lesser of the two cur-
ricula. Soon, graduates could barely compose spells and fre-

quently didn't have enough magical power to blow their noses.

Historically, the country was divided into a number of independent provinces ruled by dukes, warlords and an occasional madman. The principal occupation of these province leaders was making war on the neighbors. These constant wars provided employment for many dwarf warriors since the dukes prided themselves on the quantity and quality of their ax-dwarfs. Many dwarf families were proud of the generations of warriors who fought exclusively for Duke X or Warlord Y. These families ignored the fact that almost all the warriors died at an unnaturally young age.

ROMEO AND JULIET

Romeo Montague, a poor dwarf silver miner, walked into the market square in the town of Verbona where he bought a fortune cookie from a food vendor, a gnome who had migrated from the distant eastern provinces. Breaking it apart, he removed the slip of paper inside. It read: "Today, you will meet the love of your life."

Romeo snorted, balled up the paper and flipped it into the dirt road just as three elf riders entered the square from the opposite corner. The appearance of the Capulet brothers turned Romeo's mouth dry; too dry to eat the hard cookie. He dropped it and looked for a place to conceal himself. He didn't fear the brothers, but a confrontation would make him late for his ballet class. Before he could move away, Banquette, the middle brother, called out, "Look! A Montague!"

"A little dueling exercise will build our appetites." Puque, the youngest brother, flipped his blue cape over his shoulder, exposing the rapier on his hip. All the elves wore black riding boots, tan breeches, a blue doublet and a matching cape. House Capulet had pretensions of nobility and so had adopted blue as their color, as if a color could make folks forget about their crimes.

Led by Foberon, the oldest, they dismounted, drew their rapiers and advanced towards Romeo. The brothers possessed a bad reputation in town because of their notorious ways and constant roistering.

"Let's do this quickly before the authorities arrive." Banquette walked with a limp from a riding accident.

"I p . . . propose we each stick him twice." Foberon chuckled. "Just to see the c . . . color of a dwarf's blood."

They moved closer, waving their blades so the points whistled. Romeo backed up against a wall and drew his battle ax.

"An ax won't save you, dwarf scum," Puque said. "Not against three of us."

"Aye," Romeo replied, "but it's good enough to kill one of you before you get me."

The brothers hesitated a moment.

"He's bluffing," Banquette said. "We can kill him before he harms us."

"Foberon!" Romeo grinned at the elf. "I choose you. You're the eldest, so it's only fitting that you die first."

Foberon's rapier paused in mid-swing.

"I'm sure," Romeo continued, "Banquette and Puque won't mind splitting your portion of the inheritance." He laughed at the expression of dismay on Foberon's face.

"Hark." Foberon cocked his head to one side. "I th . . . think I hear the authorities. We must d . . . depart."

"We'll finish this another time, Romeo," Banquette said as he put up his blade.

"Anxious to get your brother killed, are you?"

The elves mounted their horses and rode off.

Romeo watched them leave. The feud had been in existence as far back as he could remember and it would continue until one side was wiped out. Fifty years ago, his family had discovered an emerald mine. Within a short time, the Capulet's had stolen it through legal trickery. Since then, a dozen members of each clan had been murdered because of the feud.

# # #

A few blocks beyond the square, Romeo came to the old warehouse used by his dancing instructor. He knew he was good enough to dance professionally, and someday soon he would begin his career as a dancer. He needed to save a bit more money, and then, good-bye to the silver mines because he had no intention of spending his entire life underground like most dwarves. Down there, a false move could mean a broken neck.

He entered the hall where most of the dancing class -- gnomes, half-pints, dwarves and elves -- engaged in stretching exercises while the five musicians tuned their instruments. He went to the lower *barre* and began his warm-ups. Holding onto the *barre* with both hands, he exercised his legs and loosened his muscles while observing his movement in the mirror behind the *barre*. He had almost finished his warm-up when a female yuk swaggered into the hall. The wide-shouldered, green-skinned creature wore leggings and a tunic. A tall elf-maiden followed. In the mirrored wall behind the *barre*, he watched them approach the dancing master. His mouth agape and stunned by her remarkable beauty, he stared at the elf maiden. Tall and willowy like all elves, she had silver hair cropped short, green eyes and translucent skin. She wore sandals and every toe had a jeweled ring. Her long dress barely rippled as she walked across the floor.

Romeo felt a shiver run up his spine. Could the fortune cookie have been correct? He left the *barre* and approached the dancing master.

The yuk saw him and growled a warning. "Pig dwarf! Take yer eyes off me ward or I'll rip 'em out of yer head and stuff 'em down yer throat." The baldheaded creature had tufts of coarse black hair scattered around her arms. Yuks had become popular as chaperones and body guards because no one wanted to fight one of the vicious creatures. Hiring them involved an element of risk because yuks often ignored orders they didn't like, and disciplining one of them could be suicidal.

Romeo opened and closed his mouth a few times, but kept looking at the maiden. Never had he seen a more beautiful female.

The dancing master noticed Romeo. "This is Juliet Capulet and her chaperone, Dreadmona. Juliet has joined our class. Mistress Juliet, Romeo Montague is the star of our class. I'm sure he won't mind demonstrating a few moves for you."

Romeo gasped for air. The most gorgeous female in the world was a Capulet! With a yuk chaperone! He gawked at her.

"Ain't no Montague gonna teach her nothin'," Dreadmona growled. "Her brothers won't allow it."

"I've never met a Montague before." Juliet stared boldly at Romeo. "You don't look like the demon that my brothers described."

Dreadmona grabbed Juliet's shoulder and shook it. Juliet turned away, but Romeo saw her looking at him from the corner of her eyes.

He went back to the *barre*, his mind swirled with strange emotions and thoughts. He was hopelessly in love.

# # #

After class, Romeo carried his work satchel and rode down the elevator bucket into the bowels of the earth. At the bottom, he walked through a maze of tunnels lit by widely spaced torches until he came to the newest one, a short tunnel ablaze with lights. Inside, the miners greeted him with wisecracks. He was the senior rock-walloper on the second shift and popular with the crew. If the Capulets hadn't stolen the emerald mine, he'd be a mine owner today instead of a mine worker.

He couldn't get the image of Juliet out of his mind. As a dancer, she was untrained but her graceful figure and elegant movements showed great promise once she had removed the toe rings. He had always dreamed of having a tall, slender lover instead of a short and squat female dwarf. He knew she was attracted to him -- he had caught her surreptitious glances whenever her chaperone's attention strayed.

The crew chief, Ocello, interrupted his thoughts by slapping him on the shoulder. "C'mon," the dwarf said. "Get ready so these lazy bums can do some work."

Romeo opened his satchel and took out a small pillow and a long scarf. He balanced the pillow on top of his head and held it in place by wrapping the scarf over the pillow and under his chin. Ocello helped him secure the scarf with a pin. Next, he took out an oversized helmet. Made of iron, it featured a twelve inch spike on the top. The helmet fastened under his chin with a thick strap.

Romeo took his place with two other similarly attired dwarves, his apprentices. He rolled his shoulders to loosen up his muscles. He nodded to the chief and forced thoughts of Juliet from his mind so he could concentrate. One mistake now could seriously injure or even kill him.

"Clear the lane!" Ocello shouted. The rest of the crew backed up against the wall, leaving a path to the end of the tunnel. The chief raised his right arm.

Romeo took a deep breath. When Ocello's arm fell, he lowered his head until the spike was horizontal to the ground, roared his battle cry, "*corps de ballet*," and charged.

He felt the spike hit the rock wall and penetrate. A shock thundered through his body when the top of his helmet slammed into the wall. His peripheral vision narrowed until it was the size of a small coin. The crew ran forward, untied his helmet strap and caught his limp body. They carried him to where he started his run, sat him down and went back for the apprentices. Ocello placed a sponge soaked in herbs under his nose. The pungent smell cleared his brain. As always after a run, his head hurt and his neck throbbed. He looked, still cross-eyed, at the helmets. His entire spike was buried in the rock and the spikes from his two apprentices were only half-buried.

The crew pried the helmets from the wall then attacked the holes with hammers and crow bars to enlarge the holes and weaken the rock face.

Romeo relaxed. He had fifteen minutes to rest before he would run at the rock again. He was supposed to coach his apprentices, but instead Juliet's image floated unbidden into his mind. She was the one he wanted to spend the rest of his life with. But how could he tell her that? The gruesome Dreadmona stood ready to remove some body parts if he tried. And even if he could talk to her, he faced insurmountable problems. He was just a lowly miner while she came from a fabulously rich family; the mine the Capulets had stolen became the largest and most prosperous emerald mine in Gundarland. Besides the feud, the eternal issue of elf-dwarf hostility had to be considered. They would be scorned by both races. Could two such different beings ever find happiness?

He made a face as he realized that Juliet's brothers would hunt him down if they found out he even talked to her. And this time, they wouldn't stop fighting until he was dead. Despite the danger, he knew he had to court the fair Juliet.

# # #

For three weeks he endured the agony of being close to Juliet but unable to touch or talk to her. Every day they exchanged looks through eyes haunted by desperation. Every day Dreadmona glared at Romeo as if daring him to try to talk to Juliet. Every day Romeo could feel Juliet's love, even across the dance hall. Every day Romeo went to the mines and tried to forget Juliet in a fog of headaches and muscle pains.

To Romeo's surprise and exhilaration, one day Juliet came to class with an elf crone instead of the yuk. The crone immediately fell to gossiping with the other chaperones and ignored Juliet. Romeo flew to her. For several moments the two did nothing except stare at each other. Her perfume made his blood boil. Romeo's heart threatened to burst from his chest. Finally, he managed to blurt, "I love you."

He held his breath until she replied, "And I you. Dreadmona has her fluxes -- you can't believe how surly she gets when that happens, as if I had something to do with it." She gave him a radiant smile. "We must make the most of today."

The musicians started the warm-up tunes and he seized her hands. Her touch sent a shock of elation coursing through his body. She seemed overcome with emotion as he led her in a dance for two known as the *pas-de-deux*. After a few twirls, she gasped, "I've never met anyone so . . . so . . . so short." She ran a hand through his beard. "Or so hairy."

Romeo clasped his hands on her slender hips and lifted her off the ground. He pirouetted twice then held her horizontal to the ground with one hand, the classic *stulchak* maneuver. "Or so strong," she moaned. "You're so different from the elves. You're everything I have fantasized about."

He placed her back on her feet. "What are we to do, my beloved?" he asked.

"I want to marry you, but perhaps you don't prefer forward females.

"I dream of marrying you."

"Woe is me. My brothers have arranged my marriage to Count Paris." Juliet's small bosom heaved. "He's old and smelly."

"How dare they marry you off!"

"They want the family to become noble and after I marry Paris, I'll be a countess."

"Can't one of your brothers marry a duchess or something?"

"They all hate females and have vowed to never marry."

"You must be rich from your inheritance. Can't you run away?"

"Alas, my brothers stole it from me."

"We must meet again." Romeo stared into her eyes. "But how?"

"Every night," she smiled at him, "I walk in the garden behind our house. In the garden, I'm away from my brothers and Dreadmona."

"After work tonight, I'll come to your garden."

# # #

On the way to work, Romeo rambled along the streets. His spirits rose and fell as he alternated between ecstasy and despair. Ecstasy because Juliet loved him and despair because he couldn't have her and still become a professional dancer. His savings would support him for the time it took to establish himself in his new career, but it wasn't sufficient to provide for both of them. Without her inheritance, Juliet was as poor as he was. To be with her, he would have to continue working in the mines to earn the money to support them both. His lifelong dreams of a dancing career clashed with his new dreams of a life with Juliet.

He continued to walk the streets, oblivious of the sounds of the people around him. Finally, he chose Juliet. Despite the end to his ballet aspirations and despite the need to stay in the mines, Juliet was worth it. He was willing to do whatever was required to spend his life with her.

# # #

Romeo thought his shift would never end. It was the longest night he had ever experienced. Finally, it ended and he cleaned up. Gulping large draughts of air because of his excitement and anticipation, he ran to the Capulet house in the wealthy part of town. He paused outside the garden to listen for signs of the brothers. After a few minutes of silence he scaled the wall and dropped down on the other side. He landed on a laurel shrub, making more noise than he would have liked. He moved away from the wall. The garden had so many trees, it resembled a forest, and the leaves whispered in a light breeze.

"Romeo, Romeo, wherefore art thou Romeo?"

Juliet awaited him! "Hsst. I'm over here, caught on a thorn bush." He tugged his cloak and felt it rip, but he was free. He hastened to her.

Juliet wore a diaphanous nightgown and her lithe beauty stood revealed in the light of a three-quarter moon. Romeo skidded to a halt at the sight of her. He stood, drinking in her magnificence. She smiled and held out her arms. He skipped forward and they embraced. Giddy with love and lust, he undid the buttons in front of his face. He parted the cloth, inhaled her essence, coughed and spit out a gobbet of bellybutton lint.

"Oh my love," Romeo implored. "Say you'll marry me."

"Yes, yes. I'll be rid of the Capulet name forever."

His hands caressed her body.

"What's in a name?" she continued. "That which we call a rose, by any other name would smell as sweet."

"What are you talking about? Have you been snorting funny herbs?" Romeo paused in his explorations. "What's this?"

"My chastity belt." Juliet sighed. "Dreadmona keeps the key on a chain around her neck. And she's very snippy when I wake up her at night to go to the outhouse. As if it was my fault."

Disappointed, but still keen, he explored higher. "Oww!"

"That's my chastity bra. It has lots of nasty sharp points that always ruin my clothes." Her hands did their own exploring. "You have one too?"

"No. That's just my iron cup. I wear it in the mines for protection in case I trip. I forgot to take it off. And it's awfully uncomfortable right now."

She looked down at him. "What are we to do, my darling? My wedding to Count Paris grows nigh."

"I have an idea." He snapped his fingers. "My cousin is a locksmith. Tomorrow night I'll return with a set of master keys. Then we'll become dwarf and wife." He embraced her and reluctantly took a step backward. He had to get rid of his cup and find a bucket of cold water. Fast.

"Parting is such sweet sorrow."

"Eh?"

# # #

Romeo suffered through the longest day of his life. He could hardly wait until it was time to return to the garden.

When Juliet didn't show up for the ballet class, he worried she might be sick. Eventually, he convinced himself that she had much to do in preparation for their meeting.

"Romeo!" the dance master yelled. "Pay attention!"

He colored under his beard. The dancing master had never before reproached him. He tried to clear thoughts of Juliet from his mind but didn't succeed. Finally, he excused himself from the class and went to visit his cousin the locksmith.

Later at work, he fingered the ring of keys between wall smashes. He pictured himself unlocking Juliet's treasures and many times his iron cup became painfully tight. Images of happiness with Juliet alternated with scenes of deadly combat with her brothers. The mood swings, from breathless anticipation to mind-numbing fear drained him emotionally just as the work drained him physically. After his last charge, he cleaned up, removed his cup and set out for the Capulet's garden almost too exhausted to meet with his beloved.

# # #

The key ring jangled when he dropped over the wall. Romeo, giddy with anticipation, stood still and listened to see if anyone had heard the noise. After a moment or two, he advanced further, avoiding the thorn bushes. In the center of the garden, he paused and looked around. "Hsst?"

"L . . . Looking for someone?" The voice came from the shadows.

The hair rose on the back of Romeo's neck when he heard two more voices chuckling. Juliet's brothers dropped from tree limbs. They carried naked rapiers and came at him from three sides. Romeo's hand reached for his ax. A knot constricted his throat. Since he anticipated an evening of love, he had left the weapon at home. All he had was the pair of metal snips in case the keys didn't work.

"J . . . Juliet has been sent away," Foberon said.

"Too bad you won't live long enough to miss her," Banquette added.

Puque, on his left, lunged and nicked his tunic.

Romeo jumped backwards and took out the metal snips. When Puque lunged a second time, Romeo caught the blade in the jaws of the snips and squeezed. The rapier snapped in two.

Puque gawked at his now two-inch-long rapier while Romeo lowered his head, roared, "*corps de ballet*," and charged. He slammed into the elf between Puque's knees and hips. His momentum pushed him forward with the brother on his back. He heard a bone crack when he ran into a wall. Puque groaned and fell to the ground.

Romeo turned to confront the other two. His attack had changed the alignment of the brothers and Foberon now stood behind Banquette who limped forward.

Using a stone bench as a launching point, Romeo leaped forward with one leg extended in the moves known as a *ballonné* with a *grand buttement*. In the midst of the leap, his fully extended right leg fully connected with Banquette's chest and drove him back. The elf bounced off a tree and stumbled forward. Romeo landed on his feet. He grabbed Banquette and hoisted the elf over his head into the *stulchak* position. He pirouetted twice then hurled the screeching Banquette at Foberon who jumped out of the way, exposing his unguarded left side. Romeo, head lowered again, charged into the elf. He drove Foberon into a tree trunk. Foberon's body went slack and slid down the tree trunk to a sitting position.

Romeo took a few deep breaths to compose himself. How was he to find Juliet? Her brothers would die rather than tell him where she was.

He clambered over the wall and walked back to his rooms. He shuddered. Where earlier, he had been filled with hot-blooded anticipation, now he suffered from cold fear for both Juliet and himself.

# # #

After a sleepless night, Romeo wandered the streets of Verbona in a brain-dead fog of desperation. His beloved was imprisoned and he couldn't rescue her until he discovered her whereabouts. For all he knew, her brothers might have advanced the date of her wedding. She might already be a reluctant bride.

He felt a hand on his arm. It belonged to an elderly elf crone who looked familiar.

"Remember me?" the crone said. "I'm Juliet's servant."

"Where is she?" Romeo's heart surged with joy. The servant could lead him to his beloved.

"She feared her brothers would kill you last night." Tears formed in the crone's eyes. "But when I saw the condition of those three, I knew you weren't dead, and I came looking for you."

"Where is she?"

"She said she couldn't live without you."

"Where is she?" He stamped his foot.

"She took poison last night, rather than marry Count Paris this morning."

"Dead?" Romeo slumped against a wall.

"Her brothers were most irate at her." The crone sighed. "She ruined all their wedding plans. They've already placed her in the family crypt. Without holding a proper funeral ceremony. They even removed her toe rings."

Romeo slid to the ground and held his head. All his dreams were dust.

"Listen to me," the crone said. "Dreadmona holds you responsible for Juliet's death and she wants revenge. She plans to hang you upside down over a fire. And cook your brains."

If Dreadmona killed him, maybe he'd find Juliet. He wanted to be with her, no matter her condition or state. She made any situation bearable. If he killed himself in the mines, it would be a lot quicker than getting caught by the yuk. He made a face. There must be a better way. One that didn't involve getting killed.

It took a while, but finally he came up with a plan. He returned home to grab the bag of coins he had saved. Romeo ran to the district populated by immigrants. He roamed the area while ignoring the vendors hawking strange foods and the hordes of children pestering him for coins. After an hour of searching the side streets and alleys, he found the shop he sought.

When he entered, an elderly dwarf eyed him suspiciously.

"Are you the wizard, MacBath?" Romeo asked the kilt-wearing dwarf. A strange plant bent long tendrils towards him. The vine sniffed his body and he could hear tiny teeth clicking behind the blood-red petals of a flower bud.

"Leave the customer alone!" The wizard whacked the plant with a wand and turned to Romeo. "You're wanting something?"

"Aye. I need something precious. Something that you can provide."

"Precious somethings cost a lot of money." MacBath combed his flowing white beard with the fingers of his left hand.

"I'm prepared to pay."

"And what is it you want so badly?"

"I want you to animate my dead beloved."

"You're wanting me to break the law? Reversing a death is illegal. The insurance companies hate it. So do the churches."

"I know it's illegal. That's why you charge so much."

"This is true." MacBath nodded. "I charge a hundred silver pennies."

"Agreed."

"Laddie, are you sure you want this lady brought back?"

"I'm sure."

"Let me get some things and we'll bring back your lover."

# # #

Outside the Capulet family tomb, Romeo steeled himself for the sight of a dead Juliet. The workers hadn't sealed the tomb yet, so he and MacBath had no trouble entering the

dark crypt. Dozens of dead Capulets lined the walls. Romeo
wrinkled his nose at the stench of mold and decay. Juliet lay
in the center on a stone catafalque wearing a white gown.
Her hands were crossed on her bosom.

"Dere ya are!" Romeo almost jumped out of his boots at
the sound of Dreadmona's booming voice. "Juliet is dead,
and it's all yer fault." The yuk stood in the entrance and
shook her fist at him. "Come outta dere."

Dreadmona's command puzzled Romeo. Why didn't she
come in and grab him? He looked around the tomb, hoping
to spot an exit. Coffins and stone statuettes filled every
nook. If the yuk came in here, he would have to elude her
long enough to bash her head with a few of the statues. He
looked at Dreadmona. "I'm busy. You'll have to come in."

"Yuks are afraid of tombs, laddie. It's about the only
thing that scares them." MacBath looked at Dreadmona.
"But, you have a big problem when you leave. That is one
very angry yuk."

"Dreadmona," Romeo said. "I came here to bring Juliet
back to life."

"Yer a magician?"

"Not me. I hired this wizard to do it. Watch."

Confusion and indecision painted Dreadmona's face.

MacBath moved to the catafalque and scattered a
powder on Juliet. The dwarf chanted softly then sprinkled a
second powder on her.

Her hand twitched.

Romeo smiled.

Seconds later, Juliet's eyes popped open and she glared
at MacBath. "Who let you in?"

Romeo moved to the edge of the catafalque. "It's all right, darling."

"Oh Romeo! I guess the poison didn't work." She slid her legs over the side.

"The poison worked. You died. I had this wizard reanimate you so we'll be together again."

"How romantic you are," she cooed as she sat up. "Hey! Who took my toe rings?"

"Juliet!" Dreadmona bellowed. "Ya selfish brat! Ya killed yourself widout thinkin' about no one else. Like me. Yer nasty brothers kicked me outta de house. Widout my back pay. Dey had a whole gang of friends to make sure me left."

"Can you move?" Romeo asked Juliet. "We'll go get a judge and have him force your brothers to give back your inheritance."

"And my toe rings." Juliet pointed to her feet. "I want them back. Can this old dwarf marry us?'

Romeo looked at MacBath.   "Aye. I'm licensed for that."

She grinned and waved a hand at MacBath. "Make it quick. We have things to do."

"I pronounce you dwarf and wife." MacBath made a mystical sign over their heads. "Kiss the bride. That's as quick as it can be done."

Romeo felt a breathtaking sensation in his loins. At last! No more chastity belts. His arms enfolded Juliet as he kissed her.

Juliet broke away and looked at the tomb entrance. "Dreadmona, I'm sorry about your troubles. I'm married now so I don't need a chaperone, but I'll need a maid if I'm to be respectable. The position is yours if you want it."

"For how long? 'Til ya throw me out like yer brothers?"

"Oh, no. For as long as you want it."

Romeo didn't think this was such a great idea, but held his tongue. Yuks didn't like to take orders and frequently ignored them. By letting the yuk decide when to quit, Juliet had possibly offered Dreadmonia a lifetime job. The only way to get rid of her was to fire her and firing a yuk was fraught with peril. One needed a platoon of body guards to protect the employer.

"All right." Dreadmona folded her arms across her chest. She had a devious smile on her face.

"Hey!" A frown flicked across Juliet's face. "Let's go someplace and do . . . you-know-what."

"I have some money left, let's rent a room." Romeo winked at her.

Juliet clapped her hands and giggled.

"Me gonna stay at da foot of de bed of me mistress." Dreadmona cackled.

Romeo stared open mouthed at Juliet.

"But . . . Dreadmona, what if I don't want you to sleep there?" Juliet gave the yuk a pleading look.

"Don't care. A maid gotta be a body guard too, ya know. Can't body guard ya 'less me wid ya."

Romeo felt an icy hand grip his guts. All his dreams and hopes were about to be crushed by Dreadmona. "You're doing this to Juliet because you can't get revenge on her brothers." Romeo pointed a finger at the yuk. "Aren't you?"

"Don't know what yer talkin' about." Dreadmona smiled. "Me gotta sleep at de foot of de bed to make sure me mistress gonna be safe." Dreadmona folded her arms. "Dat's all me know."

MacBath snickered and shook his head.

Juliet and Romeo stared at the troll, openmouthed.

Dreadmona grinned at the unhappy couple.

Romeo had an idea, one that would save the situation and taunt Juliet's brothers. "Juliet, do you have any aunts or uncles or cousins?"

"No. The Capulet name is doomed to die out with my brothers."

Romeo's stomach clenched with anxiety; so much depended on a fickle yuk. "Dreadmona, do you want to get even with Juliet's brothers? They're the ones who fired you and cheated you out of your wages."

"Yeah. Dem's on me list of things to do. Me get even someday."

"Well, the worse thing that can happen to them is for Juliet and me to have a child. Just imagine how mad they'll be. Everyone in town will hear them howling."

Dreadmona picked at a clump of hair on her arm. After a minute or so, she gave a gruesome grin. "Dat good. Me can't wait to see dere faces. Me gotta be de one to tell 'em, all right?"

"Fine, you can tell them." Romeo nodded his agreement. "But before we can have a baby, you'll have to stay outside our room."

"Uh-oh." She made hideous faces while she struggled with the problem.

After what seemed to be an eternity to Romeo, she sighed and said. "Dis a big problem, but me think gettin' even wid de brothers is bedda than getttin' even wid Juliet. Me sleep inna next room."

A wave of euphoria swept over Romeo. His child stood to inherit the emerald mine!

Juliet jumped off the catafalque and threw herself into Romeo's arms. "My hero. I knew you were short, hairy and strong. Who knew you were also smart?"

CHASING DREAMS

PART ONE: THE RETURN OF ZARRO

Zarro pulled down the black mask to cover the upper part of his face then peeked over the edge of the roof. On the hanging platform below, a trembling dwarf stood over a trap door with a noose around his neck. He had been caught stealing a loaf of bread to feed his starving wife and six dwarflings, a common event in the town of Mud Flats. A large crowd had gathered to watch the entertainment and to enjoy the fine spring weather.

He took in the rest of the platform and gulped. Three yuk guards! He expected to face only one. Two at the most. Ferocious fighters, the large, green-skinned yuks wouldn't take kindly to his interference and they were twice as tall and twice as wide as a dwarf like him. All three wore the constabulary uniform: tan breeches and shirts open to their navels because their thick, clumsy fingers couldn't handle the buttons.

Zarro stood up, smoothed his black tunic and checked that his black pants were tucked into the top of his black boots. Satisfied with his appearance, he uncoiled his bull whip and snapped it forward. The end wrapped around the stout timber supporting the noose. He put a death-grip on the handle, took a deep breath, leaped off the roof and flew towards the platform, his cape flapping behind him like a demented bat.

"It's Zarro!" a spectator yelled.

"Zarro has returned!" another screamed.

The whip unraveled and Zarro added to the chorus of screams before he crashed onto the platform and bumped the prisoner. A gasping sound came from the dwarf as he dangled at the end of the noose and scrabbled to get his feet back on the platform. Zarro dropped the whip, pulled out his cutlass and hacked through the rope. The dwarf fell into the crowd.

"Wot's this then?" a dwarf in the front row said. "No hangin'?"

"I been standin' inna hot sun for hours," another said. "I ain't gonna be cheated."

The spectators threw the sobbing prisoner back onto the platform.

Two yuks charged Zarro from different angles. He shifted his feet, got them tangled in the whip and fell on his face just as the yuks slashed with their swords. Both constables stabbed each other in the leg. Their swords clattered to the platform as Zarro scrambled to his feet and faced the last yuk.

"Zarro!" The crowd roared.

Zarro backed up. His opponent growled in anger and strode forward, his cutlass raised over his head. Zarro gulped. His sword was less than half as long as the other's blade.

"A half-penny says Zarro loses his guts," a spectator yelled.

"Done," another replied.

Before the yuk could strike, Zarro's donkey, Belinda, trotted up the steps in the rear of the platform. The wood planks shook and bounced as she ran over to the yuk and bit his shoulder. The yuk howled and dropped his sword. Zarro thanked the Fates that Belinda hated yuks even more than she hated him. He looked around for the prisoner and saw him hurrying away surrounded by a bunch of dwarflings. A female walked backwards holding a stout tree branch and threatened anyone who came close.

He fetched his whip and coiled it. Then, with rapid slashes of his sword, incised the letter Z on the yuk's chest. He crept close to Belinda from behind and leaped into the saddle.

"Zarro!" the crowd yelled over and over.

Belinda stood on her rear legs and shook herself.

"Stop trying to throw me, you stupid animal." Zarro barely held on.

The crowd cheered.

Zarro held the reins and squeezed his calves as tight as he could. Belinda leaped into the air and bucked while trying to bite Zarro's foot. He bashed the back of her head with the whip handle.

"Zarro!" the crowd roared.

Belinda jumped off the platform and ran towards the woods. Zarro's cape billowing and snapping like a loose sail.

He managed to duck in time as Belinda ran under a low-hanging branch trying to scrape him out of the saddle.

"Zarro!" the crowd screamed.

# # #

Zarro waited in the dense woods until darkness settled over Mud Flats, then he rode Belinda to the stable in the rear of his home on the outskirts of town. His dead father had won her in a card game and she hadn't done a lick of work until today. Exhilaration filled his mind. He thought of himself as a teacher and the citizens of Mud Flats as his pupils. Today, he taught them a valuable lesson on how to be free dwarfs.

He backed the donkey into a stall where she turned her head, hoping for a moment of vulnerability to exploit. Zarro unhooked his cape and threw it over Belinda's head. Instantly, the donkey leaned against a wall and began snoring. He jumped down and unsaddled the animal. After he moved outside the stall and shut the door, he reached in, grabbed the cape and jumped back while Belinda snorted and stomped in fury.

Before leaving the barn, he took off the Zarro costume and donned the garments of a dwarf peasant, becoming Andre Benoit Fabrice Herve Schwartz.

Three months ago, after his father's funeral, Andre had gone through the old dwarf's effects and found a strange, wooden chest. He broke the lock and discovered a black outfit, weapons and a diary. The pages detailed the adventures and thoughts of a dashing outlaw called Zarro who had defended the poor dwarfs of Mud Flats from exploitation by the greedy elves. Andre was amazed to learn that the legendary hero was his mild-mannered father. One entry in the diary touched a nerve: *Sometimes,* it read, *a citizen must act radically to force the government to act normally.*

Andre pondered the future. The situation in Mud Flats was as bad as when Zarro appeared a generation ago; every dwarf family in town suffered from poverty. Mud Flats was now the semiprivate preserve of the ten elves on the town council who controlled every aspect of life in town and used the constabulary of yuks to keep the dwarfs in check. The diary entry made up Andre's mind. His father had dedicated himself to freeing the town from the oppressive yuks and to forcing the elves to share political power with the dwarf citizenry. He would follow in his father's footsteps. He dreamed of a new Mud Flats and he was the ideal person to be the new Zarro since he was the most inconspicuous dwarf in town. No one would guess his secret identity.

He stashed his weapons and outfit in a hollow oak tree and entered the house unnoticed by his wife, Simone, his ten dwarflings, his lazy father-in-law or his shiftless brother-in-law. He sat down in his favorite chair and announced, "I'm home."

Only his youngest dwarfling, a two-year-old female, acknowledged his presence. She climbed on his lap and combed her tiny hands through his beard, searching for crumbs from his lunch. Her siblings engaged in roughhousing that shook the walls and sent rivulets of dirt streaming from the sod roof.

Eventually, his wife, Simone, noticed him. "We ate already. There's nothing left." She wore a house dress that fell to her knees and heavy, ankle-high boots. Unlike most female dwarfs, her beard was cut short so the dwarlfings couldn't grab it and get a ride.

"I'll get something to eat at work." He wondered if his family life would change if they knew he was Zarro.

"I suppose ya wasted the day walkin' in the woods again," his father-in-law said.

"I did."

"Iffen ya ask me," the old man continued, "ya should get a second job. Durin' the day. Then maybe we could have beer once in a while."

"I ain't had a beer in a long time," said the brother-in-law.

"If you're so thirsty," Andre replied, "why don't you get a job?"

"Don't start in, Andre." Simone wagged a finger at him. "You know my brother has a bad back."

"Pa," the oldest dwarfling said. "Zarro showed up at the hangin' today."

"Who?" Andre smiled to himself.

"Zarro. He stopped the hanging and wounded three yuks."

"Yeah. And he rides a donkey that looks like Belinda," a sibling said.

"No one rides our Belinda," Andre replied.

" Zarro could," a third said.

"Hey, Pa," another dwarfling said, "Zarro looks a lot like you. Are you Zarro?"

"Of course not," Andre replied.

"Ha! I bet," his father-in-law said, "Zarro don't waste his time walkin' inna woods."

"Ha! I bet," the brother-in-law said, "Zarro buys beer for his family."

"Ha! I bet," Andre replied, "Zarro's brother-in-law has a job."

"Ha! I bet," Simone said, "Zarro treats his in-laws with respect."

Andre picked his youngest daughter off his lap and placed her on the floor. "I'm going to work."

# # #

Two yuk brothers, twins named Rolf and Ralf, wandered up Big Muddy Street, the main road in town. They were on patrol around midnight looking for gatherings of dwarfs. Their orders were arrest such dwarfs. Considered ugly by any rational standard, they had small noses, hairless heads and black eyes. Patches of dark hair sprouted in various places around their torsos and limbs.

"Mud Flats is one borin' town," Rolf said.

"Dat's for sure," Ralf agreed. "Dis place needs a saloon." Because of their fractured speech habits, many folks thought yuks were stupid, but those who knew yuks were always amazed at their cunning ways. Few people got the better of a yuk in a negotiation.

"Needs more den one. Only place in town is dat Sylvan Arbor and dey don't serve yuks."

"Ought burn da place down."

"Can't. Da Council goes in dere." Rolf spit on the dirt road.

"Dis not like Yukburg. Dere dey got lots of saloons. Can always find a good fight in one of dem."

"Dis not wot I left Yukburg to do," Ralf said, waving his arms to encompass all of Mud Flats. "Me came here cause me ambitious. Dis job don't do it for me. Not enough money."

"Me thought us left Yukburg 'cause de mayor threw us outta the city for fightin' too much."

"Dat too," Ralf said.

"Us gonna have to work harder now dat some guys got hurt at da hangin'." Rolf shook his head at the injustice of it all.

"Oughta tell Fredek to shove it. Us work hard enough now."

"Ya got dat right." Rolf pounded one meaty fist into his palm. "Us hardest workin' yuks in Mud Flats."

"Hey! Me gotta idea. Let's volunteer to work on da buildin' site now dat the regular guys got wounded today."

"Volunteer?" Rolf stopped walking and gaped at his brother. "Ya feelin' sick?"

"Naw. Me just tired of workin' so hard. Dat buildin' job looks easy."

"Me not like idea of volunteerin'." Rolf shook his head. "Ma always said 'volunteerin' is for dummies'."

"A yuk gotta do wot a yuk gotta do."

Rolf couldn't argue with that deep philosophical observation.

# # #

"Good afternoon, Andre."

Andre gawked at the dwarf and his wife as they passed him on Big Muddy Street. The couple had never acknowledged him before. Another dwarf waved a hand in greeting. How strange. Ever since the aborted execution two days ago, dwarfs on the streets nodded to him. Or winked. Or waved.

A group of off-work miners, covered with coal dust, trudged past. The leader lifted his pickax in a salute. Andre stopped and stared after them until they marched to the Big Muddy River and jumped in to wash off the dirt.

He shook his head and entered the Sylvan Arbor, the center of social life for Mud Flat's elves. A two-story building, the Sylvan Arbor contained a bar and a restaurant on the first floor while the second held gambling tables and a meeting room. Andre worked as the busboy, janitor and general go-fer.

"Clean off some tables," the big-bellied, foul-tempered elf manager growled at him.

Andre rushed to the kitchen and grabbed an apron. He pondered the difference between elves living in Mud Flats and the ones he met from elsewhere. Occasionally, merchants or traveling elves would pass through town and get a meal in the Sylvan Arbor. These visitors were quite different from the elves living in Mud Flats. They treated the help with respect. Occasionally, he drove a wagon to the neighboring town to pick up supplies for the bar. The shop-keeping elves surprised him with their politeness. Much to his amazement, he even saw elves who were poor. He concluded that he couldn't condemn all elves because of the ones in Mud Flats, but that went against Mud Flats wisdom.

Back in the common room that smelled of stale ale and scalded butter, he stacked a pile of dirty dishes from a table and carried them to the kitchen. The two dishwashers glared at him while he poked through the dishes and gobbled up the leftover tidbits of steak and crab cake. The food here was so much better than the mush his wife made.

He ignored the vegetables and bread crusts. "Here you go." He handed the plates to the dishwashers.

"It's about time." They stuffed the remaining scraps into their mouths before dropping the dishes into the sink.

When he returned to the common room, he heard angry voices. Lithgow, the head of the council, sat at a table snarling at Fredek, the sergeant of the constables. Fredek's green skin had turned red under the elf's verbal assault. "Me find him." Fredek ground his teeth. "Me just need more time." The yuk wore only breeches and had sergeant stripes tattooed on his massive biceps. He scratched one of the clumps of thick black hair that grew in spots on his torso.

"I'm tired of excuses." Lithgow pounded a fist on the table. The silk shirt worn by the elf contrasted with Fredek's bare upper body. Lithgow's manicured nails and soft hands contrasted with Fredek's huge, calloused fists. "I want this Zarro trussed up and dumped in my office. That is the decision of the council and we want it done immediately before he does any more damage. Just to make sure everyone knows the urgency, I'm offering a hundred-copper-penny reward for anyone who captures Zarro."

"Me get him, but me workin' shorthanded right now."

"You're using the wounded yuks as an excuse? Perhaps Mud Flats needs a new sergeant."

Fredek parodied a salute, turned and stomped out the door.

Andre's anxiety spiked upward. He hadn't anticipated that the council would get worked up so fast. A chill of fear ran up his spine as it dawned on him that some of the citizenry may have guessed his secret identity. His mouth turned as sandy as the river mud during the summer dry season. Fredek could learn his name simply by grabbing a dwarf to interrogate. After a few punches, the victim would shout out Andre's name.

This revelation added more urgency to his plans. He had to rid of the yuks before they got rid of him.

He glanced at the bar where a dwarf named Pierre smiled at him. The blood drained from Andre's face. He breathed deeply to slow down his rapidly beating heart. Pierre sucked up to the elves in town and delivered most of the supplies to the Sylvan Arbor. To show the depth of his elfin sympathies, Pierre wore silk shirts like they did. He was clean-shaven because the elves couldn't grow beards. Pierre kept looking and smiling at Andre. Pierre's well-known greed made him a threat because the dwarf would stop at nothing to gain a few coins. And that greed could threaten Andre's family if Pierre thought he knew Zarro's secret identity.

# # #

After work that night, Zarro concealed himself in a stand of trees outside the town limits. It lacked a few hours until dawn and a half-moon provided enough illumination to make out objects. From somewhere in the darkness, an owl hooted. His vantage point on a hill gave him a good view of a construction site and the camp of two yuks. Both slept on the ground around a dying fire. This morning these two yuks had grabbed six sturdy dwarfs. These unlucky males labored all day building a new home for Lithgow. Without pay.

A sleeping Belinda leaned against a nearby tree with a towel over her head. Zarro, hefting a club in his right hand, planned to thrash the yuks and escape before they recovered. Just in case something went wrong, he held his sword in his left hand. He stepped towards the yuks.

Halfway down the slope, his foot slipped on a loose stone. He landed on his back, knocking the breath from his body. Gasping for air, he skidded down the hill and through the fire. His feet scattered embers onto the yuks. Both awoke roaring in pain and shock. The closest one jumped up and ran into Zarro's sword point. Still sliding on his back, Zarro yanked the blade out of the yuk's leg only to slash the second across the inside of his biceps. His feet hit a boulder, jolting him to a stop. He climbed to his feet and examined the angry yuks standing between him and the relative safety of Belinda. Both yuks cursed and brushed the embers from their clothes while favoring their wounded limbs. He circled around them and made it back up the slope.

On the top, he turned and shouted, "Leave Mud Flats! Tonight! If you are here tomorrow, there will be con-sequences." He ran over to Belinda, mounted the donkey and whipped off the towel -- always a dangerous moment. Zarro was pleased with the night's work. In order for the Mud Flatters to be free, the yuks had to be removed. That would make it easier to deal with the elves.

# # #

The two wounded brothers watched the donkey rear up on her hind legs. The rider waved his sword over his head. "Whoa! Dat some kinda rider," Rolf said.

The donkey pranced and jumped while the rider held on. "Yeah, but me hate showoffs," Ralf replied.

"Dat guy can really use a sword. Stuck both of us while layin' down."

"Don't wanna meet up wid him again."

"What 'con-se-quences' mean?" Rolf winced as he moved his wounded arm.

"Dunno. Sounds like a felony."

"Guess us bedda leave. Otherwise dat guy come back," Rolf said.

"Fredek gonna get mad when he finds us gone."

"Screw him. Me tired of workin' for him. He don't pay too good."

"Us go back to Yukburg," Ralf said. "Get some of Ma's home cookin'."

"Ma's home cookin' makes me throw up." Rolf kicked dirt on the embers of the fire.

"Forgot about Ma's cookin'. Time for us to start makin' a mark in dis world. Let's go south." Ralf made a gesture toward the east.

"Wot us do dere?"

"Start a bidsness."

"Doin' wot?

"Robbin' wagons onna Trade Road. Gotta pay bedda den dis job."

"Us bidsnessyuks? Ma'll be proud."

# # #

Golga Gemfinder gulped air as he paused outside the drawing room on the Gemfinder estate. He hadn't been this nervous in his entire life. His father and grandfather waited in the room to discuss his future now that he had graduated from Dwarfen University with a degree in Gemology. Most of his nervousness came from the unknown. He couldn't predict how the two males would react to his career decision, but they wouldn't be overjoyed. With any luck at all, he wouldn't be disowned.

After one more deep breath, he entered the room. It had a male odor of pipeweed and whiskey.

"There you are," his father said. Rotund with salt-and-pepper hair and beard braids, the middle-aged dwarf pounced and grasped Golga's hand. "The family's newest gemologist."

"Well done, laddie," the grandfather said, patting on his back. The old dwarf had white hair and a beard that was professionally curled twice a week.

"I'm sure you're dying to know what assignment we have in mind for you," the grandfather continued. The Gemfinder family owned the biggest gem mines in all of Gundarland and they also owned many silver mines. Family tradition dictated that Golga, now that he had graduated, join the family business and work his way up to the ladder.

"That's what I want to talk to you about." Golga cleared his throat. "I want to do something different. Something that doesn't have anything to do with mining."

"What is this boy babbling about?" the grandfather asked his son. "Sounds like you did a poor job of raising him."

"What you are saying, Golga?" His father glared at him. "All Gemfinders work in the family business. It's how we survive."

"I want to be a peace officer," Golga said. "I've dreamed of that ever since I was a dwarfling."

"Are you serious?" the grandfather shouted. "No Gemfinder has ever worked for the law. Some of our ancestors worked outside the law, but those were different times."

"What does a gemology degree teach you about the law enforcement?" his father sneered. "Nothing."

"I took correspondence courses all during my years at Dwarfen U." Golga returned his grandfather's glare. "And I received top grades in all my courses."

"What kind of courses?" his father asked.

"Crime Scene Deportment, Searching For Clues 101 and 102, Five Thing Not to Do When Questioning Suspects, Police Station Protocol and a lot of other subjects."

"Bah!" his father exclaimed. "How do you plan to make a living if you don't work in the mines?"

"I'm hoping you two will write an introductory letter to some of the province leaders you know."

The arguments went on for over an hour. Eventually, Golga's stubbornness wore down the older dwarfs.

"I'm sure this will end up disgracing the family," the grandfather said. "We need a way to protect our name and reputation."

"I'll agree only if there is a time limit," the father said. "Say, two years. If you haven't succeed by then you come back and work in the business."

Golga agreed. He was relieved that he didn't have to disclose his weakness; he had claustrophobia. Even thinking about entering a deep, dark gem tunnel made him break out in a rash.

# # #

Andre returned home and rolled into bed an hour or two before dawn broke. Simone was used to his late arrivals because the elves frequently threw all-night parties at the Sylvan Arbor. He had barely fallen asleep when an angry voice woke him up. Half-asleep, he stumbled out of bed and peeked out of the bedroom. His mouth dropped open. The elf-loving Pierre stood in the entranceway holding a dagger in his right hand. "Where is he?" Pierre shouted. "Get him or I'll search the house myself."

"Go away," Simone snarled. "You're walking everybody up."

"Not until I arrest Andre. He's Zarro, I tell you."

"You're crazy," the father-in-law said from the cot he slept on. "Andre's too lazy to be Zarro."

"I know he's in here. Get him."

"You leave my pa alone." The two-year-old daughter marched up to Pierre, grabbed his left hand and bit a finger.

Pierre roared in pain and raised his knife hand. The oldest son grabbed the arm and held on to it. Another son lowered his head and ran into Pierre's stomach.

"You can't take him away," the brother-in-law said. "Andre's the only one here who works." He punched Pierre in the side of the head. Pierre sank to his knees and Simone skulled him with a frying pan. The intruder crashed to the ground and remained still.

"Well done," Andre said. "This family is a terror when it gets worked up."

"No thanks to you," the father-in-law retorted. "My son, my daughter and the grandkids did all the work."

"Really," Simone said as she hauled Pierre outside by one of his feet. "I don't know where this idiot got the idea that Andre is Zarro."

# # #

When Andre showed up for work the next evening, the entire town council sat at a table. After eating dinner and drinking large quantities of wine, the ten elves always retired to the meeting room for their biweekly meeting. Andre looked forward to these meetings because the elves left lots of tasty scraps on their plates.

An hour after the council had gone upstairs, a stranger entered the Sylvan Arbor. This elf had a large dagger strapped to his leg, wore leather breeches and shirt and had weathered skin. In contrast, the flabby council members had pale, white skin. The elf climbed the stairs to the second floor. Curious, Andre grabbed a mop and bucket and swabbed his way up the stairs. He reached the second floor and mopped slowly while he listened through the partially open door.

"Only south of town, you say." Andre recognized Lithgow's voice. "Are you sure?"

"Worked it three separate times. When I pan the river to the south, I get flakes of gold. When I do it north of town, I get nothing."

"All right, spell it out for us," Lithgow's replied. "What exactly does this mean?"

"It means there is a gold field somewhere south of town, probably where all those farms are."

"How do we get those dwarf farmers out of the way?" another council member said. "I don't fancy paying those dirt diggers part of our profits."

"We own their land," Lithgow chuckled, "so we kick them off it. I'll write up eviction decrees tomorrow morning and give them to Fredek. The farmers will be gone by noon."

When this group of elves showed up twenty years ago, they had bought every property that came up for sale. Soon, most dwarfs were tenants, including the farmers, and they did what the elves dictated or found themselves homeless. The elves used their power as landlords to get elected to the council and promptly passed a law that only landowners could vote in future elections.

With turmoil and confusion swirling through his mind, Andre silently moved back down the stairs. Many dwarfs worked the coal mines. Others grubbed the river banks for shells and smooth rocks to turn into jewelry to be sold to the elves for a pittance. A third group worked the farms and they fed Mud Flats. Without the farms the dwarfs would starve. It wouldn't bother the council or the few other elves in town because they were all rich enough to buy food elsewhere and have it carted to their homes.

Only Zarro could save the dwarfs.

Before Andre could develop a plan, Pierre, sporting a black eye and a bandage on his left hand, led two thuggish-looking dwarfs into the bar. Pierre said something and the two others stared at Andre as if memorizing his features. After a few minutes, they all left.

Guessing the three dwarfs planned an ambush for him after work, Andre told his boss, "I'm coming down with a fever so I'm leaving early."

"I'm docking your pay if you leave," the boss replied.

Andre nodded, walked to the back of the building and slipped out the rear door. He took a short cut and ran all the way to the hollow oak tree. After he changed into his Zarro persona, he climbed a suitable tree, one with a stout lower limb that extended over the path and waited.   In a star-filled sky, the partial moon illuminated the path with faint, silvery light.

In a few minutes, Zarro spotted the three trudging along the path. Pierre led the club-carrying thugs who walked shoulder to shoulder. Zarro had an idea. He would drop behind the thugs, disarm them and send them packing back to town. Then he would be free to deal with Pierre and finally remove the threat to his family.

When the thugs came beneath the tree, Zarro moved away from the trunk. A loud crack shattered the silence of the night. Zarro and his tree limb plunged toward the ground. Both thugs groaned as the heavy limb crashed down on their heads. The thugs and the limb tumbled to the ground with Zarro on top. He sprang up, drew his sword and waved the blade in front of their faces as they scrambled to their feet. "Run," he told them. "Run fast, or you'll meet your doom."

The thugs hastened up the path toward town.

Zarro turned to Pierre, who had backed up against a tree and brandished his dagger in front of him. "Fool! You think Andre plays at being Zarro?" He took a few steps forward.

Pierre gasped for breath.

"Andre is too mild-mannered to fight. You should have understood that. Now you pay for your stupidity." Zarro brushed the dagger aside with his sword and, with three strokes, slashed open Pierre's shirt and carved a bloody Z on the dwarf's chest. "Leave Mud Flats. Right now. Tonight. Don't let me see your ugly face again."

Zarro watched Pierre run back the way he had come. Once he disappeared around a bend in the path, he walked to the stables and risked loosing his fingers by saddling Belinda in the dark. He mounted the donkey, waited until she stopped trying to throw him, then rode south of town to the farms. At the first one, he dismounted and awoke the family. A sleepy farmer opened the door carrying a lit candle. "Hello, And . . . Zarro. What brings you out?"

"I have news that Fredek will come here tomorrow morning to force everyone to leave the farms."

The farmer gulped and his wife, standing behind him, cried out and sobbed.

"I'll warn the other farmers. We must resist Fredek. It's time we dwarfs took a stand against the elves. We've let them push us around for too long. Tomorrow, we put an end to it. I'll be back in the morning to help."

# # #

Zarro watched from the woods. Belinda, especially fractious this morning after her midnight ride, hunkered against a stout maple tree with a towel over her head to keep her from seeing Fredek and his five remaining unwounded minions marching towards the farms.

Fifteen dwarfs, armed with clubs, spades and pitchforks moved out from behind a barn and formed a line across the dirt road.

Fredek slowed down. "Dis assembly is unlegal, like," he yelled. "Get outta da way or yer in big trouble. Right, boys?"

"Er, yeah, boss," one of the yuks replied. Zarro sensed the yuks weren't too anxious to mix it up with armed dwarfs.

Fredek moved closer to the farmers. "Last warnin'. The Council ain't gonna be happy when dey hear yer interferin' with de law."

Zarro whipped the towel off Belinda's head. The donkey turned her head and snapped at his knee. "Stupid animal." He smacked the back of her head. "Never mind me. Look at the yuks." He pointed ahead and almost lost a finger. Belinda looked, snorted and exploded out of the woods. Zarro hung on for his life as Belinda charged towards the yuks who were to her right front.

A farmer pointed at Zarro.

Fredek turned to look. "Get him," he screamed, pointing at the charging Belinda and her bouncing rider.

Zarro released one hand from the reins to uncoil his whip. He flicked his wrist and the lash wrapped around Fredek's neck. Belinda crashed like a bowling ball into the gaggle of yuks. Yuk bowling pins flew in all directions.

The dwarfs roared approval and charged.

Fredek snatched the lash in one huge hand and yanked Zarro off Belinda. He landed on his back and the air whooshed out of his body.

Belinda turned for another charge.

Zarro adjusted his mask and made a quick surveillance of his surroundings. He almost panicked when he realized he sat in the middle of the pack of yuks. He grabbed his sword hilt and pulled it from its scabbard, but the blade slashed the thigh of a nearby yuk climbing to his feet. Blood squirted over the dirt as the yuk screamed and threw down his club. "Me surrender." Zarro ignored the bleeding yuk and looked for Fredek.

Fredek growled and threw farmers aside as he rushed towards Zarro. The yuk raised his cutlass over his head just as Belinda ran into him. Fredek landed a few feet away, slamming into the ground.

The other yuks thrashed around as the dwarfs attacked their knees and ankles.

Groaning, Fredek tried to get up. Zarro's sword point sticking in his throat stopped him. "Where are the eviction notices?" Zarro said in a threatening voice. "I want them."

Moving carefully, Fredek removed the decrees from his pants pocket and handed them over. "Now," Zarro said, "you and your thugs will leave town and make sure you don't come back." He made a bloody Z on Fredek's chest.

#

The town dwarfs stood on the edge of Mud Flats awaiting news of the events. They cheered when they saw Zarro. His spirits soared. His dream of a new Mud Flats was close to reality. He walked rather than attempt to ride Belinda with her raging battle lust. He spotted Henri the blacksmith, the most trustworthy male in town and its strongest dwarf.

"Henri," Zarro called out. "We need a new sergeant of the constabulary. Do you want the job?"

Henri thought about the offer for an interval then nodded.

"Everyone in favor of Henri as sergeant, raise your hands," Zarro said to the other dwarfs.

A sea of hands shot up.

"You've been elected, Henri." Zarro grinned at him. "Come with me. We'll inform the council about the changes."

Along the way, Zarro explained his idea on how to keep the gold field from destroying the town.

They entered the town hall.

"Visitor hours aren't until later." An elf clerk waved a hand for them to leave.

"We're here to see Lithgow," Zarro replied.

The clerk rose from his chair and sneered, "Lithgow doesn't see dwarfs."

"He'll see us." Zarro partially withdrew his sword from its scabbard and the elf's sneer turned to an expression of alarm.

The two dwarfs climbed the stairs to the second floor and threw open the door to Lithgow's office.

"How dare you enter my office!" Lithgow's jaw thrust forward as he pointed a finger at them. "Town scum like you are not permitted above the ground floor." He squinted at the masked dwarf. "Are you . . . Zarro?" His eyelids opened wide.

"At your service." Zarro gave a half bow.

"You look familiar. I know you, don't I?"

"All dwarfs look alike to elves."

"This is true. Now get out of my office."

"We came to introduce you to Henri, the new sergeant of the constabulary."

"Where is Fredek?"

"All the yuks resigned to nurse the injuries they received at the farms." Zarro reached into his pocket and took out the eviction notices. "Recognize these? They weren't served." He ripped up the papers and threw them on Lithgow's desk.

"For your information," Lithgow swept a hand over the desk, scattering the pieces of paper, "only the council can appoint a new sergeant. Now get out."

"The people voted Henri in. We dwarfs are taking back control of the town. Henri will set up a cooperative so all dwarf families will share the gold if they work the mines. Part of the gold will be used to buy back property from you elves. At fair prices set by the dwarf community."

A door in the rear of the office burst open and the prospector came in, his dagger drawn. "I found the gold and a bunch of dirty dwarfs won't take it from me."

Zarro drew his sword. It was hardly bigger than the dagger. He circled to his right. The elf stabbed and Zarro jumped back. He gathered himself, lunged towards the elf and tripped over a chair leg. The sword flew from his hand as he fell on his face. The elf screamed. Zarro jumped to his feet and saw his sword sticking in the elf's shoulder. He grabbed the hilt and pulled it free.

The elf's face had gone bloodless and he leaned against a wall while holding his wound. "I. . . I didn't know dwarfs could move so fast."

"Here's your first customer, Henri. Lock him up for assaulting a citizen with a deadly weapon." Zarro smirked. "Perhaps you should lock up Lithgow also. As a material witness to the assault."

Lithgow's mouth dropped open.

"On the other hand, maybe we shouldn't stop Lithgow and the other council members from leaving town."

"They'd be a lot safer if they left," Henri said. "Without the yuks to protect them, they could be in danger."

\# \# \#

Later that day, after changing out of his Zarro outfit, Andre walked into his house and sat down. He was exhausted from his last two forays, but he had followed his father's advice. He had acted radically in order to get the government to act normally. In addition, he taught the Mud Flatters what it took for them to be free dwarfs. He hoped the lessons would last. He had achieved his dream of improving Mud Flats. His dwarflings wouldn't suffer under the yolk of greedy elves.

"Pa!" His dwarflings flocked around him. "Did you hear that Zarro fought the yuks and won?"

"No. When did this happen?"

"This morning. And we have a new sergeant. It's Henri the blacksmith."

"Well, that is a pleasant surprise."

"I suppose ya was out wastin' yer time walkin' inna woods again," Andre's father-in-law said.

"Actually, I was," Andre replied.

"Iffen the yuks are gone," his father-in-law said, "maybe you can get a job as one of the new constables. Then ya'd have money to buy beer."

Andre sighed. He doubted if anything would change at home even if they knew he was Zarro. "I'm tired from all my walking." He mussed the hair on a few dwarflings. "I'm taking a nap before I have to go to work."

PART TWO: THE LONE STRANGER

Rolf and Ralf stood alongside the Trade Road and watched the passenger carriage disappear around a bend.

"Dat was easy." Vapor from Ralf's breath formed a small cloud.

The brothers wore leather jerkins to ward off the winter weather. Each held a large dagger in one hand, and in the other, a leather sack half-filled with loot from the driver, guards and passengers. Rings, coins, jewelry and other valuables had been pilfered in another successful holdup.

"Me think us bedda take a break." Rolf kicked a clump of snow.

"Why's dat?"

"Dat wagon had two guards."

"Didn't do dem much good." Ralf chortled.

"When us start, dem wagons had no guards," Rolf said. "Den dey got one. Now dey got two. One day, a carriage gonna be filled wid bailiffs and sheriffs just waitin' for us to try to rob it."

"Why?" Ralf scrunched up his face, a sign of heavy thinking.

"Us too successful. Cops gotta tell folks de Trade Road is safe, and it ain't. Not wid us robbin' all dese carriages."

"Ya right," Ralf replied. "Us doin' dis stuff fer six full moons now. Maybe us bedda take a vacation. Where ya wanna go?" He scratched his armpit with the butt of his dagger.

"Us gotta go to annuda province so dese cops ain't got any jurisdiction where us is."

Ralf stared at his brother in amazement. "How ya know dat?"

"Me da smart brudder. Everyone knows dat."

Ralf snorted. "If ya so smart, figure out how us gonna haul all de loot."

"Gotta steal big sacks from de next freight wagon dat goes by."

Ralf scowled at Rolf. He didn't like his brother coming up with all the ideas. It could give him a big head. "Okay. Den us should find a bidsness to invest da money in. Dat way, us make more money and don't gotta do stuff."

Rolf's mouth dropped open and he gave his brother a strange look. "Ya know finance?"

"Heard someone say dat inna tavern."

# # #

Golga Gemfinder shifted his weight in the saddle on his Appaloosa racing swine. Named Argent, the sow trotted down the main street of Harcort, its hooves kicking up small clods of frozen dirt from the road. Golga fancied himself as a young eagle on its first flight from the nest. In his mind, the eagle circled the town seeking its initial prey. Here,

Golga faced his first opportunity to test the lessons absorbed during his criminology studies. He scratched his nose. The itch caused by the mask drove him crazy. It covered his eyes and nose, and wearing it was one of the family's conditions he had to accept before he left home.

He spotted a building with a sign that depicted a mug of ale. "Over there," he said to Pinto, his faithful companion. The two were a mismatched pair: Golga a dwarf and Pinto an elf. Pinto was twice the height of Golga, but only half as wide.

"I hope it has a log fire going." Pinto rubbed his gloved hands together.

Both spoke using the common language of Gundarland.

When he reached the hitching post, Golga said, "Whoa, Argent," and pulled the reins to stop his mount from going inside the saloon to forage. He slid out of the saddle and waited for Pinto to dismount from his pony. Golga tossed Argent's reins to Pinto. "Chaptiff," he said in dwarfish, "tie the mounts to the hitching post."

"Yes, Kimusabe," Pinto replied in elvish.

Golga pushed through the saloon's swinging doors and strode up to the bar. He slapped down a penny and shouted, "Sarsaparilla. Straight up."

Pinto walked into the bar and said, "Me too."

The bartender gave them a suspicious look as he poured shot glasses full of soda.

Golga threw down the drink and slammed the glass on the bar.

"What's with the mask?" the bartender asked.

Besides the mask, Golga wore brown leather breeches and a heavy gray wool sweater under a tan cloak. His black boots matched the color of his mask. A holster held his slingshot.   "To protect my identity," he replied. Unlike most dwarfs, Golga was clean-shaven, another stipulation demanded by his bearded grandfather to protect the family name. It formed part of his disguise.

"You a bandit? You gonna rob the bank?"

"No." Golga looked around the saloon. Three tables with rickety chairs sat scattered around the room. The dirt floor had suspicious dark spots in several places. A beefy man sat at one table with his head cradled in his arms. "Where can I find the sheriff?"

"Sheriff Acelin? That's him, sleepin' at that table."

Golga walked over to the table and shook the man's shoulder. The sheriff raised his head and glared at Golga. "Who're you? Why're you wearin' a mask and why'd you wake me up?" Acelin looked to be about forty-five years old and was partially bald. He had more hair on his chin and jaw than on his head.

"I am the Lone Stranger. I wear a mask to hide my identity, and I woke you up because we have business to discuss."

Acelin frowned while he digested all that information. Finally, he pointed to Pinto. "How come you're the Lone Stranger when there are two of you?"

The question startled Golga. "I'm a dwarf and Pinto is an elf. Elves don't count, so obviously, I am the Lone dwarf Stranger."

"All dwarfs are strange," Pinto said, "but this one is stranger." Pinto wore leather pants, a thigh-length tunic and a deerskin jacket, all brown in color. He also had a slingshot holstered on his hip.

Acelin shrugged. "So, what's this business you woke me up for."

"I'm a roaming bailiff commissioned by Duke Elsford. He sent me to Harcort because of a report about serial robberies. This report came from a traveler who passed through here recently."

"Stars save us from roamin' bailiffs." Acelin groaned and shook his head. "You'd think a Duke would have more important things to worry about than cereal robberies."

"Of course the Duke worries about serial robberies. They threaten the peace of his dukedom."

Acelin raised an eyebrow and gave Golga a studied look.

"What do these serial robbers steal?" Pinto asked.

"Oats mostly."

"Oats?" Golga's mouth dropped open.

"Sometimes, they get away with a few eggs."

"These serial robbers only steal oats and eggs?"

"Cereal robbers ain't much interested in stealin' furniture and valuables." He raised an eyebrow and looked at Golga.

"The sheriff thinks you are a horse's rear end," Pinto said in elvish.

"And no doubt he thinks even less of you," Golga replied in dwarfish. He cleared his throat to give himself a few seconds to think. His Enforcement Procedures course mentioned turf wars occurring between law agencies assigned to the same case. Could Acelin, a lowly sheriff in a rural town, be jealous of Golga's status as an appointee of the Duke? "Do you have a suspect?"

"Yep. Twin yuk brothers. Moved into Harcort a few weeks ago. Seems they like oatmeal. Word I got is they robbed plenty of wagons on the Trade Road over the last coupla months. They came up here when things got too hot for them."

"And you ignore them?"

"Trade Road's inna different county. I got no jurisdiction for anythin' that happened over there."

"Let's join forces and question them."

"Why bother? Widow Maud doesn't mind if the yuks take her oats once in a while. 'Sides, those yuk boys are big and mean. Most people think yuks are stupid, but I can tell you they're foxy rascals."

Golga pondered the situation for a moment; something strange was going on with these serial robberies. Acelin appeared to be blocking the investigation. Why? His reasons for not arresting the yuk brothers seemed suspicious. A sheriff shouldn't be afraid of two rogues.

Golga heard a noise behind him and spun around. An elderly man stood in the doorway pulling a sword from a scabbard. In a blur of motion, Golga's left hand drew his slingshot from its hostler while his right hand grabbed a silver slug from a pouch belted on his waist. He loaded the weapon, pulled back on the straps and fired. The sword-wielder screamed and dropped the weapon. He grasped his sword hand and moaned. "It's broke. You broke my hand."

"Why'd you shoot Cade?" The sheriff stood up and hurried over to the wounded man.

"He drew a sword. He was about to attack."

"Cade's been drawin' that sword for years." Acelin scowled at Golga. "He's real proud of it. He shows it to everyone who comes into town. I doubt if he knows how to do anythin' with it except use it as a cane."

Golga wondered if eagles made mistakes. And, if so, how they covered them up. He decided to get away from the sheriff for a while. He needed a new source of information on the serial robberies. "Where can I find this Widow Maud."

Acelin ignored him but the bartender said, "At the edge of town. She has a small farm."

# # #

While they rode to Widow Maud's farm, Golga pondered his career. For months, he hadn't done anything except file papers in the Duke's castle. This was his first investigation and he had to take advantage of it to demonstrate his ability, otherwise, he would be back to paper shuffling.

"Kimusabe." Pinto pointed to a sturdy house set back from the road. "That must be the farm." Golga rode up to the front porch. A white-haired, feeble-looking woman opened the door and stepped onto the porch. Golga dismounted to find himself looking at a bow and arrow. "You can just get right back on that pig and get off my land. You ain't stealing anything from me today."

"I'm not a thief, I'm a roaming bailiff. I am the Lone Stranger and this is Pinto. You are Widow Maud, I believe."

"What's with the mask?"

"To protect my family from reprisals from criminal elements." Golga thought the reason sounded convincing. "I want to ask you some questions about the yuk twins who have been perpetrating serial robberies."

"Ain't no cereal robberies going on that I know of." Widow Maud lowered the weapon.

"Sheriff Acelin said that they stole oats from you."

"Every so often I put a bag of oats on my porch at night. In the morning it's gone."

"So, they did steal the oats." Imitating the Duke, Golga placed his hands behind his back and paced back and forth in front of the porch. "I'll track them down and bring them to justice. Your home and property will be safe in my hands."

"If I wanted to keep the oats, I wouldn't put the bag on the porch, would I? The yuk brothers ain't stealing it as far as I'm concerned."

"But why do you put the oats where they can take them?" Pinto asked.

"So they won't steal my chickens, of course."

Golga frowned at the woman's circular logic. Being an eagle apparently meant spending a lot of time flying in circles. "If you file a complaint, I'll arrest them and relieve you of the burden of bribing the yuks."

"They ain't bothering me, and I ain't bothering them. So, I guess you're wasting your time."

Golga thought back to one of his lessons. Did Maud refuse to incriminate the brothers because she feared reprisals? He had to reassure the woman. "You needn't be concerned about the yuks. I will protect you if you press charges against the rogues."

"I got my bow and arrow, so I don't need protection from yuks. I need protection from nosy strangers."

"Let's go, Kimusabe."

"In a minute, Chaptiff.

Widow Maud's mouth dropped open and her eyes widened. "I know some Elvish and that elf just called you 'Lovey'."

"True," Golga replied. "It's a childhood joke."

"What does chaptiff mean?

"Its Dwarfish for 'skinny wimp'. It's my nickname for my faithful companion."

"Lovey? Wimp? Companion? You two are perverts, ain't you?" The bow and arrow came up again. "Get off my property. I don't hold with perversion."

An alarmed Golga jumped on his swine as an arrow whistled past his ear. "Hi-Ho Argent!" Argent snorted and meandered away while Golga urged the sow to higher speed. Pinto's pony thundered past. Another arrow flew over his head. Golga glanced at the missile and realized the feeble Maud didn't have much range with her bow. A few yards further on, he stopped and turned Argent around so he could call to Maud. "Where do the yuks live?"

"Up . . . there." Maud, red-faced and panting from her exertions, pointed towards a rocky hill a short distance away. "In . . . a cave."

Golga's forehead broke out in sweat, he felt a pang of nausea and a wave of faintness swept over him.

Golga and Pinto rode a few paces apart. The elf hummed a dirge-like elf drinking song. To take his mind off the cave and the Yuks, Golga said, "It's great being out on our own where there are no family members telling us what to do. Don't you just love roughing it?"

"It is truly wonderful to get away from a warm feather bed and to sleep on the ground in all sorts of weather." Pinto maneuvered his pony around a large rock in the path. "And then there is the thrill of catching your food every day and eating it half-raw. So much better than getting chef-prepared meals."

Golga bit his lip and pondered the sarcasm in Pinto's voice. He couldn't tell if his friend liked the adventure or wanted to be back in the family estate.

Golga and Pinto were of an identical age and had been together since they were five. Pinto's father had worked mending boots in a poor section of town, an area populated with unemployed dwarf warriors, out-of-work elves and a few homeless humans. Most folks living there didn't have money to get their boots fixed. Consequently, Pinto's family missed a lot of meals. One day, Golga's father approached Pinto's father. The dwarf offered to raise the lad in his home and pay him a salary. His father agreed, and Pinto went off to live in the Gemfinder household where he became Golga's servant. He and Golga attended classes together, played together and ate together. They were inseparable except on weekends when Pinto went home to his parent's house, now greatly improved thanks to a bag of gems the older Gemfinder had left behind.

When Golga left home to attend Dwarfen University, Pinto accompanied him, but couldn't attend classes because he wasn't a dwarf. Nevertheless, Pinto got a college education by studying the books Golga didn't need for the day's classes. Pinto could have passed all the final exams. Golga knew Pinto looked forward to the day when Golga became an executive in the gem business. The elf wanted some reflected glory and power. So perhaps Pinto was disappointed in Golga's new career.

The path climbed uphill and Golga's swine negotiated its way along a rocky path. Stunted pine trees dotted the otherwise barren landscape.

Pinto stopped humming to ask, "Why do you want to talk to these yuks? No one admits they're stealing."

"Listen and learn. Knowing the psychology of the criminal mind as I do, I'll trick them into confessing to the serial robberies. Then we arrest them and deliver them to the sheriff."

"Just like that?"

"Of course. It's so simple even an elf should be able to understand it." Golga shifted in his saddle to study the landscape. "I wonder where their cave is."

A few minutes later, a fist-sized rock whizzed over Golga's head. Heart pounding, he threw himself off his mount and scrambled behind a boulder while he drew and loaded his slingshot.

"I think we found the yuks," Pinto said as he jumped behind Golga.

Golga choked back a curse. Pinto deliberately made such obvious remarks simply to annoy him.

"Who are ya and wot do ya want?" a booming voice shouted.

Golga peeked over the boulder and saw two massive, bald, green-skinned figures standing fifty feet further up the hill. They wore canvas pants held up with greasy ropes. Leather jerkins covered the top half of their bodies. Their black, beady eyes glared with hatred.

"I'm the Lone Stranger, a roaming bailiff, and I have business with you."

"Can't talk bidsness wid you hidin'."

Golga left the boulder and advanced a few feet. "Why did you throw a rock at me?" He kept his slingshot at the ready. He saw the black maw of the cave mouth and shuddered.

"Yukland tradition," one replied. "To let ya know ya gettin' close. Who dat?" The yuk pointed to Pinto.

"This is my faithful companion Pinto. What are your names?"

"I'm Ralf," the one on the left said, "and dis me brudder Rolf."

"Me Ralf," the second one snarled. "You Ralf yesterday." He punched his brother in the arm.

"You Ralf yesterday. Me Ralf today." He backhanded his brother in the chest.

"Wait a minute!" Golga held up a hand. "What are you talking about?"

"Ma named da first one born Ralf, but den she mixed us up and didn't know who was Rolf and who was Ralf. Now us takin' turns bein' the oldest while us on vacation."

"Well, I don't care who is the oldest. I am investigating serial robberies and you two are suspects."

"Us don't rob no cereal." Rolf glared at Golga.

"Yeah. Dat old lady leave da oats out like it's garbage and us help her out by gettin' rid of it."

"Ah-ha. You admit you took the oats."

"Don't admit nothin'. Want some oatmeal? Us got plenty."

Golga realized the yuks weren't going to crack too easily. He decided to use misdirection to confuse them. It was highly recommended in his Rogue Management course. "What are you doing in Harcort?"

"Us retired from our old bidsness. Now us lookin' for a new bidsness opportunity." Rolf cackled.

"Retired? What business were you in?"

"Makin' money." Ralf smirked.

"Doing what?"

The brothers gave Golga hooded looks. "None of yer bidsness," Rolf said."Ain't gonna talk about our bidsness wid a bailiff," the other added.

Golga chewed on his lower lip. Acelin was right about how devious the yuks were. They were harder to trick than he thought they would be. "If you two are planning criminal activities, be warned I will be on guard."

Both yuks shrugged. "Big whoop," the left one said. "Dat ain't gonna stop us." He sneered at Golga. "Me wonder why dis short guy's askin' dese questions."

"Maybe him tryin' to trick us."

"Us busy," the one on the left said. "Dis meetin' is over." The brothers disappeared into their cave.

# # #

On the way back to Harcort, Golga wondered if eagles experienced the confusion and roadblocks he faced in completing his mission for the Duke Elsford. He sensed the brothers planned major mischief and he came up with an idea. He would thwart the brothers nefarious -- and nebulous -- plan and bring them to justice. His initiative would impress the Duke.

Pinto pointed to Sheriff Acelin who stood watching a construction gang. Golga rode over and greeted the man.

Acelin jerked his head towards the laborers. "They're unloadin' stained glass windows for the new church. Beautiful, ain't they?"

Golga admitted the half-dozen windows were quite pretty. "I talked to the yuk brothers. They are up to no good. I'm sure of it."

"Yuks are always up to no good." Acelin shrugged. "It's what they do. Dwarfs grub inna dirt, yuks make trouble."

Golga ignored the racial slur. "My study of the criminal mind indicates they will act under the cover of darkness. I suggest we join forces and guard potential targets during the next few nights. We can catch them in the act."

Acelin cleared his throat and spit. "I ain't losin' sleep 'cause of yuks. Besides, it's pretty cold out at night." He walked away.

"Kimusabe, maybe the yuks plan to steal the windows."

"I am always amazed at the shallowness of the elven mind," Golga said in dwarfish. "What would they possibly use windows for? They live in a windowless cave. And how can they sell their loot? These windows are custom-made and won't fit into another building. No, the brothers have a different objective in mind. I'm convinced they plan to rob the bank. After all, the bank is where the cash is. If the sheriff won't help us then there will be more glory for us when we thwart their evil plan."

"I am always amazed at how trivial your ideas actually are compared to how great you think they are."

Golga frowned, unsure what Pinto meant.

"When are we supposed to sleep?" Pinto asked.

"We'll get a room and sleep tomorrow during the day. If the yuks don't attack the bank tonight, then we'll watch the following night."

Golga rode up the street and saw Cade, with one hand wrapped in a bandage, standing in front of a shop. Golga kept his eyes fixed on the middle of the street, but, with his peripheral vision, he saw Cade make a fist with his uninjured hand and shake it at him.

# # #

As dawn broke, Golga stretched his aching, stiff muscles. The cold had seeped into his bones and he spent much of the night shivering. This was the second night of watching the bank from an alley across the street. They stopped for a fresh-baked loaf of bread at a bakery and shared it on the walk to the boarding house.

In their room, Golga fell onto the bed and sighed. Police work was much more exhausting than he believed possible. He donned a sleeping mask in case someone sneaked into the room while he slept. "This bed feels wonderful. How's the floor, Pinto?"

Pinto, wound in a blanket, peeked out at Golga and said. "Quite comfortable, Kimusabe. I'm a fortunate elf to have a master who lets me sleep in his room instead of making me go to the stables with the mounts."

"Very perceptive, Pinto." Golga momentarily pondered the hint of sarcasm in Pinto's voice then fell asleep.

A loud pounding on the door awoke him an hour later. Pinto jumped up and opened the door.

"Don't let anyone in," Golga cried out. "I don't have my proper mask on."

Sheriff Acelin stood in the doorway.

Golga rolled over to face the wall, changed masks and pushed himself up on his elbows. He had a feeling Acelin brought bad news.

"Them yuks just stole the windows from the church. In daylight, mind you." Acelin shook his head. "Each of 'em carried off three windows. They said if we interfered they would drop and smash the windows."

Pinto arched his eyebrows at Golga and smirked.

Golga ignored the elf. "Why did they steal them? They're useless to the yuks."

"This is true, but they're worth a lot to the church members. They left behind a ransom note. They want two hundred silver pennies or they'll bust 'em up. Don't know how we can raise that much money for the ransom. That's as much as I make in five years."

Golga felt a giant fist squeeze his stomach. Maybe he should have taken the advanced criminology curriculum as well as the basic and intermediate ones.

# # #

Andre strode down Mud Flat's main street. He pulled his cloak tighter against a blast of icy wind that came from the Big Muddy River. This winter was coldest one in years. He was on his way home after shutting up the Sylvan Arms which he now managed. He shivered under another wind assault. He shook his head in consternation at the many changes in town since the discovery of gold six months ago.

Then it was a peaceful town, even if the elves and yuks had made life difficult. Now Mud Flats was filled with low-lifers trying to steal gold from the unsuspecting dwarf inhabitants. Most of the stealing went on in the saloons, bawdy houses and gambling dens that filled the business section on Big Muddy Street. Six months ago, this business section had held clothing shops, butchers, greengrocers, two general stores and a doctor's clinic. Back then, folks on the street were quiet and well-mannered. Now Big Muddy Street was chaotic all the time.

He spotted Henri, the constabulary sergeant and newly elected mayor, coming out of the Lucky Charm Saloon. He looked upset. Andre thought it odd that the mayor was out so late at night.

"Henri," Andre called out. "Wait up."

Henri stopped, but from the scowl on his face, he didn't want to talk.

"You have to clean up the town. All these new-comers are cheating and stealing from the town folks."

"You're just too straight-laced, Andre. Loosen up a bit. Have some fun like the rest of the folks."

"You hired guards to protect the gold mines. Use them to patrol the town. To keep folks safe."

"Those guards stay where they are. They're doing what they were hired to do. Folks are entitled to have some fun and I'm not going to interfere with that." He nodded his head and added, "Good night." He crossed the street and disappeared down an alleyway.

Andre watched him go. Henri seemed diffcrent from when Zarro got him elected sergeant. He wondered how that had happened. Andre's actions as Zarro last spring had gone for naught. Mud Flats was even worse now then when it was under the elves. His dream of a peaceful town had mutated into a nightmare.

# # #

Late in the afternoon, Golga went into the saloon to drink away his anguish. On his third sarsaparilla, Acelin entered and collapsed into his chair. "We're truly screwed," he said. "The whole town can only raise a hundred and twenty pennies. That means the Yuks will smash all those windows."

Golga threw down his drink and beckoned for another. The town folks weren't the only ones about to get screwed. Duke Elsford would not be pleased with Golga's perform- ance. He didn't think the Duke wanted to hear a report about cereal robberies that weren't robberies because an old widow wouldn't admit she had been robbed. Then the yuk brigands robbed the town's most valuable objects almost under his nose while he guarded the wrong target. He would get a large portion of the blame if the yuks destroyed the windows and that could ruin his career as a roaming bailiff. He'd be forced to go back to the family business digging gems in the tunnels. With his claustrophobia, he'd be paralyzed with fear. He'd end up disgraced and disowned by the family. According to his extensive research, no member of the fam- ily had ever suffered from claustrophobia. His father and grandfather would interpret his symptoms as shiftlessness and would never listen to reason.

He threw down the shot of sarsaparilla. There was only one way to escape this dilemma. He would have to make up the difference in the ransom. He carried a letter of credit for five hundred silver pennies. His family provided it to cover possible emergencies. Making up the difference would give him a chance to redeem his career. He'd deliver the ransom money and trick the yuks. He would arrest them, recover the money and save the windows. An eagle couldn't ask for a more successful first flight.

# # #

Golga rode with Pinto and Acelin to the rendezvous with Rolf and Ralf. Behind them, far enough to get a running start at the first sign of danger, twelve town folks rode in two wagons to transport the windows. The wagons carried ladders and ropes because the folks planned to avoid the expense of a trial.

Golga had confidence in his plan. With Pinto playing the role of a yuk, he had rehearsed his moves in the hotel room until he could make them with his eyes closed.

The spot chosen by the brothers bordered a swamp. A layer of thick, gray clouds blocked the sun and made the frigid air seem even colder. The brothers emerged from a thicket of thorn bushes. "Which one of you is Ralf today?" Golga asked so he could negotiate with the current leader.

"Me Ralf," the one on the left replied. "Got da money?"

Golga reached into his saddlebag and took out a heavy leather pouch.

"You're crazy if you get close enough to hand 'em the pouch," Acelin said in a low voice.

Golga raised an eyebrow, but otherwise ignored the sheriff. "Where are the windows?"

"Dey safe. Tell ya after us see de money."

Golga untied the pouch, took out two pennies and tossed them to the Yuks. Rolf and Ralf caught them in midair, examined them closely and finally bit the coins. "Des two good," Rolf said. "Wot about de rest?"

"Where are the windows?" Golga repeated.

"Let's see de rest of da money."

Golga took a deep breath to calm his nerves. He knew he'd remember the next few moments all of his life; his first arrests. The eagle's first prey. He jumped down from Argent and carried the pouch to Ralf. From his case studies he knew the morale of a gang often collapsed after the arrest of their leader. With Ralf apprehended, the leaderless and confused Rolf would be easy to arrest.

Golga handed the pouch to Ralf who opened it to check on the contains. The yuk pointed to rise a short distance away. "Windows back dere." Ralf returned to examining the coins.

Pinto turned his pony and trotted towards the rise.

With both hands, Golga seized Ralf's hand holding the pouch. In a loud voice that he hoped sounded authoritative, he said, "You are under arrest."

Ralf giggled and punched Golga with his free hand. Golga stumbled backwards and landed on the ground. He skidded until a tree trunk stopped his progress. He tasted blood. With his tongue, he found three loose teeth.

Rolf and Ralf ran into the swamp, hooting and hollering as they splashed through stagnant pools skimmed with ice.

"Anyone with half a brain knew that was gonna happen," Acelin said.

Pinto reached the top of the hill and called out, "They're all here and in one piece."

Golga regained his composure and turned to Acelin. "After them!" He jumped onto the swine's saddle.

"You won't catch 'em." Acelin shook his head. "Yuks are raised in swamps. If you go in there, you'll get lost and starve or freeze to death. Unless those two ambush you first."

"They have to come out of the swamp eventually. Otherwise, they can't spend the money."

"Yeah, but that'll be on the other side of the swamp. Near the town of Mud Flats."

Golga sighed. He wondered about the relevancy of the crime-fighting lessons he had mastered. Most of them didn't apply the way he thought they should.

# # #

By the time they reached town, word had spread about the recovery of the windows. Combined with Golga's generous donation to the ransom effort, the citizenry hailed him as a hero. Golga waved to the crowds lining the main street and smiled at them. Pinto and Acelin followed and were included in the adulation. Golga's swollen mouth added to the town's admiration.

On the ride, he had mentally composed his report to the Duke. It ignored the serial-cereal robberies and concentrated on saving the windows and emphasized his injuries in the battle with the notorious yuk brothers. He was sure the Duke would be pleased with his deeds and may even reward him. Maybe he'd get a medal. All together, a good start to his career as a roaming bailiff. The eagle had completed its first flight. Golga pulled up in front of the saloon. He needed a drink to celebrate his victory.

Inside, several drinkers lounged against the bar. The bartender poured a shot of sarsaparilla when he saw Golga walked in. He threw it down and waved for another.

"You are the Lone Stranger, I presume," a voice said from behind.

Golga saw a corpulent, well-dressed man with a greasy smile.

"I am the barrister representing Cade, who was unjustly attacked by you and who suffered grievous injuries as a result of that attack." He handed Golga a paper. "We are seeking four hundred silver pennies for damages and suffering. If payment is not made forthwith, a copy of this document will be sent to Duke Elsford along with a complaint about the unprofessional conduct of some of his bailiffs."

Golga grabbed his drink and sucked it up in a loud slurp. If he didn't pay the demand with his letter of credit, the Duke would fire him and he'd end up back in the family business. "If the bank is open, I'll get the money." After the payment, he would have only twenty pennies left.

The man nodded agreement.

Golga wondered what his family would think if he asked for another letter of credit. They'd probably force him to return to the gem mine. To prevent that, he needed to recapture his portion of the ransom money. "Draw me a map, Acelin." This eagle needed another flight. "Show me where this town of Mud Flats is."

"You're out of your dwarfish mind." Pinto slapped a palm against his forehead.

Acelin drew the map and handed it to Golga who nodded and left the tavern.   Just as Golga walked through the swinging doors, he heard one of the drinkers say in a slurred voice, "Who'sh that mashked man?"

PART THREE: CLUB FIGHT AT OKIDOKY CORRAL

Golga adjusted his mask and prodded his mount forward. Argent responded with a three-step burst of energy then settled back into its former shambling pace. Pinto rode at his side and clucked his tongue to keep his pony moving. Their goal, the town of Mud Flats, lay a mile ahead of them. After months of delays, Golga hoped the trail of the fugitives hadn't grown cold.

During those months he came to realize his correspondence courses hadn't prepared him for the reality of life as a bailiff. In every instance so far, the course material had been flawed. The lessons depicted the criminals as easy to outwit, that crime solving was as straightforward as walking down the street. With the course work so inaccurate, he couldn't rely on it. To succeed in his chosen line of work, he needed his own talents. If he didn't achieve his dreams, he had no one to blame but himself.

The sun made a spectacular exit behind the mountains to the west and hid the town in semidarkness as they rode down the main street. An early spring breeze raised swirls of dust in the dirt road and sent a tumbleweed rolling past them. Further on, lanterns illuminated a section of the town filled with noisy throngs. They came upon a decent-looking eatery a few blocks before the bulk of activity. A sign proclaimed it as the Sylvan Arbor. "Let's stop here," Golga said. He rode up to the hitching post and slid off Argent.

Inside, a dwarf polished glasses behind a bar. Of the dozen tables, only two were occupied, both by elderly dwarf couples. After one glance at the masked figure, they fled the restaurant.

The bartender put down the glass and the towel. A scowl crossed his face, and he pulled out a cudgel and smacked it into his open palm.

The Lone Stranger raised his hands in a peace signal. "We're not here to cause trouble."

"Then, what's with the mask?" the bartender replied.

"I'm a roaming bailiff commissioned by Duke Elsford to ensure the peace of his realm. I wear the mask to protect my family from retaliation. I am known as The Lone Stranger and this is my faithful companion Pinto."

The bartender thought about that information momentarily, then said, "I'm Andre. I manage this place. The kitchen is closed, but I can make a cold meal if you're hungry."

"What we really need are shots of sarsaparilla and information," Pinto said. "After that, food would be good."

Andre nodded and filled two shot glasses. "What do you need to know?"

"We're after two yuk brothers," The Lone Stranger said. "Twins named Rolf and Ralf. They committed a crime in Harcort and I believe they headed here afterward."

"When did they commit this crime?"

"Over five months ago." The Lone Stranger made a face at the admission, sighed and waved a hand for another drink.

"Harcort isn't that far away," Andre said as he poured refills. "What took you so long?"

"The Duke had other business for me." Actually, the Duke had put him under house arrest for three months while another bailiff investigated events in Harcort. "Then we used an inaccurate map."

Pinto mimed turning a piece of paper upside down.

"Well, the brothers are here. They sold a pile of jewelry, bought a store and turned it into a saloon. Now it's one of the bawdiest houses in town. Mud Flats used to be a quiet place until gold was discovered. The mines attracted plenty of shifty characters. The yuks and a half-breed dwelf named Frangos are competitors." Andre slapped a hand on the bar. "The dwelf and his gang are vicious and cruel while the yuks are simply after money." He shook his head. "Unfortunately, none of the citizens care that the vulgar, disgraceful entertainment is ruining the character of Mud Flats."

"Doesn't the town have a constabulary?" Pinto asked.

"It has only one member, a sergeant who is also the mayor. Henri refuses to do anything about the situation. I don't understand him. Once I had great hopes for Mud Flats."

"Where can we find the brothers? We'll go arrest them and recover the ransom money they stole, then your town will be much safer."

"You'll need help arresting them. I know someone who can help you. Stay here and get yourselves food from the kitchen. I'll fetch my friend and send him here."

# # #

Business boomed in the noisy and noisome Foul Armpit. Good-time female dwarves in revealing costumes and gaudy braid-curl ribbons encouraged the patrons to buy more drinks by threatening to reveal even more of themselves if the males didn't drink up. An elfin floozy gyrated on a small stage to the strains of an off-key fiddle. Most of the patrons were dwarfs but one table held a group of visiting business-gnomes. Rolf and Ralf, the owners of the saloon, looked over the dozens of customers with the pride of parents watching their children. The brothers watched from a pair of chairs in a corner beyond the bar that lined the left wall.

"Us gotta grow da bidsness some more," Rolf said. "Us don't grow it, it gonna wither and die."

"Die?" Storm clouds rolled over Ralf's face as he pondered the meaning of Rolf's business treatise. "How us do dat?"

"Clem's place." Rolf jerk a thumb to the left. "Him too independent. Him need good advice."

"Like what?"

"Gotta convince Clem to join us 'fore that half-breed gets ideas about cuttin' in on dis side of da street."

"Screw Frangos. Him a dumb dwelf." He stood up and fetched two cudgels from behind the bar.

The twins swaggered out of the saloon, turned left on the wooden sidewalk and walked down two doors to the Superior Tavern. They barged through the swinging doors and stopped, surveying the small crowd of drinkers. Clem, the dwarf owner, worked behind the bar. He turned pale beneath his full, black beard when he spotted the brothers. Anticipating trouble, he grabbed a large wooden truncheon and assumed a fighting stance.

"Clem," Ralf sneered, "ya need protection from dat bad guy 'cross da street. Us gonna give ya a good deal. Only twenty copper pennies a week ya can join our association and ya get protected."

"I don't need you two to protect me." Clem tapped the truncheon on the bar. "I'll do it myself."

"Hah!" Rolf replied. "How ya gonna protect yerself from Frangos when ya can't protect yerself from us." He swung his cudgel and shattered a stack of dishes on the bar. "I love dis part of da bidness."

Rolf stomped on an empty table. Splinters flew through the air as the patrons raced to abandon the tavern.

"Now ya unnerstand?" Rolf said. "If dat dwelf come over here, him break a lot more den tables and plates."

"If ya join us, den when Frangos come here, us chase him back." Ralf crossed his arms on his chest. "Wotta ya say?"

After ten minutes of negotiating, the brothers went back to their chairs in the Foul Armpit. "Dat was fun." Ralf grinned at his brother. "And dat nice Clem guy gonna pay us twenty-five copper pennies every week."

"Yeah. It's like Ma always said, 'No evil deed goes unrewarded'."

"Dis a great town since Zarro chased Fredek away."

# # #

An excited Andre ran home. Conditions in Mud Flats had appalled him for months. Every day, it seemed the lowlifes commanded by Frangos committed another outrage against the dwarf society. They insulted and harassed old folks. They mugged dwarflings on the way to school. They pillaged shops, even in daylight. Several males had been murdered. Andre knew it was time for Zarro to reappear, but he hesitated: conditions weren't the same as before. When Zarro had overthrown the elf council, he had the support of the town dwarfs because they all suffered. In the present environment, Zarro would have to fight alone because most dwarfs liked the rowdy entertainment. He could even be betrayed by one of those citizens. Tonight, everything changed. Zarro would join forces with the Lone Stranger and Pinto. Together, they would clean up Mud Flats and return it to normalcy.

When he approached his wood and sod house, he slowed down and made his way to an old hollow oak tree where he hid his Zarro costume. From inside the house came the frantic noise of his ten dwarflings playing a game of pile-on. He dressed inside the stable and took a deep breath before facing Belinda. He hoped the fractious donkey was asleep.

She wasn't.

The noise from the dwarflings ceased with the roar of an outraged animal.

"Hey Ma," one dwarfling yelled. "Pa must be saddlin' Belinda."

Andre winced. He had hoped to change persona in secret.

His wife Simone shouted, "If any of you let on we know he's Zarro, I'm gonna dent my skillet on your head."

"I don't know why he's startin' this Zarro foolishness again," Simone's father said. "He could be out workin' a second job."

"Pa, don't you start in," Simon snarled.

Zarro sighed. So much for keeping secrets from his family.

# # #

Frangos sat in his office in the rear of Lucky Charm saloon and gambling parlor. He ignored the noise from the crowd at the bar and the angry snarls of two gamblers accusing each other of cheating. His dwelf henchmen kept a modicum of order in the place while he concentrated on developing a plan to drive his competitors out of Mud Flats. The yuk brothers were getting too big and powerful. He had to act before they got ideas about eliminating him.

Frangos had a dwarf mother and an elf father. He was thirty-five years old, had black hair and eyes and wore a Van Dyke beard. When something pleased him, he grimaced, the closest he ever came to a smile.

Conceived at a drunken orgy, he was raised by his mother and never knew his father. He suspected his mother hated him because his arrival had ruined her chances for a better life. Growing up without love, he expected hatred from others and gave it out to everyone he met.

As a dwelf, Frangos had all the bad features of both races and none of the good ones. Taller than a dwarf, he lacked the natural agility of an elf. Wider and stronger than an elf, he didn't have the stamina of a dwarf. He had neither the grace and beauty of an elf nor the shrewdness and hardiness of a dwarf. In his heart he was convinced that he had the right to extract retribution for his unloved childhood. Consequently, his only ambition was to outsmart and rob everyone he knew. His only joy came in cheating others.

He had arrived in Mud Flats soon after the gold fields opened up. He bullied a butcher shop owner into selling the business at a reduced price, changed it into a saloon and began offering a lot more services than drinks. The locals, flush with new money, flocked to his saloon and Frangos soon had a large and growing stash of coins hidden under his office floor. All his life he had dreamed of becoming so powerful that he could act with impunity and he had achieved that dream in Mud Flats. Life was good. Or as good as it gets for a dwelf.

One of his first acts was to terrify the mayor, a mild-mannered dwarf named Henri. Frangos promised that he, Frangos, would carve the letter F into both cheeks and forehead if Henri interfered with the business. Frangos also promised Henri his wife would be next.

Success bought competitors. He bought, bribe or threatened all of them until most left town or pledged allegiance to him. Except for the yuks and a few independent, smalltime operators. Rolf and Ralf laughed at his threats, scoffed at his bribes and sneered in his face. Frangos was convinced that he owned the right to monopolize the local sinning. No outsiders, especially a pair of stupid yuks, were going to challenge or change that.

The time had arrived for a showdown between his righteous forces and those reprobates across the street.

# # #

The Lone Stranger rode on the left of the three while Pinto rode his pony between the two masked dwarfs to keep Belinda and Argent from attacking each other. Even separated, the animals eyed each other and snorted challenges.

Argent made a hostile noise and tried to run under Pinto's pony to get at Belinda. Golga sawed at the reins to pull the sow back.

The further they rode up Big Muddy Street, the louder the ruckus became. Fights, snatches of bawdy songs, the clinking of breaking bottles, curses and cheers all came through the open doors of saloons, brothels and gaming dens.

"Hey Kimusabe," Pinto said, "I didn't know dwarfs liked unwholesome entertainment. Maybe you can pick up some bad habits while we're in town. That would make our lives more interesting." Pinto looked at Golga and laughed. "You should see the expression on your face."

Two blocks further up the street, they came to the Foul Armpit and dismounted. The Lone Stranger's stomach verged on the edge of rebellion and his tongue unconsciously ran over his still-loose teeth. Even with Zarro at his side, his plan to confront the brothers was fraught with peril, but he really had no choice. For the first time in his life, he didn't have any money and he desperately needed to regain his share of the ransom. The eighty silver pennies would provide a cushion of financial safety. He also needed an accomplishment to keep the Duke from withdrawing his commission. The eagle desperately needed a successful flight.

He loaded his slingshot, pushed through the swinging doors and stopped while Pinto and the sword-carrying Zarro, formed a line with him in the center. Together they advanced to the middle of the saloon. The activity in the bar amazed him. Three card games were in progress and each table had piles of coins on it. A half-dozen female dwarfs in low-cut and high-hemmed fancy dresses flirted with males.

Each female sported an elaborate hair-do with matching beard curls. On a small stage, an elf chanteuse belted out an obscene love song accompanied by a male who played a fiddle missing two strings.

All activity in the saloon ceased. Several patrons gasped, "Zarro! He's back."

"Who's the masked man with him?"

"Zarro?" one patron said. "What are you doing?"

"We're cleaning up Mud Flats, Henri," Zarro said in a harsh voice. "Since you won't."

"You don't know what you're doing," Henri said in a quavering voice.

The Lone Stranger recognized the stark fear in Henri's eyes and wondered what caused it.

A female saw the loaded slingshots and screamed. The others looked and scrambled behind husky males.

"Hey!" one twin yelled. "What's goin' on?"

Rolf and Ralf stood up from their chairs at the end of the bar. "Looky," Ralf cried out. "It's dat Zarro guy. Us gotta get even from de last meetin'." Both grabbed cudgels.

"And dere's dat other guy." Rolf laughed out loud and pointed with his club. "Da one from Harcort."

The Lone Stranger drew himself up and said in a loud voice, "Who's the oldest today?"

"Us don't do dat anymore," Rolf replied. "Us too busy to worry 'bout who da oldest."

"You two are under arrest," he announced. "I'm taking you and the two hundred penny ransom back to Harcort."

Ralf bent over from laughing so hard. He slapped his thigh.

"Ya musta scrambled his brains when ya punched him," Rolf said.

The Lone Stranger bit his lip. This wasn't going the way he had hoped it would. He tried again. "Surrender and no one will get hurt."

Both Yuks continued to laugh. Finally, Ralf stopped, wiped the tears from his eyes and said, "Screw ya."

"That's it," The Lone Stranger said. "You had your chance." He fired a silver bullet at Ralf.

Ralf swung his club, hit the bullet in mid-flight and sent it bouncing off a wall.

Pinto fired at Rolf who swatted the bullet through an open window.

The customers dove to the floor and quick-crawled towards the front and side doors.

"Hey," Ralf yelled. "None of ya bedda leave widout payin'."

Three hands rose above table top level, dropped coins and withdrew.

"Dat's bedda."

Rolf hefted his club and advanced on The Lone Stranger who was fumbling with his pouch in an attempt to reload.

Zarro saw the danger and knew he had to move quickly. He jumped on a table to get the proper height to whack the yuk in the head with the flat of his sword. Just as he started to swing, his foot slipped on loose playing cards. He screamed. His sword sliced through the rope supporting a heavy chandelier. It crashed onto Rolf's head, knocking him to the floor. A dozen lit candles rolled around. Zarro's follow-through tumbled him from the table and he slammed into the floor. The edge of his sword ended up pressed against Rolf's throat. His eyes bulging in surprise and pain, Rolf cried, "Me surrender."

"No him don't," Ralf roared as he moved to help his brother.

Zarro jumped up and retreated to stand by The Lone Stranger.

Ralf pulled Rolf out of the wreckage and both stomped out the candles. Ralf faced the lawmen. "Us not surrenderin'," he snarled. "Ya bedda get outta da saloon."

The Lone Stranger sensed his plan had gone awry, but he had to brazen it out. "Know this," he said. "I'm not leaving Mud Flats until I accomplish what I set out to do."

"Guess ya gonna die here from old age." Ralf laughed out loud and slapped his brother on the back.

# # #

In the morning, Golga woke up in the Sylvan Arbor and looked out a second floor window. A heavy rain turned Big Muddy Street into a good imitation of the river itself. He silently thanked Zarro for letting them sleep here. Without any money, he and Pinto would have had to camp on the outskirts of town. It seemed strange that Zarro had told them to stay. It implied that Zarro and Andre were close. They both had the same physique and mannerisms. He wondered if they were related. He dressed and changed to his alter ego, the Lone Stranger.

Andre, dripping wet, arrived and began making breakfast.

"Zarro said we could stay here," the Lone Stranger said before Andre could question why he was here.

"Not a problem," Andre replied.

"Where is he?" Pinto asked.

"Probably at home, where ever that is. No one knows and he shows up when no one expects him."

The Lone Stranger wasn't convinced that Andre didn't know more about Zarro. "I hoped we could get together and plan our next moves."

"I'm afraid you'll have to do that without him. If I see him, I'll tell him what you plan to do."

"The yuks are much more confident and even smarter then when I last encountered them," the Lone Stranger said. "Getting the ransom money back will be tough."

"We should let someone else do the dirty work," Pinto said.

"What's that mean?" Andre asked.

"You said this Frangos was in competition with the yuks. Perhaps we can set up a fight between the two sides and we just watch while they finish each other off."

The Lone Stranger gave Pinto a surprised look. Why didn't he think of that?

"How do we do that?" Andre asked.

"I don't think it'll be too hard to arrange," Pinto said.

# # #

Frangos inventoried his supplies of liquor. Last night had been busy and he noted several items that needed replenishment. Despite his booming business, he didn't feel satisfied. During the night, he had peeked across the street a few times and saw that the yuk brothers were even busier. Since moving into town, they had taken away a good amount of his business. After they refused to back down and leave town, he ignored them, figuring a pair of yuks were too dumb to present any serious competition. That was a mistake. The yuks were clever and wilier than he was. He prided himself on his innate criminal ability, but Rolf and Ralf were a source of embarrassment to him with their superior villainy. More importantly, they threatened his dream. If he didn't do something, the yuks could get more powerful than he was and that would cramp his ability to act with impunity.

He walked to the door and gazed on the yuk empire. Their saloon seemed more festive and inviting than his. Their bawdy house more cheerful. Everything about the yuks made his business look shabby and sleazy. Frangos knew it wouldn't be long before the two sides had a showdown. Winner take all.

A dwarfling, breathless from running, barged into him. "Watch where you're going, you little brat." Frangos pushed the youngster away.

"Mister Frangos. I just heard the yuks sayin' they was gonna move into your side of the street."

Frangos felt as if someone had punched him in the stomach. He grabbed the lad by his shoulder. "How did you hear this?" He wondered if this was a yuk trap.

"I was behind their saloon lookin' for stuff that got dropped last night by the drunks. The window to their office was open and I heard them talkin'. They said it was time to run you outta business."

Frangos digested the news and decided it wasn't a trap. He smiled at the dwarfling. "You done good. Here's a half-penny as a reward. You keep your ears open and if you hear anything else, you come and tell me."

The dwarfling grabbed the coin and took off running.

Frangos smiled. Today was as good a time as any to destroy the yuks.

#

Rolf and Ralf lounged around in the empty saloon eating egg sandwiches. Broken mugs, overflowing spittoons, chicken bones, empty bottles and even a set of wooden false teeth littered the floor, indications of the success of last night's business.

A young female burst through the swinging doors, skidded to a halt and looked around the gloomy room. She spotted the yuks and ran over to them. "Got news for you," she said.

"Wot dat?" Ralf replied.

"Frangos is out to get ya. I heard him tellin' his crew it's time to take over this side of the street."

"Told ya us can't trust a dwelf," Ralf said. "Maybe us get rid of him."

"Someone always tryin' to break de peace." Rolf shook his head. "A bidsness gotta protect itself from predatory competitors. Dat's the way of the bidsness world. Gotta hit or be hit."

His brother's weighty pronouncement stunned Ralf.

"Look," the dwarfling shouted. "He's comin'." She pointed to the street where Frangos and two of his crew stepped off the sidewalk.

"Kinda early to have fun," Rolf said, "but it's wot us gotta do when us own a bidsness."

"Yeah," Ralf said. "A bidsness sure puts a lotta demands onna guy."

Frangos reached the middle of Big Muddy Street, the unspoken neutral zone, and stopped. Fearful citizens ran a dozen steps out of the way then halted to watch the entertainment. By the time the yuks stepped out of their saloon, a mob of folks blocked both ends of the street.

"Heard you're planning to invade my territory," Frangos sneered.

"Got dat wrong," Rolf replied. "Us mindin' our bidsness when us gets word dat you da one doin' de invadin'."

"I think this town isn't big enough for you and me," Frangos said.

"True." Ralf grinned at Frangos. "Need help packin'?"

"Let's settle this like gents," Frangos said. "We meet privately and discuss this until one side gives up."

"No knifes or swords," Ralf said. "Cowards use dem things. Real guys only use clubs."

Frangos nodded agreement.

"When?" Rolf asked.

"Today? High noon?"

Both yuks nodded.

"At the Okidoky Corral? It has lots of room."

Both yuks nodded again.

"Just you and one other dwelf," Rolf said. "Us have a fair discussion."

# # #

The Lone Stranger looked up when Pinto returned from listening to the confrontation. The elf grinned as he said,

"We can arrest the yuk brothers after the fight. Whether Rolf and Ralf win or lose, they will be too beat up to able to resist arrest. Then we take them back to Harcort to stand trial."

"I think you two should go to the fight," Andre said from where he polished the bar. "To keep the peace. Frangos can't be trusted and those yuks are too shrewd for their own good. There's going to be trouble there, I just know it." Andre dropped the towel and walked towards the door. "I'll try to find Zarro. I'm sure he'll want to meet you at the corral."

After Andre left, the Lone Stranger pondered the possible outcomes. If they did arrest the yuks, he could recoup the ransom money and then repay the folks in Harcort. Of course, escorting Rolf and Ralf back to Harcort to stand trial was fraught with peril. If either one managed to get loose, he and Pinto would be in a lot of danger. This wasn't exactly the scenario he had envisioned when he rode towards Mud Flats. That dream always ended when he recovered his share of the ransom money. He never considered the aftermath.

Ten minutes later, Zarro entered Belinda's stall. The donkey had her back turned as she munched on hay. Zarro got close and tossed his cape over her head. She stopped chewing, leaned against the wall and emitted a snore. After he saddled her, he mounted up, whipped off the cape and hung on as Belinda bucked and jumped, trying to smash his head against the roof of her stall. During one jump, she turned toward the door. He dug in his spurs and hung on for his life as she exploded out of the stable.

"Hey, Ma," one of Andre's dwarflings said as Belinda thundered past the house. "Pa's at it again. I wonder where him and Belinda are goin' this time."

"That fool is jeopardizing his job," Andre's father-in-law yelled. "Someone has to work in this family. I'm too old and my son has a bad back."

"Shut up!" Simone banged a skillet on the cook stove. "All of you."

Zarro rode Belinda towards the Okidoky Corral and wondered how his family had discovered he was Zarro. He also stewed over possible outcomes of the fight. Either Frangos or the brothers would prevail and drive the loser out of business. If Frangos won, he would step up his bullying and could end up as powerful as the old elf council. A slightly better result would be for the yuks to win. They were more interested in making money than in committing crimes. Unfortunately, the Lone Stranger planned to arrest the yuks and take them to Harcort. That would leave an entertainment vacuum in Mud Flats and Frangos could still end up in business even if he lost the fight.

The citizens would object if the entertainment ceased altogether. They might even riot. Certainly, if he forced both sides to leave Mud Flats, the town dwarfs wouldn't support him like they had in the past. Besides, some other nefarious crook would simply move into town and the new deadbeat could be even worse than Frangos and the yuks.

All these results were unacceptable to Zarro, but he didn't see how could he change the outcome.

# # #

The Okidoky Corral sat on the northern edge of Mud Flats between Big Muddy River and Big Muddy Street. It consisted of a large clapboard stable and a much bigger corral enclosed with a split log fence that penned in a dozen animals.

By the time the Lone Stranger and Pinto arrived, noisy crowds of Mud Flatters milled about. Bookies worked the crowds, calling out the latest odds. Females from the two gangs, dressed in their finest and most revealing gowns, warmed up the crowd by leading cheers for their employers. All wore ribbons laced through their beards. The ones working for Frangos romped near the river while the yuks' employees frolicked in the main street. Bartenders from both sides sold dippers of ale or hard liquor from big tin buckets.

Rolf and Ralf walked toward the Corral on their side of the street while Frangos and his dwelf sidekick, Kontos, marched on the opposite side. Kontos was bigger and more muscular than Frangos. Each combatant carried a hefty club.

Soon, the Lone Stranger and Pinto were joined by Zarro. The crowds muttered at his arrival.

"Why you here, Zarro?" one yelled. "We don't need ya."

"Ya ain't gonna stop all the fun in town, are ya?" another called out.

"Who you bettin' on?" a third asked.

Zarro bit his lip. He was concerned at how strongly the town-folks felt about the sleazy entertainment provided by Frangos and the yuks. The reaction to losing all their amusements would be unpredictable and might even turn violent. He would have to consider the citizens possible reactions in any decision he made. He spotted Henri nearby. The mayor's eyes never stopped moving from side to side while he made hand-washing motions. Zarro wondered what made Henri so nervous these days.

Frangos and Kontos insisted on fighting with their backs to the town. Rolf faced off against Frangos and Ralf took on Kontos. The combatants took their positions and all four offered the usual pre-brawl insults.

On Frangos' sideline, his females linked arms and performed a dance that involved a lot of high leg kicks while they sang,

> "Frangos, he's our dwelf,
> No one's more top-shelf.
> Watch him pound the yuks,
> And bruise the green-skinned bucks."

Meanwhile, the yuk females clapped hands in a rhythmic manner and cheered,

> "Let's go, yuks!
> Let's go, Rolf!
> Let's go, yuks!
> Let's go, Ralf!"

"Something's wrong here," Pinto said.

"What?" Zarro asked. "What do you mean?"

"Look how much bigger and stronger the yuks are. Frangos should be worried about that. He's going to get clobbered. So, why is he smiling?"

"You're right," Zarro said. "Frangos is up to something."

"He must plan to cheat," the Lone Stranger said. "But how?"

The combatants opened the brawl by trading exploratory blows to test their opponent's defenses. With each swing, the clubs clacked and the fighters grunted. The cheerleaders picked up the beat of the fight and clapped and cheered in rhythm with the strokes.

Over time, the more forceful blows of the yuks took a toll on their smaller opponents and drove them back a step with each swing.

Frangos suddenly jumped backward, stuck two fingers in his mouth and whistled shrilly.

Zarro looked around to see what the signal meant. Six club-carrying dwelfs ran out the stable door and turned towards the street. Scattering cheerleaders, they positioned themselves behind the yuks who continued to bash away at Frangos and Kontos.

"Oh no!" Henri whined. He grabbed Zarro's arm. "Don't let Frangos win."

Zarro tapped the Lone Stranger's shoulder and pointed towards the six. "This isn't right," he said. "It ought to be a fair fight."

"Why should we interfere?" Pinto asked.

"I don't think Frangos should be allowed to win by cheating." Zarro loosened his sword in its scabbard.

"You're right," the Lone Stranger replied. "The Duke detests cheating. We must act." He drew his slingshot and loaded it. Walking into the street, he aimed at a dwelf in the middle of the line. His silver bullet hit the target below the knee. The dwelf screamed in pain and fell to the ground kicking up a small cloud of dust as he rolled around. Pinto hit another in the hip. That dwelf dropped his club and doubled up, groaning. Zarro ran towards a third with his cutlass drawn. He slipped and sprawled on his stomach. The sword thrust forward between the legs of the charging dwelf. He tripped, smacked his head on a rock, groaned, rolled over and passed out. Zarro jumped up to look for another opponent.

"Keep 'em busy," Rolf said. "Me see wot's goin' on."
He half-turned to look behind him. "Frangos cheatin'," he
said to his brother.

"Dat's not good." Ralf swung a mighty blow that bought
Kontos to his knees even though the dwelf blocked it.

"Yuks don't like cheatin'," Rolf said as he swung at Frangos. The dwelf tried to block the blow, but Rolf twisted his
wrists at the last moment, and the cudgel smashed into Frangos' ribs. He screamed in pain as he flew sideways a few
feet. He sank to his knees and then flopped on his back.

Kontos, after a glance at Frangos, skipped backward a
few steps, dropped his club and held his hands away from
his sides. "I quit."

Frangos' cheerleaders gasped in surprise. The yuks' females squealed in delight and jumped up and down.

The Lone Stranger reloaded his slingshot, but not before
the three uninjured dwelfs fled towards the stable. He let
them go.

Zarro walked over to Kontos and pointed his sword at
him. "Get Frangos on his feet."

Frangos groaned and sucked in his breath as he stood up
with Kontos holding an arm.

"You two leave town," Zarro said. "Right now."

"My business," Frangos croaked. "I can't leave it."

"Leave town and hire an agent to sell it."

Frangos leaned against the side of a building while Kontos scurried off to hire a wagon.

The Lone Stranger and Pinto, with loaded slingshots,
confronted the yuks.

"No one ever help us before." Rolf shook his head in
disbelieve. "Thanks."

"Yeah," Ralf added. "Dat real nice. Ma always said, 'Don't expect help. Gotta do things on yer own.' Wait 'til she hears 'bout dis. She ain't gonna believe it."

"Yeah," Rolf added. "Us got help from de law. Ma gonna be surprised. First time it happen in da family."

"We're placing you under arrest and taking you back to Harcort," the Lone Stranger said.

"Dat's a long time to keep us from escapin'." Ralf grinned at the Lone Stranger. "Ya ain't gonna get much sleep along de way."

"They're right you know," Pinto whispered in the Lone Stranger's ear. "We can't get them to Harcort by ourselves."

Zarro walked up. He sensed the crowd growing unruly as word spread that Frangos was out of business, and the yuks were getting arrested. "We have a problem," he said in a low voice. "The citizens are working themselves into a riot. I don't think they'll let you take the brothers out of town."

The Lone Stranger looked around and saw the unruly, muttering crowd. The hair on the back of his neck rose. Besides the difficulty of getting the brothers to Harcort, it looked like they couldn't get them out of Mud Flats. He chewed his lip as he pictured himself grubbing in a gem mine.

"Tell ya wot," Rolf said. "Us like Mud Flats. 'Cause ya got us outta da trap, us promise us gonna be responsible bidsness yuks from now on."

"Yeah," Ralf said. "No more funny stuff if ya let us stay. Us'll be legal like."

"I need to talk to Henri." Zarro walked over to where the mayor stood. The Lone Stranger and Pinto joined them.

"The brothers promise to keep the law if we let them stay," Zarro said, "but I think we should make them pay a penalty for their past misdeeds."

"They also have to repay the ransom money to Harcort," the Lone Stranger said, "plus a penalty."

"What about their Trade Road thefts?" Pinto asked. "They're wanted for robbery."

Henri shrugged. "The Trade Road is in a different county and it's not our problem or jurisdiction. If someone wants to arrest the yuks for Trade Road crimes, they'll have come here to arrest them. We can't do it for them."

"I have an idea," Zarro said. "Let's make them beautify Mud Flats." He beckoned to the yuks. When they approached, he said, "If you want to stay, you have pay two thousand silver pennies which will be used to build parks and playgrounds in the town. Henri will supervise the construction so you won't be able to cheat."

"Two thousand?" Rolf looked angry. "Dat's a lotta cash."

"It's pay up or leave town." Zarro crossed his arms and stared at the brothers hoping they wouldn't sense he bluffed about leaving town.

The brothers exchanged glances. "Okay. Us build da stuff," Ralf said, "if ya let us stay."

The Lone Stranger said, "I need to recover the ransom money you took from Harcort."

"More money?" Ralf scowled at the Lone Stranger.

"Pay up," Zarro said. "You have to start out with a clean slate. Pay back the ransom if you want to stay."

"All right. Us give de money back," Rolf said. "One hunnert twenty pennies, right?"

"No. It's two hundred pennies. Silver ones."

"Us gotta try, ya know." Rolf grinned.

"I promise you I'll watch very closely," Zarro said. "Any criminal activity will be severely punished."

The yuks nodded. "Us turn over new leaf or new bush or new wotever."

The yuk cheerleaders cheered and danced in the street because now they could keep their jobs.

Henri shook his head. "I'm glad to see the last of Frangos." He seemed almost cheerful to Zarro. "Now I can do my job."

# # #

Zarro rode Belinda away from the Okidoky Corral. He pondered the mixed results of the day's activities. On the one hand, he had followed his father's advice and acted radically to get the government to act normally. Henri had disclosed the threats he received from Frangos. On the other hand, his actions had almost precipitated a riot. Apparently, when acting radically, it was dangerous to get between folks and what they considered necessary fun. He promised himself to remember that last bit in the future.

Nevertheless, he had accomplished his dream. Again, Mud Flats was a law-abiding town in which he was proud to raise his dwarflings. He mentally retired his Zarro persona. He would be Andre permanently from now on. No more risking injury saddling Belinda; no more sword fights; just a quiet family life.

# # #

Outside of Mud Flats, Golga removed the mask sighed and scratched his nose. While he had survived the mission, he hadn't arrested the yuk brothers. Explaining that inconvenient fact to the Duke would be tricky. Perhaps, he should tell the Duke the brothers had been apprehended and sentenced to stay in Mud Flats performing community services. That may work although it stretched the truth a little. On the plus side of the ledger, he had recovered all the ransom money and folks in Harcort would be pleased. That must count for something with the Duke.

No matter how he analyzed it, he had to admit that his eagle had lost a few tail feathers on its first flight.

Nevertheless, recovering the ransom money meant he had a success to put on his list of accomplishments and he had also learned a few hard lessons. His dream career was well-launched and he had safely eliminated the need to work in the mines. Turning to Pinto, he said, "I'm guessing that you'll soon have a new job. After I put a few more success on my resume, the Duke will have to consider me for a permanent job. Like an appointment as a county bailiff. You can then become my chief clerk."

"I want to be in charge of your schedule so I can decide who gets to see you and who doesn't. That should be very lucrative for me."

Golga frowned. Was what Pinto suggested illegal? Or shrewd business?

Maybe it didn't matter, as long as he didn't have to go back to the family gem mines.

# # #

Ralf lean his chair against the wall of the Foul Armpit and looked fondly at the clubs Frangos and Kontos used. Mounted in a place where all the customers could see them, the clubs served as a not-so-subtle reminder that the brothers could be violent when required. "Dis town gonna be pretty dull widout Frangos."

"Yeah, and us promise not to do any fun stuff anymore."

"Us gotta find somethin' to keep us busy," Ralf said. "Maybe dis a good time to start anudda career."

"Huh?" Rolf looked puzzled.

"First, we gotta spread da word dat us buildin' da parks. Us don't want folks thinkin' Henri doin' dem."

"Why us care?"

"'Cause us gonna go inna politics." Ralf grinned at the expression on his brother's face.

"How us do dat?" Rolf stared at his brother. "And why?"

"Henri not doin' a good job as mayor. Us oughta run against him."

"Run for mayor?" Rolf wondered if Ralf had a brain fever.

"Sure. Folks gonna love da parks and dey'll get us a lotta votes. Den us gotta spread a lotta money around. Especially to da poor families inna town. Us gotta kiss a lotta babies too."

"Dwarf babies?" Rolf looked stunned.

"Dey de only kind in Mud Flats."

"Yuaccchh!" Rolf spit on the floor. "Kissin' dwarf babies and keepin' legal-like? Me hope Ma don't hear about dis stuff."

"Us get elected for sure," Ralf chuckled. "Den us can do all sorts of fun stuff."

"Yuk mayors? Ma'll be proud. She always said us was too big fer our britches."

"Us take turns bein' mayor and assistant mayor."

BOGGERTS BLUE

Burga, gnawing his lower lip, stood beneath a clump of oak trees and surveyed the walls of the ancient, nondescript castle, situated in the middle of nowhere. A wretched chanting came from somewhere within the castle precincts. He tried to ignore the stench emanating from the green-slimed moat.

Where were the guards? he wondered. Even the stingiest castle warden could afford a contingent of dwarf warriors to guard a kidnapped princess. Could it be a trap?

Time to go to work. He untied the apron that identified him as a Warrior-Cook. Festooned with dozens of small pockets that held spices, condiments and implements such as a corkscrew and a zester, it was a graduation gift from the College of Combat and Culinary Arts. He stowed it in a saddlebag. While walking to the moat, he stretched his six-foot-four-inch frame to loosen up his muscles. He straightened his leather breeches and bearskin, sleeveless shirt. He had been taught that princesses preferred to be rescued by appropriately dressed heroes.

At the bank of the moat, he unwound a rope with a grapnel attached to one end. He tossed the grapnel onto the wall, grasped the rough surface of the rope and swung over the moat. He scaled the wall, looked around and frowned while coiling the rope. Why was no one defending the castle? It was too early for lunch. If it wasn't for the singing, he would suspect the castle was abandoned.

He squelched a burp from his breakfast -- two pounds of bacon, a dozen eggs scrambled with morels and a stack of blueberry pancakes. It depleted most of his supplies but he needed the big meal because castle defenders rarely agreed to a luncheon truce. That made for a long, hungry day.

He grasped his oversized spatula and skillet. The spatula, named Flippa, had razor-sharp edges along its two long sides. Frya, his large, heavy skillet doubled as a shield and made an excellent blunt instrument.

He jumped from the wall and ran across the inner yard to the keep, his head in constant motion looking left and right, searching for an ambush. At the base of the keep, he launched the grapnel toward an upper window with a tunic airing on the sill. The hook sent the garment fluttering across the yard. A woman appeared in the window, hand to her open mouth. Burga winked at her just as a warrior rounded the keep. The surprised dwarf hesitated long enough for Burga to whack him in the head with Frya. Like a broken bell, the skillet and the dwarf's helmet clanged together loud enough to alert anyone not sound asleep.

Burga scurried up the rope and stepped into the princess' room. Below, a mixed squad of dwarfs and men appeared, cursed and shook their fists before running to the entrance.

Burga glanced at the room. Sparsely furnished, it contained a pallet, a stool, a small table and a princess. He smiled. "I'm Burga. I'm here to rescue you." He picked a few rope fibers out of the palm of his hands.

"I'm Princess Gerhilde." She was young and attractive with reddish-brown hair. Of medium height and build, she placed her hands on her hips, stamped her foot and said, "What took you so long? I've been captive for over three weeks."

Her acerbic tone irked him. "Where is everyone?" He hooked a thumb towards the window. "I thought I would have to fight my way through a battalion of soldiers to reach you."

"Over there." Gerhilde pointed to a different window. "Count Lazlo makes them attend services every day. He's a religious fanatic."

Through the window, Burga saw a tall, thin, richly dressed man standing on a platform by the far walls preaching to the assembled staff and soldiers. They responded with frequent hosannas.

"Lazlo thinks he's been touched by a god named Lester." Gerhilde sniffed in disdain. "He has started a religion to worship this god. He even wants me to convert and become the bride of Lester. Whatever that means."

"What's this mess?" Burga examined a tray containing green-molded cheese, glue-like porridge and stale bread.

"It's what they call a meal in this dump."

He grinned as he recalled the tales he had heard at school. The professors told how bad the food was in captivity and how grateful kidnapped princesses were to be fed a gourmet meal after their rescue. Frequently, they accepted marriage proposals on the spot.

Burga heard a stampede of shod feet on the stairs. "Time to go, Princess." He pushed a heavy table against the door. "That'll slow them down."

"But --"

"C'mon. Wrap your arms around my neck and hold on while I climb down the rope."

"But --" Gerhilde pointed to the door.

"No time for chitchat." Burga pulled her close. "Hang onna my neck."

The soldiers banged axes on the door and the upper half swung open, missing the table by several inches. Dwarfs and men swarmed onto the table.

"Uh-oh."

"I tried to tell you it's a split door," Gerhilde hissed in his ear. "Did you listen? No."

Burga made a face and choked back a reply. "Here we go." He pushed off the window sill and rappelled down the rope.

A dwarf stuck his head out the window and hacked at the rope. Burga slid faster, wincing in pain at his rope burns.

Gerhilde shrieked so loud his eyeballs bulged.

The rope parted, and they fell the last ten feet with the princess screaming even louder. Burga landed on his feet, but Gerhilde's weight threw him off-balance. They tumbled to the ground in a heap.

"Get off me, you oaf," Gerhilde snarled.

Burga jumped to his feet, grabbed Gerhilde and threw her over his shoulder. He raced around the keep towards the drawbridge, but skidded to a halt when he saw the castle troops streaming towards the gate. "Too late," he said. "We can't use the drawbridge. We'll have to go over the wall."

Burga dashed back to the wall. Panting from carrying the extra weight, he climbed the stone stairs, took a deep breath and looked back. Soldiers ran towards them.

Gerhilde slid off his shoulder. "Do you know what you're doing?" A sneer contorted her face. "We're trapped between the soldiers and that." She pointed to the moat. An ominous shadow beneath its surface disclosed a pocket sea-dragon.

"Not for long." Burga scooped her up and leaped off the wall.

She screamed again.

Burga thanked the stars when they went underwater; it stifled Gerhilde's noisemaking. He kicked off the bottom of the moat and shot to the surface. He pushed her onto the bank just as the red-scaled monster surfaced alongside of him. He pulled Flippa from its scabbard and sliced off an ear. The creature retreated and Burga climbed out. He gazed at the wet, smelly princess and her clinging kirtle. "You're free." Splotches of green slime decorated her hair.

"Who are you?" Anger flashed in her eyes and water dripped from her nose.

"I told you my name." Her response to the rescue puzzled him.

"What are you, then?" Her face turned red.

"I'm a Warrior-Cook."

"You have an accent, so you must be foreign-born. And I'll wager you're not a nobleman. Am I right?"

"Well, uh --"

"How dare you rescue me!" Gerhilde slapped his face and stormed off towards the drawbridge, trailing a wake of mud from her wet clothes. "This is so embarrassing. I'd never be able to show my face in court again if you saved me."

"Hey! Where are you goin'?"

"Back to Count Lazlo until a suitable nobleman can free me. If you ever come near me again, I'll rip your guts out, you . . . you peasant."

\#\#\#

A disappointed and angry Burga returned to the campsite where his horse grazed: disappointed because Gerhilde rejected him and angry for the same reason. Her refusal to be rescued held devastating consequences for his career. Upon graduating, he entered a probationary period. He had six months to accumulate a resume of four adventures. He was almost out of time to gain the credits necessary to finish probation.

He threw himself down and sat with his back to an oak tree. His resume held two accomplishments and only a week remained out of the six months. Even worse, he was out of flour and capers, had only a few drops of olive oil left, precious little oregano, and no money to replenish his supplies.

Hoping to get some money, he had spent a week organizing, preparing and cooking a feast for Duke Rudolph, the Province Chief. The Duke loved the food, but the notorious cheapskate hadn't given him a cash bonus. Instead, Rudolph made him a roaming bailiff charged with freeing the province from evildoers and bad cooks.

He fell asleep dreaming about a shopping spree in an exotic spice bazaar.

\#\#\#

Burga imagined a tiny hand whacking his right shoulder. He shrugged it away to get back to his new dream in which he achieved his ultimate career objective: promotion to the rank of Hero-Chef. With that rank, he could pick the choicest adventures and nobles would shove money at him to develop special recipes named after themselves.

The hand punched him again, and Burga opened his right eye to squint in the direction of the disturbance. His left eye popped open an instant later. A small creature stood on top of two others to reach his shoulder. Blue fur covered their scrawny bodies. Burga blinked a few times, but the apparitions didn't go away.

"You look like a warrior," the blue apparition said. "My name is Big Jeanne. I am the war-chief of the Boggerts Blue and my tribe is in trouble. Will you help us?" A belt around her waist carried a small war-hammer.

Burga considered. This could be a chance to fill in part of his probationary resume. Besides, the motto of the Col-lege was, 'Don't overcook the food and protect the weak.'

"All right." He had never heard of a boggert cuisine so perhaps he could discover some new recipes. "What's the problem?"

"A greedy noble wants to seize our tribal lands. Come. It's not far."

Burga stood up and noticed that Big Jeanne didn't come up to his knees.

# # #

"We live underground." Big Jeanne pointed to a tunnel-pocked hill. She led him to a clearing on the crest that acted as a social hall and included a view of the entire area.

"All these oak trees." Big Jeanne waved her hand in a circle. "The man wants to cut them down. We have lived on this hill for centuries as you big-feet count the years."

"Who's this guy?"

"Pick me up."

Burga bent down, held out a hand and Big Jeanne sat in it. Her fur was soft and downy. "He lives there." She pointed to a castle.

"Count Lazlo?" Gerhilde called him a religious fanatic. How could he protect the boggerts from a land-hungry count with a small army at his command? While he mulled the situation, a chirping noise came from the base of the hill.

"The signal from our sentry. He comes," Big Jeanne said. "Prepare yourself."

Burga made a face. He leaned against a stout tree while he figured out what to do. Big Jeanne scampered away.

In a few minutes, a mounted Count Lazlo came into view escorted by two armed riders. A dozen workers followed on foot carrying axes. The Count ignored the keening of the boggerts. On the crest, he turned to the workers. "Start clearing the trees." To the warriors, he said, "Get rid of the boggerts."

The two warriors dismounted.

None of them noticed Burga. His spleen rose. He wanted to protect the little buggers from a horrible death from the soldiers's swords. "Halt!" He stepped forward. "The boggerts are under my protection."

The workers froze.

"Who dares to interfere with the work of Lester's Supreme and Exalted Bishop?" Lazlo squinted at him. "Are you the fool who tried to rescue Gerhilde?"

"I dare and I am."

"The Great and Only God Lester has decreed that I build a temple on this hill to become the center of His temporal empire. He who stands in Lester's way will be condemned to eternal punishment. For you, that eternal punishment starts now. Kill him."

The two warriors fetched shields from their horses and spread out.

Burga drew Flippa from its holster and lifted Frya from its hook on his belt. He moved sideways to his right to confront one warrior. He screamed the battle cry of the day, "*Asparagus*!" The man slashed at him. Burga blocked the sword with Flippa and swung an overhand blow with Frya. The warrior threw up his shield and the cast iron skillet smashed into the top edge crumpling it into scraps. The warrior dropped the useless shield. He didn't look quite so confident when he swung his sword again. Burga ducked under the stroke and, while in a crouch, moved forward a pace. He swung Frya a second time and the skillet connected with the man's knee. He screamed and the sword fell out of his hand as he fell to the ground. He balled up holding his knee with both hands and groaned.

Burga turned to face the second assailant.

"Oh Great Lester! Strike down Thy enemies! " Lazlo sprayed spittle in all directions. The warrior stood warily and awaited Burga's attack.

Burga struck with the spatula and the warrior blocked it. Burga feinted with the skillet. The warrior reacted to protect the shield. Burga stepped into the opening provided and whacked his opponent's sword arm with the flat side of Flippa. The sword fell to the ground.

Burga turned to Lazlo. "Maybe Lester went out to have a snack."

"Blasphemy! The penalty is death. For you and the boggerts. Prepare your souls, for I will return." Lazlo turned his horse and rode down the hill. The workers ran after him while the two injured warriors barely managed to mount their horses.

# # #

Later, as the sun descended behind the trees, Burga sat down beside Big Jeanne who tended a fire in the clearing. Burga didn't look forward to another meeting with Lazlo, but Big Jeanne didn't seem too concerned. "What are you cookin'?" he asked her.

"I'm toasting fir twigs." Big Jeanne rotated the twigs.

"You folks eat twigs?" That didn't sound like a promising recipe, but the smoke from the burning twig reminded him of the many steaks he had grilled over a pine fire.

"Try one." Big Jeanne handed him a smoking twig.

Burga accepted it and brought it close to his face. He had to admit it smelled delicious. He took a small bite and tried not to grimace. It tasted like charcoal and made his mouth dry. He gave Big Jeanne a false smile, chewed and, with some difficulty, swallowed the morsel. He handed the rest back to the boggert. "I'm not that hungry."

"You are the first big-foot to ever try our food." She laughed. "You're a brave one."

Boggerts sat in groups around the clearing. Some devoured branches and twigs while others gnawed on a thick log they had dragged from the woods.

A pompous, older boggert, accompanied by two young ones, strutted to the fire and helped himself to a twig. Gray streaks mottled his blue fur. Unlike the other boggerts, he wore a vest and a plaid kilt. His paunch was too big for the vest to button and the kilt threatened to fall off his hips. The boggert took a bite and examined Burga. "He's a big one, but what good is only one of these big-feet? We need a dozen at least."

"This is The Royal," Big Jeanne said. "King Kirk the Twenty-third."

"Where is Duke Randolph?" The Royal said. "Does he know this evil man violates the land treaty we have?"

"What land treaty?"

"Duke Billy, Randolph's da, gave us this land as a reward for supporting his army."

Burga wondered what a bunch of tiny boggerts did to earn a land grant.

The Royal snapped his fingers. "Fetch the treaty." The two attendant boggerts bowed and ran off. They returned with a small chest and put it down at The Royal's feet. Kirk opened it, extracted a parchment roll and handed it to Burga. The text granted Kirk the Twentieth and the tribe of Boggerts Blue a tract of land forever and one day. At the bottom was a sketch of the land. Burga stood, looked around and found the two landmarks the map used to identify the land.

He sat down and grinned at Big Jeanne. "This treaty means Count Lazlo is a lawbreaker. I'll have to arrest him the next time I see him 'cause Duke Randolph made me a roamin' bailiff."

"Excellent," The Royal said. "See to it," he added as he walked away.

"What did the boggerts do to earn the land treaty?"

"We helped Duke Billy crush a rebellion."

"But how?" Burga frowned. He had trouble picturing the boggerts in battle.

"I'll show you." Big Jeanne whistled a two-tone note and a dozen boggerts fetched small bows. She found a piece of loose bark from a white birch tree and propped it against another tree on the far side of the clearing. In turn, each archer shot an arrow. Every missile pierced the bark, but none stuck in the tree behind the target.

"Good shootin'," Burga said. "But what harm'll those little arrows do to Lazlo's troops?"

"Not his troops," Big Jeanne replied, "his horses. The animals get flighty when we shoot the arrows at their withers. Often, the horses throw their riders. Or stampede away from the fight."

"Ahh." Burga smiled.

Big Jeanne ordered an archer to fetch an acorn. When the boggert returned and placed the nut on the ground, Big Jeanne pulled out her war hammer. "Imagine this is a soldier's toe or instep." She smashed the nut and pieces flew in all directions. "We hide alongside a path and jump out to attack the soldiers' feet. They don't fight very well on one foot." She looked Burga in the eye. "Our problem is we can't do it alone. We need big-feet to draw the attention of the enemy away from us. Without big-feet, the enemy will look for us and that makes it hard to surprise them."

Burga beamed and slapped his knees. He knew how to finish plumping his resume, and, for good measure, to get Gerhilde to grovel.

# # #

With the sun not yet over the treetops, Burga waited on the hill while Big Jeanne organized and positioned the boggert warriors. She placed a contingent of boggerts alongside the path to the crest. Further up, she positioned a dozen archers in the lower branches of trees.

While the boggerts prepared, Burga faced the possibility of defeat. The boggerts were convinced they could make a difference in the outcome of the battle; he wasn't so sure. Today would end either with his promotion or his death. He took his apron from the saddlebag and donned it. If he fell today, he'd fall wearing the apron to say that here lies a Warrior-Cook. He loosened the stoppers on a few spice jars as a precaution.

Success would bring different problems. Princess Gerhilde would be furious and accuse him of making another attempt to rescue her. If she didn't recognize the reality of the situation, he wouldn't accumulate the necessary credits to finish his probationary period.

A chirping sound from below alerted him. He shook his wrists to loosen them up and seized Frya and Flippa. He stationed himself in the middle of the clearing and prepared his mind for battle by recalling the recipes for his favorite dishes: meals he would never prepare again if he died. Slowly, a great rage at Lazlo built up. How dare that fanatic threaten to shorten his culinary life?

He pawed the ground like a war charger.

Two mounted soldiers appeared at the edge of the clearing riding in front of Lazlo. Six horsemen and a dozen foot soldiers followed the Count. Burga raised an eyebrow. Big Jeanne better be as good as she claimed.

"There he is," Lazlo yelled. "He who would deny Lester His temple. Seize him and bring him back to the castle. I'll question him about his faith before I put him to the sword."

The leading riders pushed forward.

Burga calculated attack angles.

Behind Lazlo, curses and shouts erupted. The half-dozen riders bounced and floundered as their mounts sidestepped, whinnied and jumped. Two riders fell out of the saddle and another mount broke from the column and charged into the woods with its rider sawing at the reins.

Shouts and screams came from the foot soldiers. Their formation became ragged.

"*Rutabaga*!" Burga roared the day's war cry and attacked the horse on his left. He cracked the animal in the head with Frya. The stunned horse collapsed on its front forelegs, throwing the rider. He crashed onto the ground and groaned.

"You fools!" Lazlo roared. "Get him! For Lester's greater glory."

Burga whirled on the second rider. The skillet blocked a sword stroke. He thrust Flippa forward and its blunt front edge connected with the pit of the rider's stomach. The rider gurgled and doubled up. A blow to the back of his head from Frya knocked the the rider out of the saddle.

More screams came from the foot soldiers.

Burga glared at Lazlo and strode forward. He shoved Flippa into its holster.

"You dare to strike Lester's defenders?" Lazlo drew his sword. "Your fate is sealed."

Lazlo hacked with his sword. Burga swatted the thrust away with Frya, grabbed his bottle of cayenne pepper and thumbed off the stopper. He threw the spice into Lazlo's face. Lazlo screamed in pain. Burga jumped, bear-hugged him, pulled him out of the saddle and threw him to the ground. "Yield."

"Spare me," Lazlo gasped between sneezes. "I must be about Lester's divine mission." He knuckled his streaming eyes.

"I arrest you for violatin' the treaty between the Boggerts Blue and the Duke."

"Lester's needs . . . (sneeze) . . . take precedent over an earthly treaty. Especially . . . (sneeze) . . . a treaty with creatures who are unworthy of . . . (sneeze) . . . Lester's grace and love."

Burga grabbed Lazlo's collar and yanked him to his feet while he pulled out his spatula. "Order your men to disarm." Burga jammed the razor-sharp edge of Flippa against his neck. He applied enough pressure to open a cut. Blood trickled down Lazlo's neck.

"Cease and . . . (sneeze) . . . desist!" Lazlo's voice cracked as he gave the order.

"Throw down your arms," Burga yelled. "Or I turn your count inna steaks and chops."

After some hesitation, the men dropped their swords and Burga relaxed slightly. One problem – the easier one – solved. Now, for the tough one: Princess Gerhilde.

\# \# \#

Burga crossed the drawbridge and rode into the castle courtyard. Lazlo, red-faced and swollen-eyed, rode with his hands tied at the wrists. Behind Burga, the disarmed soldiers trudge across the bridge. Many needed assistance to walk. The castle guards, confused by the procession, gathered in a ragged formation and awaited developments.

"Disarm them," Burga said to Lazlo.

"Sergeant," Lazlo called out. "Lester demands that your men ground their arms."

The sour-faced sergeant gave the order and the guards dropped their swords and axes.

Burga spotted a servant. "Collect the arms and lock them up."

Princess Gerhilde walked down the steps in front of the keep. "Why are you back?" she said in an icy voice. She stood with her hands on her hips.

"I arrested Count Lazlo and I'm securing the castle." Burga had trouble concealing his agitation. What would she do? How would she react to his plan?

"That's a rather desperate way to rescue me." She glared at him.

"I'm not rescuing you, Princess. Count Lazlo violated a ducal treaty. Since I defeated and arrested him, I'm the warder for the castle until Duke Rudolph appoints a replacement." Burga took a deep breath. "As warder, I'm releasing all Lazlo's prisoners, including you. You are free to return to your father's castle without paying the ransom. Good day,

Princess." He found the chief servant and said, "Release any other prisoners."

He spurred his horse towards the stables.

"Wait," Gerhilde's voice sounded unsure.

"Yes." Burga halted the horse, took a deep breath and turned his head.

"How am I supposed to get to my father's castle?"

"I don't know." Burga shrugged. "I'm too busy to help. I have to deliver Lazlo to the Duke."

Gerhilde chewed on her upper lip.

"I have an idea." Burga reached over and took a purse from Lazlo's waist. He shook out three silver pennies and handed them to Gerhilde. "There's a village about a mile down the road. This money will buy a room for the night and, in the mornin', you can hire a cart to take you home."

"A cart? You jest."

"Ride a cart or walk. Those are your choices."

"I'd be disgraced in either event. Going home without an escort is . . . so ordinary."

"I can't think of anythin' else to do."

"I can. Take me with you to the Duke and then escort me home."

"Me?" Burga managed to look surprised. "I'm just a foreign-born peasant."

"I . . . spoke rudely and in haste. I apologize." Gerhilde gave him a blazing smile. "Please?"

Burga pulled a face, stared into space and rubbed his chin while he counted the number of drops of olive oil needed to fill a tablespoon. When he finished, he said, "All right. I'll have a horse saddled and we'll ride out after I take care of a few chores."

Gerhilde smiled.

"But only if you swear that I rescued you."

She started, frowned and hesitated a few seconds before nodding her acceptance.

He dismounted and followed a servant into the kitchen, where he restocked his dwindling supplies. He also chose a few bottles of wine. Once he got rid of Lazlo, he planned to prepare delicious meals for Gerhilde while they traveled. The wine could lead to a marriage proposal.

When he returned to the courtyard, Big Jeanne and a dozen boggert warriors trotted over the drawbridge.

Burga hoisted her up and put her on his shoulder. He faced the castle staff and guards. "Until I return, Big Jeanne is in charge of the castle. Everyone kneel and swear an oath to obey her orders as if they came from me. When I return, anyone who violated the oath'll answer to me."

While the staff and soldiers dropped to one knee, he whispered to Big Jeanne, "Don't eat all the furniture."

THE BIG BANG

Brodwin stood up and bumped his head on a ceiling beam. While rubbing the back of his head, he held out his new wand for the other wizards to see. "Developed it myself." As if to emphasize its power, he slammed the table with the butt of the four-foot long, shillelagh-like hunk of blackthorn wood sending the wine cups and pitchers jumping and wobbling.

Five wizards including Cenwig, the Grand Wizard, sat in a dimly lit tavern in the city of Dun Hythe. They squinted through the gloom to make out details of the wand. "It's ugly," said a plump wizard.

"I prefer a short, slender wand," said another. "They're more elegant and they speak of sophistication."

"Why is it so bulky?" Cenwig asked.

"It can store more spells and hold more magical power," Brodwin replied, "because it's much thicker than the usual model."

"I don't see any reason to break with tradition," Cenwig said.

Brodwin bristled at the man's belittling voice. But then, Cenwig's jealousy always led the man to disparage Brodwin's accomplishments. "It has other advantages."

"Like what?" the plump wizard asked.

"It can be used as a walking stick and it makes an admirable blunt instrument."

Cenwig pulled the two wine pitchers close and peered into them. "Two more empties." He waggled a hand over his head with two fingers extended and looked at Brodwin. "There is no place for radicalism in wizardry. The conservative ways are best."

"Bah! Stuck in the past." Brodwin sneered at Cenwig. "All of you."

A shapely serving girl carrying two pitchers of wine, dodged a groping hand, and, with an astonishing display of agility, stuck an elbow into the ear of the hand's owner. She placed the pitchers on the table and stomped her heel on the groper's foot as she left with the empties.

"Whose turn is it?" a wizard asked.

"Brodwin's," the would-be-groper said as he massaged his ear.

"What vintage and year do we want this time?" Brodwin moved the two pitchers to his side of the table. The wizards always bought the dregs of the wine kegs, the cheapest wine available.

"Surprise us," Cenwig said. "Use your powerful new wand."

All the wizards laughed.

Brodwin pushed his belly button-length white beard to one side and stuck the wand into a pitcher. He swirled the burgundy-colored wine and hope the immature and still erratic wand would respond properly. He did the same with the second pitcher while Cenwig stared at him to ensure he didn't mumble a spell to help the wand.

"Green wine?" the plump wizard pointed to the first pitcher.

Cenwig sniffed it and cackled. "Tea." He tested the second pitcher and grinned at Brodwin. "Prune juice. You never were any good at magic and your wonderful new wand is no better."

"It just needs more experience." Brodwin felt annoyed that he had to defend his wand, but then Cenwig somehow always managed to get under his skin. "So it'll know which spell to launch."

"I know the very thing." Cenwig snapped his fingers. "A quest to season the wand. It's a Trade Road problem. Bandits, as you might expect."

Brodwin gnashed his teeth because Cenwig had him cornered. He couldn't openly refuse the quest offered by his superior without losing a great deal of prestige. The man deserved an enchanted enema, but there were too many witnesses. Still, he pictured Cenwig running for an outhouse with his robe flapping about his rotund body. He smiled at the image.

"The road's been cut by a bandit chieftain called Heafoc." Cenwig smiled at Brodwin. "There's no need to tell you how dependent our fair city of Dun Hythe is on the Trade Road. The alternate routes are so much longer that Dun Hythe will soon run out of supplies. Many taverns are already out of mead."

"What!" A wizard exclaimed. "No mead. I pour it on my oatmeal every morning."

Brodwin raised an eyebrow. Cenwig never cared a fig about Dun Hythe in the past. Why the sudden clamor over supplies? Something didn't smell right.

"I charge you to eliminate this menace," Cenwig continued. "Immediately. Lest the women and children suffer."

"Sorry. I'm, booked." Brodwin felt relieved as he recalled a previous appointment. "I have to stop a war between two princes down south." He filled his wine mug with tea and took a sip. It tasted like dish water spiked with vinegar.

"Overruled. This is a priority assignment. Besides, wars take time to organize and this mission will only take a day."

Brodwin weaved his fingers through his beard. Cenwig always gave him assignments like this one because he knew that Brodwin's magical talents didn't extend to field magic. Set-piece magic was his forte; spells he could memorize and practice. Like pulling a rabbit out of a hat. He simply couldn't master the impromptu and creative spell casting needed to survive in the field. It would be a dangerous mission made doubly so because he knew from the past that Cenwig always concealed vital information about the assignments. "What haven't you told me?"

"Nothing," Cenwig replied. "I've told you everything the mayor told me when he asked for the Guild to help."

"What do you know about this Haefoc?"

"After he captures the wagons, he demands a ransom from the drivers. If they don't -- or can't -- pay up, the wagons are burned." Cenwig shrugged. "Other then that, Haefoc is just another thug as far as I know."

Brodwin didn't like the smirk on Cenwig's face while he talked about Haefoc. He was sure Cenwig lied.

"Oh, bye the bye," Cenwig said. His smile sent a dagger of fear stabbing into Brodwin's heart. "There is a food convoy leaving for Dun Hythe in the morning. It'll use the

Trade Road, so make sure you eliminate the gang by early afternoon. That will ensure the convoy gets through."

# # #

Early in the next morning, Brodwin paused deep into the forest on the west side of the Trade Road. He scanned the underbrush for signs of bandits. Midges and greenbottles swarmed around his head. Perceiving no danger, he edged further along the game trail, careful to place his sandals to minimize noise. Each step released an earthy reek of mold and decayed leaves. The air in the forest smelled musty as if it had been trapped by the ancient, sinister-looking oak and hickory trees. Canopies of interlaced leaves kept the sunlight from reaching the ground and the area glowed with a preternatural green light. Whenever a ray of the late morning sunshine eluded the leafy filters, a golden shaft shimmered brightly.

After ducking under a half-fallen tree, he stopped to knead his aching thigh muscles. "Plague take Cenwig for getting me into this mess," he groused aloud. The ignominy of it all. He, a famous wizard-arbitrator who had negotiated the end of numerous wars and prevented plenty of others from starting, assigned to carry out a foray that should be handled by a squadron of knights.

He clutched the rough, burled shaft belted at his waist, but it didn't offer an comfort. Someday, songs would be written about his wand. Right now, it was too magically unpredictable to be relied upon.

Near his head, a round portal appeared. "Hey," a voice said as the wooden door swung open. "Need anythin'? I'm goin' out for a bite to eat."

"You can't leave," Brodwin said in a whisper. "I suspect I'll need your assistance before long. And do lower your voice. Bandits and fell creatures live in this forest."

"Drat." The door slammed shut and the portal disappeared.

He rounded a clump of white birches and spotted trouble. A hag leaned against a hawthorn tree in a small clearing. "Good day, Madam." Brodwin drew his wand and watched her, alert for hostile activity.

"Looking for someone?" She wore a ragged, knee-length brown dress and wood-soled sandals. Her gray hair stuck out in random spikes, an indication of magical power leakage. Her wrinkled face formed into a gap-toothed smile.

"Bandits, actually. You wouldn't know where Haefoc is would you?"

"You really don't want to meet him." She shook her head. "Trust me."

"I have to meet with him." Brodwin drew his wand. "Are you going to help me?"

"No." She stared into his eyes, challenging him.

Brodwin aimed his wand and a fiery comet exploded from its tip. The fire ball left a wake of sparks, but just before it reached the target the sparks changed to a wake of yellow petals and a dozen butter-colored roses smacked into the crone's chest. She caught the bouquet with one hand, winked at Brodwin and snapped her fingers.

He heard a loud crack over his head and jumped to his left, but not quick enough. A large tree limb landed on his

right foot. Brodwin howled in pain and hopped in circles –
sunwise – with his injured foot in the air. When the ache
subsided, he faced a seductive, much younger woman
clothed in a clinging green dress. In her left hand she held a
porcelain vase with the roses.

The beauty of the raven-haired woman dazzled Brodwin
momentarily and he almost didn't notice the brick whizzing
toward his head. He ducked and the missile brushed his ear
as it whistled passed.

Her shape change and the quickness of her spells indicated that he faced a powerful sorceress. He muttered a spell
to check her magical signature and gasped at the intensity of
her aura. It indicated a strength equal to his own. His reputation depended on reducing or eliminating her power. So
did his life.

A desperate ploy came to mind. Advanced theoretical
occultism held that black and white magics possessed opposite polarities and offered the potential for spontaneous com-
bustion. According to this theory, if a quantity of unspelled
magic of one persuasion encountered an unspelled quantity
of the opposite polarity, the magics would annihilate each
other in a process called the Big Bang. No one knew just
what the Big Bang entailed because no wizards were insane
enough to volunteer to test the theory. Until now. It was his
only chance to neutralize her and it didn't require field magic, only mental and magical fortitude. It would be his white
magic against the hag's black.

To achieve the annihilation, he had to organize his magical reservoir into a single lump and release it before she
launched a retaliatory spell to divert the lump. He had to
hold her attention for the few moments he needed to gather

his magical resources. He tucked the wand under his left arm and limped to his right. She moved sensuously in the opposite direction. Both stared into the others eyes. "What's your name?"

"Carla, not that it's any of your business."

"The earth is round, you know."

"Twit. Everyone knows that."

He pushed his magical power into a glob. It squirmed and tried to burst through the fissures in the boundaries.

Carla extended her open hand.

Brodwin flinched even though no brick flew at his head.

"Nervous, aren't you?"

"The earth revolves around the sun."

"One of them moves and I don't care which one it is."

He continued to shape his magic and the mass became more compliant. He was almost ready! "The moon is made of dirt and rocks."

"What rot!" Carla raised her eyebrows. "Everyone knows it's made of yogurt."

Brodwin unleashed a tsunami of unspelled magical power.

"What the--" Carla held up a hand to stem the onrushing power.

Brodwin sensed the awesome power he had unleashed. It gathered speed as if attracted by her opposite polarity. It had a shape of a monstrous bird of prey and was solid enough to leave a shadow on the ground as it flew toward its target. A moment later, his world filled with a collage of bizarre hues and sounds that threatened to shatter the confines of his brain. He soared backward, landing on his back. He struggled to catch his breath and get his eyes in focus.

Wisps of flames licked at parts of his beard. He smothered them and ran a hand over his face to check for damage. His eyebrows were burned off. Again.

Over the site of the Big Bang, an untidy rainbow of unprimary colors hung in the sky. Embers of occult particles filled the air with a stench like Limburger cheese and gave it an acidic taste. A large oak tree carried daffodil blossoms instead of leaves while another dripped with heavy bunches of lilacs. Many small trees stood upside down with their roots waving in the breeze and the grass in the clearing swirled with red and blue hues.

Without a reservoir of magic, he felt strange, almost hollow.

Carla, back in her hag shape, lay in a heap. The smoke from her scorched hair produced a black halo around her soot-covered face and her eyes rolled independently of each other.

He smoothed his charred beard. His new problem was what to do with a shape-shifter. He needed her as an escort, but once she regained some magical power, she could escape, leaving him lost and isolated in the forest. He'd have to try a novel approach and hoped it worked.

Brodwin snapped his fingers twice before the portal reappeared and opened. "I need my old prayer rope."

"Be right back," the voice answered. For the next few minutes, Brodwin heard drawers opening and slamming shut. "Here it is." A two-foot hunk of thin cord filled with small knots sailed out of the portal as the door closed and it disappeared.

Carla, now conscious, watched him as he tied her hands together. "Do you think this will hold me?"

"If you shape-shift, you'll lose your hands." It was all bluff because he had no idea what would happen if she changed. He hoped Carla didn't have any experience with prayer cords and so wouldn't be willing to risk changing. "Pity you didn't stay as the younger woman. Travel would have been more pleasant."

"Liked her, did you?" Carla cackled. "Maybe you'll see her again later on."

"Now, take me to Haefoc."

"Are you sure? Most people, even wizards, don't want to meet a dragon."

Brodwin opened and closed his mouth a few times. "Dragon? Haefoc is a dragon?" Cenwig had neglected to mention that fact. That was the meaning behind Cenwig's smile when he talked about Haefoc being just another thug.

He stared at Carla, bewildered. On the assumption that dragons verged on extinction, he had skipped most of the dragonlore lectures in Wizardry College. As a consequence, he possessed a negligible knowledge of dragons. The only way he passed his final exams was to use an out-of-body spell to read what the smartest student answered on the dragon questions.

#

Brodwin followed Carla along a forest path while he pondered Cenwig's elegant trap. Quitting the mission would severely damage his reputation, but would save his life. Not that it would be worth living after Cenwig spread an exaggerated account of his failure over the scryer network; his reputation would be ruined. Continuing the mission could mean his death, but there was a slight chance he could pull it off. The spiteful man had been unusually clever in designing this snare. Caught between the two ridiculous conclusions, he chose possible death over the certainty of watching Cenwig gloat about his failure.

That decision made, he dredged his mind for bits of dragonlore.

"Where'd the rope come from?" Carla held up her hands to show the prayer cord.

Brodwin shook his head to clear his thoughts. "I once saved an imp from a dreadful, but much deserved, death. He's served me ever since. Balthasar stays in my tower and uses an enchanted portal to follow me around. Whenever I need something, he fetches it."

He trailed Carla along an animal trail for what seemed miles. His toe grew worse as he walked and eventually, he could no longer match Carla's pace. "Slow down," he called out to her.

She laughed and continued to draw away, forcing Brodwin to use his wand as a cane to help him negotiate the rough trail.

A bit further on, she stopped and waited for him to catch up. She pointed ahead and cackled, "My coworkers."

"Stars above!" Brodwin gawked at a pair of sword-wielding trolls. He snapped his fingers and held out his hand. "My sword please. And do hurry." His mind seethed, searching for a plan to trick them, the only way he could survive this encounter.

The door appeared and a skinny, green hand reached out with a sword. "Two trolls? I need a new master, 'cause you're dead meat." The portal disappeared.

"Ya finished foolin' around?" a troll asked.

Brodwin, his mouth too dry to answer, nodded.

One troll moved forward while the second circled behind him. Barely five foot high, both possessed huge shoulders and thick arms. A greasy length of rope served as a belt to hold up their ragged pants.

He tried to think of a stratagem, but their closeness made it difficult to concentrate. Their body odor alone made his brain cells freeze up.

Carla whistled encouragement to the trolls and snapped her fingers.

The first troll closed and swung his sword. Brodwin parried the blow, but an electric-like shock of pain surged throughout his arm and shoulder.

The second charged. Brodwin squealed in terror, dropped to the ground and rolled away. The sword whistled over his head so close it gave him a partial haircut. It thwacked into an oak tree. Brodwin scrambled to his feet and raised his weapon.

The first troll watched the second who had both feet against the tree, his body parallel to the ground while he worked the sword hilt to free the blade wedged into the tree. When the sword came free, the troll thumped onto the ground. He leaped up, screamed in rage at Brodwin and charged.

Brodwin couldn't fend off another blow, not with his still quivering arm. A cunning strategy came to mind. Despite overwhelming evidence to the contrary, trolls believed themselves smart creatures and were always trying to convince people of their intelligence. He stuck the point of his sword into the dirt and held up his right hand. "Truce?"

The charging troll skidded to a halt, his blade poised to decapitate Brodwin, and looked at his companion. Both looked puzzled.

"I have a problem. Everyone knows how clever trolls are so I think this problem will be a snap for you two."

"Clever?" Carla gasped. "These two?"

"Me fix problem," the second troll said. "Me cut off yer head." He drew back his weapon.

"If you kill me before I solve this problem, I'll come back and haunt you." Trolls were known to fear ghosts.

The troll dropped his arm and glanced at his companion. Both showed plenty of white around their eyes. "What kinda problem?"

"Arithmetic. I have to add seven and nine and I can't get the right answer. After we solve the problem we can go back to hacking and slashing."

The trolls dropped their swords and the second one said, "Hold up fingers."

Carla sat down with her back to a tree trunk and took a nap.

The first troll held up his fingers and the second started counting. "One . . . two . . . four . . . three . . . seven." As he ticked off each number, he turned down one of his partners fingers. "What da next number?"

"Nine."

"One . . . two . . . five . . . er . . . three . . . two." After exhausting his mate's fingers, he turned down his own using his chin as a pointer. "Six . . . four . . . nine." Then he mis-counted the fingers not turned down. "Da answer's five."

"No." Brodwin shook his head. "I tried that number."

"Stupid troll!" The first troll backhanded the second across the face. "Ya too dumb ta do numbers."

The second responded with a wicked punch to the stomach. "Me not stupid."

The first, his yellowish skin turning red, landed a fist on the other's nose.

While the two grappled, cursed, kicked, punched, bit, snarled and yelped, Brodwin snapped his fingers a number of times before the portal appeared. "I need two lengths of rope."

Two ropes sailed out of the door before it slammed and disappeared.

One troll slumped to the ground.

"Congratulations," Brodwin said to the semiconscious winner. He gave the troll a whack in the head with his wand. After tying their hands, he woke up Carla.

Carla looked at the trussed up trolls. "Maybe you're not so dumb."

"Shall we push on? We'll leave these two behind."

# # #

While they marched, Brodwin analyzed his situation. Besides his lack of dragonlore, he no longer possessed any magical power and it would be more than a day before his magic reservoir replenished itself. The power stored in the wand was too unreliable to be useful. From the troll fight and the traveling, his physical state bordered on exhaustion. He had an injured foot and numerous aches and bruises. All he had left was his negotiating skills. He vaguely remembered hearing that dragons were intelligent creatures. If so, perhaps he could reason with Haefoc. If so, he could still complete the mission and foil Cenwig's diabolical plan. Provided the beastie wasn't hungry.

With his inward focus, he didn't notice that Carla had stopped until he bumped into her.

"Oaf! Watch where you're walking."

"Why did you stop?"

"We're here." Carla pointed to a cave in the side of hill.

Brodwin gulped. He shivered because the back of his neck felt as if an icy hand gripped it. His stomach felt as if he had swallowed a few rocks. He stood up straighter and squared his shoulders; better to face a hungry dragon than a triumphant Cenwig. He waved Carla ahead. "I'll be right behind you." He drew his wand.

Using his wand to support himself, he climbed the hill with the last of his energy. Gasping for breath, he passed through a low opening. Inside a few torches burned in holders and provided enough light to see all the roomy cave. It had a nauseating stench of rotten garbage and what he assumed was dragon spoor.

"Whatzis!" The sleeping Haefoc roused himself and looked around. He flicked his tail sending pebbles and garbage hurtling around the cave. "Why are you tied up?"

"I captured her, defeated your trolls and now I have come for you." Brodwin hoped his voice didn't betray his false sense of bravado.

"A wizard! A skinny one at that." Haefoc tapped a claw on the ground.

Brodwin sought a negotiating edge. Ignoring the dryness in his mouth, he examined the red and green dragon. About twelve feet long with small, thin armor plates, Haefoc could be either a mature small one or a young large one. He recalled another wizard bragging about tricking a young and inexperienced dragon, but if Haefoc was mature, that same trick would result in a fatal disaster.

Haefoc stood up and shook himself. His armor plates made an unearthly din as they banged around.

Brodwin saw a few coins scattered beneath the dragon's stomach. Even he knew dragons made beds from their treasure. Since Heafoc had hardly any wealth at all, he must be young. Finally, information he could use.

"Good-bye, wizard." Haefoc turned his snout towards Brodwin. Black smoke leaked from the beast's mouth and flames licked at the edges of his teeth.

Brodwin sobbed. He wouldn't live long enough to use his new knowledge. He instinctively held up his wand as a protective shield. He gave a startled cry when it launched a spell. The recoil almost caused Brodwin to drop the wand. A ball of water flew at the dragon and disappeared into his maw. A hissing sound came from Haefoc's stomach and steam replaced the black smoke. The dragon blinked several times and belched.

"You have managed to add a few minutes to your life span which you will regret." Haefoc moved closer. "Because your death will be that much slower."

Brodwin realized the inadvertent spell had gave him the few seconds necessary to save himself. "Sorry about the spell, but I had to stop you from making a bad business decision. Actually, from making a second bad business decision."

"What are you talking about?"

"First, I have to explain a thing or two."

"Make it quick. I am famished and if you're merely stalling I will chop off your legs and arms first to prolong your agony."

"On my way here, I didn't know if you were young and inexperienced or old and stupid. Now I see your problems stem from youth."

"A wizard should know better than to insult a dragon." Haefoc scratched a claw on the stone floor. The screeching sound sent shivers up Brodwin's spine. "Now I'll eat your arms and legs in small bites."

"An experienced dragon wouldn't be in the predicament you're in."

"What do you mean?" Haefoc's tail cleaned a portion of the floor.

"Why are you attacking wagons?"

"To get gold, of course. I am starting out and have to build up my horde."

"Ahh, gold."

"You are stalling and this conversation is irksome."

"I suppose when you first started out, this was a lucrative enterprise?"

"Very."

"And business has slowed down, has it?"

"Actually," Haefoc stopped swishing his tail, "we haven't seen a wagon in almost a week."

"That's because the merchants are using different routes to ship their goods."

Haefoc scowled at Brodwin.

"You got a bit of gold early on, but you missed the main chance. If you had set up a business to protect the merchants on the Trade Road instead of robbing them, your cave would be filling up with gold."

"What are you talking about?"

"The Trade Road is the quickest and cheapest route for merchants to get their products to and from Dun Hythe, but it runs through a forest seething with bandits. I'll offer my services to negotiate a deal with the merchants because I think there is still time to get you a deal."

"You better explain."

"Of course."

# # #

Three days later, Brodwin chuckled at Cenwig's fury.

Brodwin had just finished describing how the merchants now paid Haefoc one gold coin for every wagon that used the Trade Road. In return, the dragon and his minions guaranteed the wagons would be free from bandits attacks throughout the length of the forest.

"Actually, I must thank you for giving me this assignment. I'm now Haefoc's business manager and I'll get a fee from all his new ventures." He snapped his fingers twice and portal appeared. "Give me a copy of the flyer."

A hand extended out of the portal holding a small piece of parchment. "Careful. The ink may not be all dried," Balthasar said before slamming the door.

Brodwin handed the parchment to Cenwig. "Our newest venture."

Cenwig glanced at the flyer. "What the stars is 'Deconstruction Services'?"

"The city has lot of decrepit buildings and it started a program to knock them down and build now ones. It takes a lot of time and labor to knock down an old house, but Haefoc can do it in less than an hour. He lands on the roof, stomps down the whole structure then burns the debris. His minions see that the fire doesn't spread. This service will mint money for us. And of course, because of you, I met Carla."

Carla, in her eye-popping younger form, smiled at Cenwig. "Isn't he the smartest wizard you ever met?"

Cenwig made a sour face.

"Shall we go?" Brodwin turned to Carla.

"Where are you going?" Cenwig growled.

"To stop the war before it starts." Brodwin winked at his adversary. "Then, Carla and I will take an extended vacation."

"While on vacation, we plan to write a paper on the Big Bang." Carla grinned at Cenwig. "We'll jointly present it at the next Advanced Theoretical Occultism Symposium."

"I'll send you a ticket to the Symposium," Brodwin said with a chuckle.

THE QUEEN'S HERO

PART ONE

Enric Knef, captain of the brig *Rosebud*, climbed to the quarterdeck and surveyed the Sea of Gundarland. Two-foot waves rocked the ship in a gentle motion as it sailed east toward the island of Bermid. From what he could see in the predawn half-light, the sea was free of other ships. He smoothed his lemon-colored caftan. Tucked into his belt were a pair of throwing axes. Like many dwarfs, he braided his beard and dyed each of the three braids a different color. He checked on the lookout. The sailor had one arm wrapped around the mast and studied the eastern horizon.

Ragazza, his navigator, stepped out of the hatchway onto the main deck. She sniffed the air in all four directions then climbed the stairs to join Enric. She was an elf, tall and slender. Her six-foot height doubled Enric's and her silver hair contrasted with his dark brown, her green eyes with his brown. She wore sea boots and a sky-blue robe decorated with weather symbols: the sun, storm clouds, rain and snow. "We're about to have a visitor," she said by way of greeting.

Enric glared at her. His broad nostrils flared and he clenched his fists.

"No," she added, "it isn't Egor. As far as I can see, the pirate is nowhere around here."

"Ahh," Enric chuckled. "I was about to have the crew load the cannon." The *Rosebud* possessed four small cannons mounted in pairs at the bow and the stern. "So who's the visitor?"

"I don't know." Ragazza shrugged. "Whoever it is, he's still over the horizon. He's adrift in a small boat."

"Let's see who it is. Perhaps, we'll earn a reward. The Fates know we deserve it."

Ragazza sketched runes in the air with both hands. The wind shifted direction and the ship curved to the south.

# # #

Knuben Bullard raised his head and glanced around the horizon. He shuddered at the pain caused by turning his sunburnt neck. His face, neck and hands were blistered and raw. He saw nothing, but then he couldn't see very far from his current position, flat on his back in a small rowboat. He feared the rising sun. This was his third day without food and water and he knew he wouldn't see the sun set. His will to live ebbed as fast his physical strength did. At least, he wasn't seasick, probably because his stomach had been empty for so long.

What an inglorious end to his short career. A week ago, he had taken a position in the court of Queen Sheena, the ruler of Sulvaria. Given an assignment by her, his efforts had ended in a disaster. The only good thing about his present situation was that it spared him the embarrassment of telling the queen about his non-achievement.

He dozed off for a time and, when he awoke, he spotted a shadow on the horizon. Knuben frowned. It looked too square to be a storm cloud and it was purple, not black. He decided he was hallucinating. Not a good sign.

When he awoke the next time, the shadow had moved close enough so that he could see a sail. What kind of ship flew a purple sail? He squinted and discerned a pink hull.

The bizarre ship sailed straight at him, and, at the last minute, dropped its mainsail. It flew a strange flag that looked like it was made of needlepoint. The ship coasted to a stop and a scruffy-looking, partially bald dwarf appeared at the rail. "Ahoy the boat," he called out. "Anyone alive down there?"

Knuben forced himself to sit up and almost fainted from the pain. He flapped a hand, unable to answer because his mouth was so dry.

"Catch the rope," the sailor yelled. He twirled a rope over his head a few times and hurled it. The rope landed across Knuben's body. He grasped it, groaning at the intense pain of curling his fingers around the rope. Three more dwarfs joined the first and pulled on the rope until the rowboat was alongside the ship. One of them dropped a rope ladder and scrambled down it to help Knuben slowly climb to the deck. He moved and felt like an old man. He reached the deck with the last of his strength and sat down as if his bones were made of liquid. The first dwarf handed him a ladle of water. Knuben slurped it up, spilling much of down his chin. The water felt glorious against his tongue and cracked lips. He felt the terrifying specter of death walk away.

"I'm Ardnt, the bosun," the dwarf said, refilling the ladle from a bucket. "Drink this one a bit slower." Ardnt was taller than the other crew-dwarfs and clean-shaven except for a line of dark hair around his mouth and chin.

Knuben sipped the second ladle while examining his surroundings. The sails really were purple although much of the dye had been leached out by the sea and rain. Close up, they appeared speckled.

"Ardnt," a deep voice called from the stern. "Bring him aft."

The bosun waved a hand in front of his face in a parody of a salute. "Need any help standing up?" he asked Knuben.

Knuben grasped the rail with one hand and pulled himself up. The water had revived him wonderfully and he felt alive for the first time since his disastrous meeting with the pirate admiral, Egor. He took a few steps and managed not to fall on his face despite his staggering gait. He climbed the stairs to the quarterdeck and froze at the sight of the dwarf standing by the wheel.

"What's your problem?" the dwarf growled. "You never see a dwarf in a yellow caftan before?"

Besides the bright caftan, the dwarf had three earrings in each ear and enough bejeweled, gold bracelets to buy a castle. "Er . . . no." Knuben forced his brain to work. "It's the beard."

"What about my beard?" The dwarf eyed him suspiciously and Knuben sensed he was about to get thrown overboard.

"The colors. I've never seen such brilliant colors in a beard."

"Ahh. I make the dye myself." He patted the red, blue and white beard curls, setting his bracelets jingling. "Welcome aboard the *Rosebud*. I'm Captain Enric. And you are?"

"His name is Knuben," the female elf said.

Knuben was surprised she knew his name. He studied her for a moment as a vague memory stirred in his mind. "Ragasi? No, it's . . . Ragazza."

"So, you remember me." She gave him a radiant smile. "I'm Enric's navigator and weather witch."

"Where do you two know each other from?" Enric asked.

"When I went to Sorcery School, Knuben attended the college across the road."

"And what college might that be?" Enric asked Knuben.

"The Academy of Combat and Mechanical Arts," Knuben replied. "I'm a warrior-tinker and part of Queen Sheena's court. Or I was. I'm not sure of my status right now."

The crew raised the mainsail and the ship resumed its journey. It heeled against a wave and Knuben dashed to the rail and threw up most of the water. He wiped his lips and turned back to the dwarf.

"Come." Enric turned towards the stairs. "We'll go to my cabin and you can tell us the tale of why you were sun- nin' yourself in the rowboat."

Knuben followed Enric and Ragazza into a small, dark cabin beneath the quarterdeck. Light came from a large win- dow in the rear. Various weapons and nautical implements lay scattered around the room. On one wall hung a large portrait of a female dwarf and four dwarflings. Enric cleared a space on a chair by dumping a pile of clothes on the floor. The three of them sat at a table and Enric roared for a meal to be prepared for Knuben. "So," he chuckled. "Tell us your story."

"The Queen charged me to go to Bermid and collect her tax revenues. I did just that. My ship was anchored in the harbor, ready to sail in the morning. My orders were to sail the taxes across the Bermid channel to the mainland and hand it over to a wagon and a squadron of cavalry. That was a faster and safer way to get the taxes to her capital." He paused for a moment. "During the night, two small pirate ships sneaked up and attacked my ship. The crew and my soldiers surrendered. I fought alone until I was jumped from behind and taken down. The pirates tied me up and threw me at the feet of their leader."

"Who was a huge yuk named Egor, I'm sure," Ragazza said.

"You know him?" Knuben blinked in surprise.

"Egor?" Enric laughed. "He's the scourge of the Gundarland Sea. No ship is safe from him."

"This Egor stripped me of my armor, my sword, my shield and my boots. All he left me was my breeches and the tunic I'm wearing. He had his pirates lower the ship's boat and put me in it and cut it lose on the tide." Anger flooded Knuben's mind. He pounded a fist on the table and winced at the pain. "Someday, I'll teach him some manners."

"Many ship captains have sworn the same oath," Ragazza said. "In vain."

"How many soldiers did you have on the ship?" Enric asked.

"A dozen. I was supposed to have twenty-five, but the army minister only gave me a dozen. He said he couldn't afford to send more. They didn't do me much good."

"You needed a lot more than a dozen to protect the tax money from Egor." Enric smiled at Knuben. "In any event, you survived and the important thing about survivin' is that you have an opportunity to learn from your mistakes."

"I have to get back to court and tell the Queen what happened. Will you take me there?"

"Nay." Enric shook his head. "I'll not go further east than Bermid."

"Why not? I'm sure the Queen will give you a reward."

"Egor has a stronghold on an island southeast of Bermid. From there, he controls the whole eastern part of the sea. Only ships with a strong guard can get through without being captured or sunk."

A dwarf entered with a tray containing a bowl of broth and a plate of salted fish. Knuben didn't realize how famished he was until he smelled the food. Even with the rocking of the ship, he wanted to eat everything in sight.

"After you finish eating," Ragazza said as she stood up, "I'll show you around the ship. Meanwhile, I'll make a salve to put on your sunburn."

"I'll leave you to the food," Enric said. "I'll be on the quarterdeck." He followed Ragazza out of the cabin.

The fish and broth restored Knuben and allowed him to take stock of his situation. His plan to leverage a court position to gain career promotions was dust. He had naively hoped to advance in record time from his current rank of warrior-tinker to knight-tinker to knight-mechanic and then to the ultimate rank of hero-inventor. Now he'd be fortunate if the Queen didn't throw him in jail for losing her tax revenues.

# # #

PART TWO

Egor sat in his private quarters on the island of Ancora. In the sheltered bay of his stronghold, a dozen corsairs rode at anchor. He scratched a clump of dense black hair on his chest. The yuk pirate admiral stood five feet high, had green skin and was bald except for patches of hair scattered randomly about his body like raisins in a bowl of mushy peas. He had a large skull-and-cross-bones tattooed on his left biceps and a bloody sword on his right. He wore a pair of breeches made from old sailcloth and held up by a rope. His chest and feet were bare. Cruelty radiated from his black beady eyes and anyone caught in their glare felt like a rodent trapped by a snake.

He reached down and opened the chest he had stolen in Bermid. He cackled and ran a hand through the mass of silver pennies. It wasn't just the monetary value that elated him. The coins represented another step in his long-term plan to become the king of Sulvaria. Without Bermid's taxes, Queen Sheena would be hard-pressed to pay her troops and soldiers who weren't paid didn't stay in uniform too long. Meanwhile, he'd use the coins to hire more pirates and build more ships. As Sheena became weaker, he became stronger.

Egor stood, stretched his heavily muscled body and snorted as he recalled the ignorant puppy Sheena had sent to collect the taxes. Named Knobbin or something like that. Inexperienced, he hadn't posted enough guards to prevent a surprise attack. Then he had the gall to challenge him to a duel as if to make up for his errors. If the puppy had shown more respect, he'd still be among the living. He would have been released in Bermid with the rest of the crew. But Knobbin's lack of respect called for a penalty. By now, he must be dead from thirst and exposure.

He walked to a wall map depicting the Sea of Gundarland, his own private lake. Few captains sailed this sea without his permission, and he gave permission rarely these days. His strategy was to starve Sulvaria of customs duties and taxes to weaken it.

Everything was going according to plan, except for a single problem. He smashed a huge fist into a palm thinking about Enric. The dwarf openly defied him. Someday, soon, Enric would stand in these quarters wearing chains. It still rankled Egor that the dwarf refused to join his fleet even though he would have command of a squadron of corsairs. Despite orders to capture him, Enric had evaded his pirates because of his weather witch and his skills in ship-handling.

Egor disdained the large, slow brigs favored by merchants like Enric. He preferred the smaller, faster corsairs. Two or three of these nimble ships could easily run down and capture a much larger vessel, except Enric's. He always sold the captured ships to get cash to build more corsairs.

His success was a tribute to his earlier struggles. When he was only eight, Egor had signed on a fishing boat and he quickly developed a love of the sea. It was so much cleaner than the fetid marshland where he was born and raised. By age fifteen, he was captain of the boat, the previous captain having mysteriously disappeared. At first, he supplemented his fishing income with a bit of piracy, but it didn't take him long to realize that piracy was much more lucrative than fishing. It was also a lot more fun.

He forced his mind back to the map and reviewed his strategy. His corsairs were gathering in the harbor. Twenty more should be here in a day or two. Then they would all sail as a mighty fleet and capture the city of Bermid. Once the city fell, the rest of the island would capitulate as well. With Bermid in his hands, he planned to attack and conquer Sheena's capital and install himself as king. Then an interesting diversion would crop up. Sheena's three daughters were reputed to be beautiful even if they weren't yuks. He'd use them to stock his harem. Reports said Sheena was still attractive. Maybe he'd let her join the harem.

# # #

"These are called backstays," Ragazza said. She and Knuben stood together on the main deck as she pointed out various features of the two-masted brig. His chalky skin appearance had disappeared after she cast a mild seasickness spell on him.

"It isn't very different from the ship the queen gave me to collect the taxes. This one is a little bigger, I think."

Most of the crew-dwarfs ignored them and went about doing nautical chores such as tightening the rigging, stowing gear and cleaning the deck. Off-duty dwarfs sat in twos or threes in out-of-way spots.

Ragazza sneaked a look at Knuben. Taller than the elven males in her clan, he had broad shoulders and light brown hair. His handsome face featured blue eyes, a strong chin and a long straight nose. She had covered his bright red face, neck, feet, ankles, hands and wrists with a grayish paste. The paste gave off a strong odor of rotten fish guts, one of the primary ingredients.   Unlike most males she knew, including Enric and the crew, he spoke softly and politely, unusual traits in a trained warrior. Even after his horrid experience with Egor, he smiled easily and often.

"What are they doing?" Knuben's frown caught her by surprise. He pointed to two dwarfs sitting near the capstan.

"Knitting shawls." The needles flashed in the sun as the dwarfs manipulated them with blinding speed.

"Sailors do that?"

"Most don't. The ones that do tend to end up on the *Rosebud*. Enric is one of the few captains who tolerates his sailors knitting in their spare time." She indicated the flag flying from the mainmast. "The crew made that. And those three," she indicated another group sitting on the forward hatch, "are making a quilt. That one is carving an animal. The crew donate the stuff to an orphanage in Bermid."

Knuben grabbed a backstay and leaned back to study the rigging. "When I sailed to Bermid, that was my first time on a sailing ship. The sails and rigging, the block and tackle are fascinating to me as a tinker. Sailing ships really are incredible machines. Even if the motion makes me sick."

"I love the sea. Since I left home, the *Rosebud* has become my new home and the crew is now my family. I don't think I could ever live on land again."

Ragazza continued her guided tour of the ship. Near the bow, he said, "What kind of cargo does the *Rosebud* handle?"

"Almost anything that can be traded profitably and Enric needs lots of profits to feed a wife and four dwarflings. Right now, with Egor controlling the seas, there is a shortage of everything. Any cargo we carry will fetch high prices.

"I'm glad he's an honest merchant."

"Well, we're mostly honest, but the really big profits are in smuggled, illegal goods. Folks are willing to pay top price for pipeweed and yukeste."

"What's yukeste?"

"The national drink of yukland. It's so powerful that all the other countries ban it entirely. Naturally, that makes it even more desirable. A smuggled case of yukeste can fetch the crew's wages for an entire voyage." Ragazza saw Knuben's discomfort. "Very few folks in this world aren't guilty of some minor lawbreaking. Or perhaps I should say, law-bending."

"Still, the idea of being on a smuggler's ship bothers me."

"If governments didn't make stupid laws telling folks what they can do and can't do, there wouldn't be the need for smugglers. What makes our smuggling so lucrative is that the *Rosebud* is the last honest, well semi-honest, ship on the Sea of Gundarland. Egor has captured or sunk all the rest. We are the last free ship in this area of the world. Egor has sworn an oath to sink us and Enric has sworn an oath to defy Egor. Those two don't like each other."

Knuben wondered if the feud would affect him.

#

Queen Sheena sat in her dressing room pondering a host of problems. The one that most annoyed her at the moment was the crow's feet around her eyes. Lately, the wrinkles were harder than ever to disguise. She made a face. She didn't have time to worry about her looks. Sulvaria

plummeted towards bankruptcy. The treasury stood empty --
again! -- and would remain so until the taxes from Bermid
reached the capital. The island specialized in wool produc-
tion, both for export and for making cloth. In addition, a
small state-owed gold mine produced enough metal to keep a
dozen goldsmiths busy. Their artistry was renowned
throughout Gundarland, and fetched premium prices. Alas,
with Egor controlling the Sea of Gundarland, Bermid's trade
had decreased to a trickle. Nevertheless, even the dimin-
ished amount of taxes from there were crucial to Sulvaria's
survival.

In normal times, the bulk of the money flowed into the
treasury from customs dues collected by the port of Cintri,
largest city in Sulvaria and her capital. Egor's presence had
cut the customs dues to almost nothing. Trade goods, instead of leaving on ships from Cintri, now traveled up the
length of Gundarland and shipped out from a port in the
north. Egor's pirates had deprived Sulvaria of its trade income and the taxes collected from the citizenry weren't
enough to run the country.

Sheena counted again on her fingers. It took a week for
a ship to reach Bermid from Cintri and load the tax money.
Once across the channel and on the wagon, it was a two day
trip. So the money, five thousand silver pennies, should get
here later today. Knuben's ship should be back tomorrow.

The first bill to be paid was the military payroll for the
troops on the Yukland border in the west. The presence of
yuk brigands required a large, costly presence to prevent
them from pillaging the nearby country.

"My lady?" Her maid entered the room. "Your advisors
have assembled in the council chambers."

"Thank you." Sheena stood and smoothed out her kirtle and surcoat, both pale green. Her reflection in the mirror showed that she still retained an attractive figure at forty-three. She turned from the mirror and paced the room, mentally preparing herself for the aggravation of the council meeting. Her advisors were a major part of the county's problem. A group of old men who claimed their ministry positions by right of inheritance and nobility, they never gave her any useful advice and their solution to every problem was to spend more money. The council chose to ignore the impact Egor had on the treasury.

Sheena sighed. After three years, she still missed her dead husband. She missed his strength in the council room and his warmth in the bedroom. Queens ruled Sulvaria and and few of them ever had a helpmate like she had. Most consorts grappled with their spouses for power.

Thoughts of her husband made her think of her three daughters. One of them would succeed her on the throne. Whoever that was, she needed a strong husband to support her. One who would stand behind the queen and help her. Where was this marvelous man to come from? The court nobles were all arrogant fops. They flirted with her girls hoping to increase their own power.

The only possible candidate to come to mind was Knuben and he was still of untested mettle. His grandmother had been Sheena's wet nurse. His mother was the daughters' nursemaid. Knuben had grown up with the girls and attended the same classes they did. When he came of age, he went away to begin arms training. His recent return to court was like getting a prayer answered. He was someone she could trust.

# # #

Knuben and Ragazza stood on the quarterdeck letting a breeze wash over their faces.

"Ahoy the deck" The lookout's voice had a nervous edge to it. "Corsairs! Three of them. Aft. Onna port side."

"Blast the luck!" Enric peered through an eye glass. "We'll never make it to Bermid without gettin' cut off. Our only chance is to keep goin', and hope they give up the chase." He handed the glass to Knuben. "They're Egor's ships."

After examining the pirates for a moment, Knuben said, "They're awfully small." Without the glass, they looked like water-bugs, except for the sail.

"Aye. Small, swift and maneuverable. They have sails and oars so they can go against the wind."

"Can they catch us?" Knuben asked.

"They're faster than we are," Ragazza said. "No matter what sort of wind there is."

Knuben's emotional roller coaster took another plunge. He hadn't recovered from the last meeting with pirates and he was about to have another.   "What are our chances of beating them off?"

"Not so good. I've got thirty sailors, but some of them have to sail the ship and can't get into the fight. Each corsair carries sixteen rowers and usually has another twenty fighters. We're badly outnumbered, but since you're a warrior that helps our odds a bit. I can get you a sword and shield from our armory."

"Any armor?"

"No, and you don't want any, laddie."

"Why not?" Enric's reply puzzled Knuben.

"Sailors fall overboard durin' sea battles. If you're wearin' armor, you go straight to the bottom."

Knuben blanched at the idea. "What happens if we lose?"

"They often let the crew go free." Ragazza crossed her arms. "But Egor hates us. We're for the slave markets. Unless he wants us dead."

Knuben shuddered. He had betrayed Sheena's trust by losing the taxes, and now he stood to lose his freedom. Maybe he had been born under an unlucky star. In frustration, he grabbed a stay and squeezed it. Suddenly, an idea blossomed in his mind. He turned to study the lower spar on the mainmast. It extended a few feet past the side of the ship. "Enric. When I was attacked, the corsairs lashed themselves to the middle of my ship. Do they always do that?"

"Aye. The main deck is the one closest to the water, so the middle of the ship is the best place to try to fight your way on board. Why?"

"Does the *Rosebud* have spare blocks and tackles?"

"Of course."

"How about empty water barrels?"

"Got plenty of them." Enric raised an eyebrow.

"You have an idea, don't you?" Ragazza squeezed his elbow.

Knuben chewed on his lip before answering. "I think so. I need a lot of spare rigging. I also need a pen and some paper to draw up my plan."

"Arndt," Enric called out. "Assign two dwarfs to get whatever Knuben wants. Then break out the weapons and distribute them." He turned to Knuben. "Whatever you're plannin', you don't have much time to get it done."

##

Sheena's three daughters sat in their lounging chambers directly over the Queen's council chambers. Aileen, the oldest at twenty-one, stood in front of a wall mirror and admired herself. Using a hand mirror to see the back of her blonde hair, she made a minor adjustment. Bridget, nineteen, lay on the floor with her eye to a peep hole she had drilled two years ago. Her light brown hair cascaded over her head and covered the floor. Christel, seventeen, sat in a chair reading a treatise on calculus, the latest craze among alchemists and natural philosophers. She curled a twist of black hair as she read.

"Whath Mama doing?" Aileen asked. "I heard a thcream."

"She's screaming at the Defense Minister," Bridget replied. "Mama isn't having a good day, it seems."

"Ithn't Knuben due back thoon?" Aileen turned the mirror to get a different angle.

"Why are you asking about him?" Bridget looked up from the peep hole and raised an eyebrow to her sister.

"No reathon. But he doeth liven up the court. You have to admit he turned out rather fine. Tho different from the noblemen around here." Many court fops hoped to make points with Aileen by talking with a slight lisp like she did.

Christel marked her place in the book with a finger and giggled. "Aileen, I do believe you're smitten."

"You're thuch a brat." Aileen threw the mirror on a sofa and smoothed her green dress. "Ath if I would care about thomeone not noble born."

"Still, Mama sent him on an important mission." Bridget rolled into a sitting position. "She could have sent one of the noblemen like she did in the past." Bridget wore brown riding breeches under a blue kirtle. "Perhaps, she has plans for him."

"Well, he's certainly more interesting than the other noblemen." Christel picked a thread from her ratty, worn yellow sweater. "They're all so . . . ordinary. Not one of them knows anything other than how to ride and hunt. Knuben has schooling. I bet he could teach me some mathematiks."

"Oh, to be young and innothent again." Aileen smirked at her sister. "Mathematikth, indeed."

"You want Knuben to teach you something different?" Bridget guffawed, her whole body shaking. "Me too."

"Your mind ith alwayth in the gutter." Aileen stomped her foot. "I want to hear of fashionth in other courtth. Or perhapth a new dance."

"It's not likely a warrior-tinker would bring news of court fashions or dances," Christel said.

"Thath true." Aileen sighed. "Especially one ath poor ath he theemth to be. Hith thword hilt doesn't have a thingle jewel on it."

"Maybe that's because he uses his sword for something besides display," Bridget said. "Unlike our noblemen. I doubt if any of them has ever been in a real fight."

"I'm tired of talking about a hired thword," Aileen said. "We have important issueth to talk about, like what thhould we wear to the Anniverthary Ball. We better prepare a litht for Mama before the tax money cometh from Bermid. Otherwithe, the'll thpend it all on thome dreary project."

# # #

Enric retreated to the quarterdeck where he fumed over his bad luck. He needed to land in Bermid and sell his cargo to pay his crew. Not many of them would stay on the *Rosebud* if they weren't paid. With three corsairs after him, it was possible he could lose everything: ship, cargo, life. Getting captured would be the worst possible fate, even worse than death. Egor would torture him as repayment for refusing to join up with the pirate.

Over a year ago, he and Egor had met under a flag of truce. Sitting in a port-side tavern, Egor had pitched his offer.

"Me need squadron commanders." Egor paused to down a mug of ale. "Ya de best captain on de Gundarland Sea. Me offerin' ya da job."

"Sounds like a lot of trouble. Runnin' the *Rosebud* is much easier."

"Ya get a share of de loot, ya know."

Enric had thought about the offer for a few seconds while brushing his beard with a hand. "Let me tell you my counterproposal." He drained his mug and signaled for refills. "I'll join up if I have joint command of the pirate navy. And you and me split the loot equally."

"Ya outta yer mind." Egor smashed a huge fist on the table. "Me da only boss. Ya work fer me and ya don't get a equal share."

"Then I'm not interested inna job." Enric stood up. "I don't take orders."

"Ya walk out, me gonna see you dead, real quick. Me gonna sink ya ship."

"I'm walkin' unless you reconsider my offer."

Egor crossed his arm on his massive chest and glared at Enric. "Ya dead, dwarf."

"I'll make it easy for you to find me. I'm dyein' my sails purple and I'm paintin' the hull pink. Just so you won't get me confused with another captain."

Enric shook his head. Pissing off Egor wasn't the smartest move he ever made, but he never knuckled under to bullies. Not after the childhood he had. As the youngest dwarfling -- and the only male -- among twelve siblings, his sisters made him wear dresses and attend their never-ending, make-believe tea parties when he was small. And with no one but older sisters, the only hand-me-down clothes were dresses. His toys were dolls and trinkets. In school, he quickly learned to defend himself because the other young male dwarfs made fun of his clothes and the costume jewelry he wore. Before long he was the most feared street fighter in town.

Growing up with all those females also taught him to think for himself. It was the only way he could push back at his sisters. Faced with the family tradition of a mining career, he ran away and joined a ship. Using talents he didn't know he had, he rose to captain before long and bought his own ship from his mostly legal profits.

He stopped thinking about the past and turned to Ragazza who sketched runes to keep a steady breeze blowing them eastward.

"What does your foretellin' say?" he asked her.

"It's murky. All I can see clearly is a pearl choker."

Enric watched dwarfs fasten new rigging lines to the main mast spar. Another pair lashed ropes into some sort of net while still more hauled empty water barrels up from the hold. He wondered what kind of contraption Knuben had in mind. He didn't care as long as it helped beat off the pirates.

The corsairs had halved the distance and he could see individual pirates now. They were the typical mixed lot: yuks, humans, dwarfs, a few elves, an occasional scrawny half-pint. While he watched, the oars were shipped and amid great shoving and pushing, a new set of rowers took their places on the benches. The oars began beating again with stronger force.

"Can you get the wind to blow against them?" he asked Ragazza.

"They're still too far away. When they get closer, I can set up a cross wind that'll slow them down." Ragazza held onto a stay and didn't take her eyes off Knuben.

Enric noticed and wondered what that was all about.

He watched dwarfs wrestle a barrel into a netting they had lashed together. Others threw buckets with ropes attached into the sea. They hauled them back and emptied sea water into the barrels. Enric frowned. The fresh water barrels would have to scoured with vinegar before they could be used again, but that was a small price if Knuben's plan worked. Enric squinted at the new rigging and could only surmise that Knuben wanted to give the pirates a shower.

Not that they couldn't use one, but there were more important issues right now than pirate hygiene. The corsairs drew
even closer. Time to go below and get ready for battle.

# # #

"What do you think?" Knuben asked Ardnt as he tugged
on a line to check the tautness.

"That scum is in for a big surprise. I can't wait to see
their faces." Ardnt looked over the stern. "They're getting
close. I better get the lads into their battle positions. Then I
can break out the pipeweed."

"Pipeweed?" Knuben started. "You let the crew smoke
pipeweed before a battle?" The brown weedy material was a
mild hallucinogenic drug. After graduation, Knuben had experienced a few battles while in the employ of a duke who
was at war with his neighbor, but he had never heard of al-
lowing the troops to smoke weed before a battle.

"Aye. It settles their nerves and makes the battle more
fun. Except for the enemy." He pointed to the forward hatch
cover. "I put your sword and shield over there."

After Ardnt left, Knuben climbed on the rail. Holding a
backstay, he examined the corsairs. Pirates not engaged in
rowing brandished swords or axes. He heard curses in a
number of dialects. All three corsairs were identical, as if
built from the same design. They had a single mast with a
square sail and eight oars per side. He estimated the ships
sideboards were only half as high as the Rosebud's main
deck. The pirates would have a steep climb to get on board.
Made more difficult by his invention, he hoped. After the

battle, he could write a paper on the idea and send it to his college for publication in its technical journal.

The *Rosebud* crew, all puffing on pipes, pranced around, climbed ropes and flung obscene gestures at the pirates. Others piled squares of cloth on the deck near the rail.

Knuben took several deep breaths. He faced his first battle at sea and the activities of his battle mates didn't do anything to calm his jittery nerves or the knot in his stomach. Fortunately, Ragazza's seasickness spell still worked. Fighting a battle while throwing up didn't sound like much fun.

Since his rescue this morning, he found life more beautiful than previously and he didn't want it to stop. His senses were keener and everything looked delightful after facing death by exposure. He glanced to the quarterdeck. Ragazza sketched an air rune. Dark clouds gathered over the corsairs and the waves around the small ships grew higher and rougher. The craft tossed and pitched. With another symbol the clouds dropped fist-sized hail on the pirates. They yelped in pain.

Knuben went aft and stood alongside Ragazza. "Can't you make the winds stronger so we can go faster?"

"It won't do any good. If I make the winds stronger, we'll have to take in sails so the masts don't snap." She smiled at him. He noticed her smile lit up her entire face. "You'll get to use your new weapon before long. I hope it works the way you think it will. Otherwise, today will end badly."

Enric emerged from his cabin. He wore a padded doublet and a blood-colored kilt. His feet and the lower parts of his hairy, thick legs were encased in leather seaboots. A dagger stuck out of the right boot top. Besides the two throwing axes stuck in his belt, a large battle ax was draped over his left shoulder. His beard curls were tucked under the doublet to prevent pirates from grabbing them, and the bangles had been removed from his wrists.

"Ardnt," he called, "are the cannons loaded with grape?"

"We're all ready, sir. Just waiting for the buggers to get closer." Ardnt stood on the quarterdeck between the two small brass cannons mounted on the rail behind the wheel.

Ten minutes later, Enric said, "They're close enough, now. Fire when ready, Bosun."

Ardnt adjusted the aim and touched a slow match to each cannon. Both disgorged a large cloud of grayish smoke accompanied by a loud bang.

The grape shot rippled the sea near the closest corsairs like falling raindrops. The pirates jeered.

"Arrgh," Enric growled. "The only thing the cannons ever hit is water."

Minutes later, two of the three corsairs pulled alongside the *Rosebud*, one on each side. Grappling hooks snaked skyward and fell over the railings.

Led by Enric on the starboard side and Ardnt on the port, the *Rosebud* crew, many armed with a knitting needle besides an ax, sliced at the ropes attached to the grapples. Hands and heads appeared on other ropes. Dwarfs slashed with axes and jabbed with needles. Still more pirates climbed the side of the *Rosebud*. A few dwarfs grabbed squares of cloth and dropped them on the heads of the climbing pirates, blinding or distracting them. The dwarfs followed up with ax strokes.

Knuben ignored the dryness of his mouth and took up a rope coiled at the base of the mainmast. He and a dwarf helper hauled on the rope and a barrel rose to the height of the lowest spar. When it reached the spar, it stopped its upward movement and ran out along the spar on the starboard side until it hung over the sea. While the dwarf lashed the rope to a cleat, Knuben grabbed a second rope attached to the netting that encased the barrel. He pulled and the netting upended. The barrel hurtled downward. Knuben heard a loud crack followed by screams and curses. He raced to the starboard railing and looked down after dodging a cutlass stroke. The force of the barrel shattered the keel of the slightly built corsair, breaking the ship in two. Waves forced the sections away from the Rosebud, straining the remaining grapple ropes. They snapped and sent the climbing pirates into the sea. The stern section was already awash and the forward section wallowed on the waves. Pirates jumped off both halves.

With the threat gone from the starboard side, Enric ordered six dwarfs to reinforce the port side. He ran past Knuben and clapped him on the arm. "Well done, laddie."

Knuben grabbed a second coiled rope and hauled another barrel up the mast. This one slid out to the port side. Just as the barrel fell out of the netting, a loud roar startled him. A huge yuk threw himself into the defenders, and sent three of them sprawling. The pirate jumped up and faced Enric. The yuk swung a huge sword at Enric's head. The captain blocked the blow, but the sword hewed through the haft of his ax. Enric dropped the handle and drew his two throwing axes. He hurled one at the yuk who swatted it away with his sword. The pirate grinned and advanced on Enric.

Knuben snatched up his sword and shield.

Sounds of splashing and confusion came from the second corsair.

Knuben yelled a challenge and charged the pirate. The yuk slashed at him. Knuben took the blow on his shield. He pushed forward, ramming the yuk with his shield held high. He jabbed the sword underneath the shield. The yuk screamed and clutched his thigh. Knuben stepped back a pace and hacked at the distracted yuk. The pirate collapsed to the deck.

Enric picked up an ax dropped by a wounded dwarf. "Once again, well done, laddie."

Both rushed to the port rail. The barrel had smashed through the port gunwale, ripping a large hole in the side of the corsair. The small craft listed sharply.

Within minutes, the *Rosebud* was safe with all the pirates dispatched or knocked into the sea.

"C'mon," Enric called to Knuben. "Let's see where the third bugger is." The two ran to the quarterdeck where Ragazza steered the ship. Knuben had time to reflect on his mental agitation. The yuk was his first known kill. In previous battles he had never been sure what happened to the soldiers he faced.

Ragazza let go of the wheel momentarily to hug Knuben. Embarrassed at first, he soon hugged her back and forgot about the dead yuk.

"Ragazza!" Enric interrupted the hugging. He pointed to the remaining corsair, now retreating. "Let's drive him towards the shore on one of those islands." Three small islands broke the surface a mile to the starboard side. "Ardnt!" Clean up the deck and get the crew ready. We're goin' pirate huntin'."

Ragazza released Knuben and sketched a wind command. The corsair heeled to the starboard as the strong wind caught the sail in its wrong alignment. Another command set the waves leaping at the boat, driving the corsair beachward.

"Ha!" Enric said. "This will be easy. I love sinkin' Egor's ships."

Enric invited Ragazza and Knuben to join him in his cabin while most of the crew-dwarfs danced and sang songs. Others stood around smoking more pipeweed and grinning. Ardnt preceded Enric carrying a strong box found in the beached corsair. The pirates, after their ship had been driven ashore, fled to the other side of the island. Ardnt led a landing party to destroy the ship and found the chest.

Inside the cabin, Enric rubbed his hands and grinned at the others. "I love this part of the job."

Ardnt inserted an iron bar between the lock and the stout chain that secured the strong box. The lock groaned before splitting apart. Enric stepped forward, threw the chain to the deck and opened the lid. He gasped and thrust both hands into the chest. He picked up a double handful of riches. Jewels, coins and gold spilled through his fingers.

The others pressed close. "Those corsairs had good hunting," Ragazza said.

"Aye," Ardnt replied. "It's our good fortune they tried us last."

"There ain't enough ships left to get this much loot," Enric said. "They have to be raidin' coastal villages and towns now."

"We only survived because of Knuben," Ragazza said.

"This is true." Enric pulled his beard curls and frowned. "Without his great idea, we'd all be shark food. Or worse. He's gotta be rewarded for this battle." He scratched his bulbous nose. "By the *Rosebud's* rules for loot-sharin', I'm entitled to thirty percent of this loot. Ragazza and Ardnt each get ten percent and crew shares the other half. Since Knuben's not enrolled on the ship's rooster, he ain't entitled to a share of the loot. As your reward, Knuben, I'll give you half of my share."

Enric enjoyed watching Knuben's reaction, especially his mouth hanging open in the fly catching position.

"I'll add half of my share also." Ragazza placed a hand on Knuben's arm. He turned red.

"Me too," Ardnt said. "Gotta encourage people who save my life." He winked at the still-stunned Knuben.

"N . . . now I can replace the tax money."

"Are you daft, laddie? Forget the queen." Enric stomped his foot on the deck. "You're rich and you have a fine future sailin' with the *Rosebud.* We can go anywhere we want now and we can beat Egor."

"My honor depends upon completing my mission." Knuben stuck out his jaw. "I have to return to Queen Sheena and hand over my share of the treasure to replace the money I lost."

"Let's take him back," Ragazza said. "I've never been to a court."

Enric thought about her idea. The *Rosebud* was already past Bermid. Going to Cintri would mean bigger profits. He nodded then plunged his hands into the chest again. This time he came up with a choker necklace. "By the gods of the sea, Ragazza, you were right. Look at this!" The choker had three strands of matched pearls and a large emerald in the middle. "I claim this as part of my share." He held it against his neck. "How does it look?"

"We can't see it," Knuben replied. It's covered by your beard."

Enric pulled a face and seized a hand mirror. "You're right. Now what do I do? There's no sense wearin' this thing if I can't make everyone jealous."

Knuben left the cabin feeling as if his feet didn't touch the deck. His career dreams were back on track. His honor was restored. He had a paper to write. And then there was Ragazza. Life had never been better.

PART THREE

Knuben gazed at the capital city of Cintri, less than an hour's sail away. Knuben and Ragazza stood on the quarter-deck and gazed at the roofs of buildings sparkling in the morning sunlight. Two points of land wrapped around the bay leaving only a narrow passageway into the harbor. Near the entrance, the color of the water changed from deep blue to green.

The ship rolled on a wave and Ragazza's hip bumped Knuben's. Both smiled. The last two days had been the most splendid in his young life. He and Ragazza spent all their waking hours together. She was gentle, unassuming, had a pointed humor and a keen intellect. At night, alone in his small cabin, he dreamed of spending even more time with her. The only time he didn't think of her was when he made notes or calculations for the paper on his new naval weapon.

While he enjoyed her company, he hated the crowded conditions on the ship. Wherever he went, he tripped over someone. Without her seasickness spells, he'd be on the edge of death by now.

"I wish the voyage could last longer. For the first time since I joined the *Rosebud*, I have someone to talk to who isn't a dwarf. They all have pretty strange world views. At least, they're strange to an elf."

"How did you end up on the ship?" He looked into her face and smiled. "There must be a tale here, but maybe you don't want to talk about it."

"I usually don't talk about it, but I'll tell you." She sighed. "My father is a rich merchant. He signed a marriage contract for me without asking my permission. The wedding was to take place the day after I graduated. My future husband was another merchant, already old. I pleaded with my father to get the contracted voided, but he wouldn't. At a family gathering to celebrate the betrothal, I refused to marry the old goat, set his hair on fire with a spell and fled. I left school before the family could come and fetch me back. Later on, I heard my father disowned me and the clan kicked me out. I came south and found out that no one wanted to hire a weather witch who didn't have a graduation certificate. Except Enric. So, here I am. A disowned, tribe-less elf maiden working for a part-time smuggler."

"How sad." Knuben hugged her.

"There are compensations." She gave him a wan smile. "I love the freedom of the sea."

# # #

Angus MacLeod raised an eyebrow and asked, "And what does her Majesty plan to do now that the Bermid taxes are lost?" The elf's voice dripped with sarcasm. MacLeod was the Minister of the Treasury. Tall and skinny with a large paunch, he wore a silk green tunic and black breeches. He stared boldly at the queen who sat at the head of a large walnut table in the council chamber on the upper floor of the castle. Stained glass windows let in sunlight and colored it in all the hues of the rainbow.

"We don't know for sure the taxes are gone," Sheena replied. "Possibly the wagon lost a wheel, or one of the horses got hurt." In her heart, Sheena knew she lied. The tax wagon should have arrived two days ago, and Knuben's ship was overdue. Her heart plunged in despair.

"If the ship is also lost, it will be heavy blow to the navy," added Nelson Bidwell the Commodore of the Fleet. A chunky human, he wore a blue uniform a size too small and excess flesh bulged in many places. He wore his long hair pulled back into a club in the fashion of the sailors. "Since we had only six ships to begin with, this will be a serious blow to the fleet's ability to combat piracy."

Sheena resisted the urge to grab the man's queue and drag him around the chamber. He had the arrogance to talk about combating piracy when the fleet had yet to engage the pirates. The Commodore would use the lost ship as another excuse to avoid a naval battle. In his most aggressive movement, he sailed a squadron of ships down the coast on a voyage lasting two days. At the tip of Sulvaria, he turned around and sailed back to port. As soon as he docked, he announced he had cleared the coast of pirates. He had yet to see a pirate ship let alone engage one in battle. To emphasize the ineffectiveness of her fleet, new reports told of pirate raids on coastal towns and villages.

"The most pressing problem right now, Majesty, is the Army payroll," General Claus Groner said. "We must raises taxes immediately." Groner eschewed beard curls, one of the few dwarfs who didn't spend large numbers of hours on his beard. He had a dark brown uniform festooned with medals and braids. "I suggest you authorize my soldiers to seize property in order to get money to pay the troops."

"We will not raise taxes." Sheena glared at the dwarf. "They are already too high. And we certainly won't seize private property. What I need from my ministers is ideas to address our problems. Ideas that don't involve raising taxes, unless those taxes are on the nobility."

"Majesty! Please! Don't joke about abandoning an ancient tradition." Pierre Dubois, a half-pint, had a horrified expression on his face. As short as dwarfs, half-pints were only half as wide. Dubois was the Court Administrator and he wore a white tunic and brown breeches. Unlike the other ministers, he didn't wear boots. His bare feet displayed an elaborately coiffed toe-hair. For some reason, half-pints considered toe-hair displays very sexy.

"I do not joke," she replied. "It is time the nobles paid for their privileged life. The farmers and merchants and craftsmen shouldn't be the only ones supporting the government."

"I object, Majesty." Dubois looked indignant. "We pay our dues by serving. Many military officers serve without pay as do your ministers in this room."

Sheena almost replied that serving without pay was the only way many nobles could get and hold a position. She gnashed her teeth. Yet another meeting degenerated into useless squabbling.

The queen believed her mission was to protect the throne and the common folk from assaults by the predatory nobles. The ministers, all from the nobility, fought to preserve their hereditary rights and to increase their strength while decreasing the power of the throne. Sulvarian tradition called for the ministers to come from the most powerful noble houses. There were seven such houses and these families supplied all the ministers. When a minister retired or died, a noble house not represented in the cabinet supplied the replacement. How she would love to break the tradition and appoint ministers who weren't from those families. Appointing someone from the merchants, farmers or artists in Cintri would transform the cabinet and offer a way to lessen the power of the nobles. Unfortunately, she wasn't strong enough to accomplish that. The noble cabinet ministers would block her attempts. Her primary weakness was that they controlled the military. Another weakness was that a minister controlled the treasury, but since it was frequently empty, that wasn't as big a problem as the military. Nevertheless, she vowed to keep looking for opportunities.

A page burst into the room. "Majesty!" The lad, gasping for breath, said. "A ship! It approaches the harbor."

Sheena rose from her chair and waved the lad closer. "Is it our ship from Bermid?"

"No, sire. The harbor master says he's seen the ship before, but he thinks its been captured by pirates and they are
attacking."

Pandemonium broke out. The Ministers wailed and
called on Sheena to do something.

Sheena felt disgust for the ministers. She gave them a
withering look. "Silence!" When she got it, she said, "The
navy is to prepare to attack this ship. Just in case. And the
army is to take up positions to defend the port."

Both ministers eyed her with misgivings. Groner, the
Army minister, bit his lip. Bidwell made washing motions
with his hands.

"Don't just stand there. Get on with it." Sheena stamped
her foot.

After the two military ministers left the room, she ignored MacLeod and Dubois and the secretary who took
notes. The ship had to be more bad news, she thought. Perhaps it carried a ransom demand for Knuben. She had sent
him on the mission so she had a duty to pay the ransom. Unfortunately, she didn't know where the money would come
from.

#

Ragazza went to her cabin and puttered around. She
now had second thoughts about taking Knuben back to court.
He had told her about the queen and her daughters. She
didn't like the way Knuben talked about them. Ragazza saw
all those women as competitors, even though he viewed the
queen as an aunt and the princesses as sisters. Knuben had
grown up with the princesses. They attended the same

classes, played together, ate meals together. He was all too familiar with those fancy women. Her foresight indicated they would be a threat to her happiness.

The closer the *Rosebud* sailed to Cintri, the more nervous she became. The problem wasn't clear-cut. It was nothing she could identify or focus on, but she knew the court meant trouble for her and Knuben.

The thought of competition for Knuben made a knot in her stomach. These last few days had been wonderful. Full of companionship and laughter. Knuben's weapon bought a sense of security to Enric and the crew; they no longer worried about Egor. The crew believed the weapon enabled them to sail anywhere they wanted to go. That meant they would all get rich as the only trading vessel on the Sea of Gundarland. She had never seen Enric or the crew so happy.

She didn't have much experience with courts, only what she had heard about them in school, but, with its reputed pleasures and intrigues, she pictured the court as sharks swallowing Knuben like a tasty morsel. He was honest and idealistic, traits that were probably despised in an imperial court.

She wanted to go topside and conjure up a strong off-shore gale to blow the *Rosebud* out to sea, but she couldn't betray Enric's trust by doing that. She plopped down on her cot and put her face in her hands.

# # #

Egor kicked a table in his office. A pile of coins and a gold necklace bounced around and fell to the floor. Three of his precious corsairs! Most of two crews! And all that loot!

All lost to the *Rosebud*! He decided that Enric would spend at least a week dying after he caught him. He waved a hand dismissing the corsair captain who had just arrived in port carrying the marooned survivors of the battle.

He paced his office. What to do about the strange weapon the *Rosebud* carried? Did it exist or had the survivors concocted the story to cover up their own incompetence? How could a corsair be destroyed in an instant? How did this weapon affect his plans? Why was the *Rosebud* last seen sailing toward Cintri? Did Enric plan to join forces with Queen Sheena? Or sell the plans for the weapon?

He stopped in front of the wall map. The news held too many uncertainties. He hesitated and mentally debated his options. Should he postpone his attack on Bermid to deal with the *Rosebud,* or continue as planned? He paced in front of the map and finally pounded a fist into his open palm. He had spent too much time preparing for the invasion of the island. He couldn't delay it because a ship brought in a report about a new weapon that may or may not exist. He made his decision.

He threw open the door and yelled, "Orderly!" He tapped a toe until a pirate finally stood in the doorway.

"Aye?" The elf stood in a position of slouched attention.

"Tell da captains to begin loadin' da corsairs. We attack as planned."

# # #

Knuben stood in the bow of the cutter as it approached the wharf where a pretentious-looking, obese man awaited. A half-dozen soldiers stood behind the gray-robed official.

Enric and Ragazza rode in the stern of the cutter, one on each side of the tiller. Ragazza had told him that customs officials were pompous oafs, and Knuben could only deal with them by being even more pompous. To help him, she and Enric gave him a crash course on pomposity.

The boat banged into a wharf piling and Knuben hauled himself up a rope ladder. He looked down his nose at the shorter official and said, "My name is Knuben Bullard. I am on a mission for the Queen. I need an escort for myself and my two companions." He snapped his fingers and added, "See to it."

"You dare to suggest," the official replied, "that you are a royal agent? Not likely the Queen's agent would dress in little more than his underwear." The official pointed to Knuben's feet. "And walk barefoot."

"For your information," Knuben glared at the man, "I escaped from the clutches of the pirate admiral Egor. He stole my armor and weapons. And my boots. Now organize an escort before I give you a thrashing."

He turned his back on the official and offered a hand to Ragazza. She gave him a heavy wooden box and climbed out of the cutter. Enric followed taking care not to soil his chartreuse caftan. His beard curls had been sheared down to stubble to allow the pearl choker to be displayed around his thick neck. On his sandaled feet, he wore ten toe rings. The gaudy effect was somewhat muted by the throwing axes tucked under his belt.

Knuben turned back to the customs official. "Are you going to stand here all day? You risk your career."

The official stared at Enric before replying, "My orders are to arrest everyone who comes off your ship."

Knuben had a bad feeling about the contents of the box getting looted in the royal jail.

"I think we can come to an arrangement," Ragazza said as she stuck her hand under Knuben's arm. "Why don't you have these soldiers escort us to the palace where you can get further instructions about what the Queen wants you to do. I assure you, she wants to see this man very badly."

The man pondered the proposal for a few seconds, gulped and nodded his assent.

"Along the way, I have to stop to buy boots," Knuben said.

# # #

Aileen, Bridget and Christel ran into the audience room and shoved several court fops out of the way so they could get a good viewing position. After hearing of Knuben's imminent arrival from a maid, the princesses had no time to primp. Already, rumors had traveled through the palace about Knuben's strange adventure and his exotic companions. The girls knew Knuben's future could change for the better, making him even more desirable. In their haste, they wore what they called peasant garb: a kirtle covered by a mantle. Clips held their long hair bunched behind their backs.

Sheena saw her daughters and said in mock amazement, "A court appearance? So early in the day?"

The girls made faces at their mother.

"The thinkth the'th funny," Aileen said.

"Strange," Christel said. "Why is she suddenly in a good mood?"

"Because," Bridget replied, "Knuben must have the tax money. Money always puts Mama in a good mood."

"Money?" Aileen smiled. "Now Mama won't have an excuthe not to buy me a new ball gown."

"She may prefer to pay the troops rather than buy you a dress." Bridget grinned at Aileen's sour expression

"I need a book on Optiks more than you need a dress," Christel said.

"Oh, bother you and your bookth," Aileen replied.

A commotion at the entrance interrupted their discussion of priorities.

Knuben entered the throne room carrying a box under his left arm. His right hand held the hand of a tall elf wo-man. A dwarf in a splendid caftan walked behind the pair.

The princesses all sucked in their breath at the sight, but each kept an eye on her sisters in case one of them tried a preemptive strike to grab Knuben.

"Look at the color in the dwarf'th caftan," Aileen said. "It'th thplendid. I want a ball gown in that color."

"Who's the elf with the ugly robe? And sea boots?" Bridget asked. "And why is she holding Knuben's hand?" She had penciled in Knuben as her consort when she became queen and she didn't like the idea of a competitor.

"Never mind the caftan, look at the dwarf's choker." Christel's mind boggled at the pearls and the emerald. She could buy the worlds' greatest library with the price of the choker.

"Holding handth in court ith unstheemly," Aileen sniffed. "I have tho much to teach him before he'll make a thuitable match for me."

"I bet she's a witch," Bridget observed. "Look at the symbols on her robe." Maybe she could get Mama to throw the elf out of the country on a charge of witchcraft.

"She's awful plain looking," Christel said. She slipped behind the taller Aileen so Knuben wouldn't see her looking like a peasant woman.

# # #

The crowd in the Queen's throne room astonished Knuben. The customs official must have sent a messenger ahead while he ducked into a shop to buy a pair of sea boots and a tan cloak. On a dais across the room, Sheena sat on a large, elaborately carved throne. Behind her, windows allowed sunlight to illuminate the room and her. In a white tunic, she seemed to be on fire from the brilliant sunlight. Knuben gulped in anxiety. To get to the throne, he would have walk up an aisle formed by a two phalanxes of people who stared at him like he was a new and strange type of bug.

He squeezed Ragazza's hand to steady himself and stepped forward. As they moved up the aisle, the eyes of the crowd shifted from him to Ragazza and then to Enric. Knuben fancied he could hear their eyeballs swiveling back and forth. Gasps of surprise came from the crowds and Knuben knew most of them came because of Enric's chartreuse caftan, choker necklace and jewel-studded toes. The guards at the door had forced him to leave his throwing axes behind.

To take his mind off the crowds, Knuben examined the queen as he approached. Short and in her forties, she had short blond hair and green eyes. Her silk tunic accentuated her slender, but curvaceous frame. He stopped at the foot of the dais and bowed. Ragazza followed his lead and bowed with him. While in his bow, he noticed a table to the left of the dais. Four old males sat in chairs and frowned. They must be Sheena's advisors, he thought.

Knuben raised his head and said, "Your Majesty. I have returned from Bermid in an unexpected manner."

"I see you brought visitors to my court," Sheena smiled at him, "but as long as you have the tax money they are welcome."

"Alas, the taxes were stolen by Egor --"

Angry exclamations came from the old males at the table. The queen held a hand in front of her open mouth.

"Egor attacked my ship before dawn while we waited for the tide. He overcame the guards, stripped me of my armor and weapons then set me adrift in a rowboat. After a few days, these two rescued me with the *Rosebud*, their ship."

A male in a blue naval uniform pounded the table. "Twenty-five soldiers overcome by a handful of riffraff? That is incompetent leadership."

"I only had twelve soldiers, not the twenty-five I was promised." Knuben stared at the naval minister. The army minister squirmed on his seat.

Sheena scowled at Groner before saying in a small voice, "No taxes?"

"No taxes, but I have something to replace them."

The queen started, then a wan smile played across her face.

"Soon after I was rescued, the *Rosebud* was attacked by three pirate corsairs. We defeated them and discovered a treasure chest in one. I give you my share of the loot as compensation for the lost taxes."

Knuben lifted the lid on wooden box and showed the contents to Sheena. She gasped aloud and beckoned him closer.

The four ministers stood and craned their necks to see better. They held a whispered conversation among themselves.

Knuben mounted the dais and held the box where the queen could examine the contents.

"Well done, Knuben." The queen stuck a hand in the box and picked up a handful of coins and gems. She let them spill back into the box. "You have repaid my trust in you."

"Majesty," an elf minister said. He had a large paunch and wore silk clothes. "If this came from the pirates, it is legally considered loot and your ministers are entitled to a share in accordance with ancient tradition."

Anger washed over the queen's face. She stood, her fists clenched. "Listen carefully, MacLeod. This treasure replaces the taxes and will not be shared by the ministers. Is that clear?"

MacLeod locked eyes with the queen briefly before breaking off and sitting down.

Sheena glared at the ministers for a few more seconds as if challenging them. She turned to Knuben and said, "Introduce the visitors."

Knuben presented the two of them.

"Tell me, captain. Is the *Rosebud* a pirate ship also, or perhaps a smuggler?"

"Well," Enric coughed into his fist. "You see, Your Majesty . . . "

Sheena laughed at the dwarf's discomfort. "Since you returned Knuben and defeated Egor's corsairs, I grant you a full pardon for any and all crimes you may or may not have committed against Sulvaria."

A naval minister groaned aloud then said, "Majesty. We should make an example of this one to discourage others."

"Keep quiet, Commodore Bidwell."

Enric and Ragazza exchanged smiles.

"In three days," Sheena said, "I am having a ball to celebrate the twentieth anniversary of my coronation. I invite the three of you to attend as my honored guests. My staff will find rooms in the castle for you to stay in."

Knuben sighed in relief. Losing the taxes had been forgiven. The queen was pleased with the substitution. He was back in her good graces and that could lead to opportunities for promotion. Life was good.

Ragazza felt self-conscious standing in the throne room. Her robe looked like a rag alongside the gowns and kirtles of the nobles. The three beautiful young women standing near the dais wore kirtles that looked more costly than a set of new sails for the *Rosebud*. They had to be the princesses and she didn't like the way their looks devoured Knuben. They reminded her of snakes trying to hypnotize their prey.

Her ability to read people's integrity -- part of her wizard's training -- showed nothing but cupidity in the three women. Folks in the crowd and especially the four old males at the table calculated how to manipulate Knuben for their own ends or to get rid of him. Only the queen seemed to appreciate Knuben and what he had done.

Knuben was in danger as long as he stayed at court. She feared for his integrity and his honor, but how was she supposed to protect him? The folks in this castle were like an unknown species to her. She had never before experienced such avarice. Life was not good.

# # #

Enric smoothed his caftan and grinned at the queen. A pardon meant he didn't have to leave the *Rosebud* anchored outside the harbor where Ardnt could beat a hasty retreat in case of an attack by port officials who suspected the ship carried contraband goods. Despite the paint job and dyed sails, one port official had recognized the *Rosebud*. Enric and the customs officials had experienced misunderstandings in the past, but now he could dock her and unload her. The cargo of cloth, copper bars and wine would be easy to off-load and sell. The rest of the cargo required some finesse. It consisted of three barrels of prime pipeweed, a highly taxed substitute for tobacco. Not paying taxes on it meant big profits. He also had a dozen cases of yukeste, a liquor that was almost pure alcohol and banned in every province in Gundarland. That made it highly exotic and much in demand. Perhaps he would donate a few bottles to the anniversary ball. No party was dull when yukeste was served. At least, not until everyone passed out. After he sold his cargo, he'd go legal and respectable. With Knuben's water barrels, he didn't have to fear Egor's corsairs. He could sail wherever he wanted to go. He had an advantage no other merchant ship had. It wouldn't be long before others figured it out, but until then, he had an edge and he had to exploit it.

With Sheena's court open to him, he also had a lock on a very lucrative market: fashions. Once he got measurements, he could have custom-made dresses and gowns made up for the females. Zears, a large island off the coast of Yukland, was renown for its fabrics and he now had the freedom to sail there and back. He'd give the gown measurements to his wife and have her supervise the sewing.

Selling the dress fashions could be even more lucrative than pipeweed and yukeste. And it was legal. Life was good.

# # #

Egor stood near the steering oar of his corsair as his fleet sailed into Bermid harbor. Night gradually gave way to the semidarkness that precedes dawn. His ships slid forward using muffled oars. Already, he could make out the wharfs that jutted into the harbor. His ship and one other would secure the wharfs and ensure that no ship escaped out to sea. The remainder of his fleet would beach on the sandy shore, disembark and head for the city's gates. His spies assured him the gates would be open this early to allow farmers to bring in the day's produce to the market.

He moved up to the bow while his ship curved into the port and headed for a wharf. He jumped onto it before the ship stopped moving. Two ships were tied to the wharf, but he didn't see any of the crew. They were probably all in town.

Cutlass at the ready, he and a dozen other pirates ran to the land end of the wharf and checked for activity. Nothing moved in the port area. Good, he thought, complete surprise. With hand motions, he gave directions to some pirates to inspect other wharves and secure them. He glanced back at his fleet just as three corsairs slid onto the beach.

"Who goes there?" a voice cried out.

Shivers ran up Egor's spine. The voice came from the darkness near the beached ships. He peered in the direction for a few seconds then gasped. A group of horsemen rode into view with lowered lancers and stopped a few feet from the water. From their bulkiness, Egor surmised the riders wore armor under their outer garments. Knights! From the lack of uniforms, he guessed they were out for some practice before the heat of the day. What rotten luck!

Pirates jumped out of the ships, but hesitated instead of advancing, baffled by the appearance of horsemen.

"Get movin'!" Egor roared. "Move! Get to da gates."

One rider broke from the group and galloped toward the city. The others fanned out and formed a line along the shore.

More boats hissed onto the beach. The early arriving corsairs backed off the beach and rowed away from the shore to make room for others. The crews from the first three boats advanced slowly until the knights charged. The pirates ran back to the water.

Egor cursed. The success of his plan depended on surprise, and these knights had ruined it. His only chance to take the city now was to get to the gates while they remained open. He ran from the wharf to the landing area. When he got there, he grabbed a pirate standing in water up to his ankles and hauled him onto land. He pushed the pirate forward and yelled "Charge!" He ran toward a knight, dodged the lance point and attacked him with his cutlass. Around him, several pirates screamed in agony.

More corsairs beached.

The knights broke off the attack and retreated toward the city. They moved slowly and made frequent sorties to disrupt the pirates and keep them off-balance.

Egor pushed pirates forward. He cursed and smacked others with the flat of his cutlass. His surprise attack had failed. Now he would have to besiege the city.

Ragazza hummed a childhood ditty while she and Knuben strolled arm in arm through the streets of the city. A gust blew in from the harbor sending dead leaves and dust swirling around. They had spent the last two nights together in Knuben's room and she never felt as joyful as she did today.

They entered a small park and sat down on a bench. Flower beds displayed vibrant spring flowers in every possible hue. Shore birds squawked and wheeled overhead. Ragazza watched two squirrels chase each other around the base of a tree. Despite her happiness, she couldn't shake the feeling that the old men at the table represented a danger and that the princesses were cooking up a disaster. How to tell Knuben? She hoped she didn't make the situation worse by talking to him. Finally, she said, "They're after you, you know." She held her breath awaiting his response.

"Who?" A puzzled Knuben looked at her. "Who are talking about?"

"Those four old males at that table? They're dangerous. They all want to use you for their own needs and then get rid of you."

"They're the queen's ministers. Why would they want to get rid of me?"

"Because you succeeded. They're afraid the queen will use you to weaken their power."

Knuben picked at a fingernail. "You think so? I never considered that. I was just trying to complete my mission."

"Life on the *Rosebud* and life in court are completely different. Don't make a mistake thinking that the courtiers are like the crew. Sailors work to survive. In the court, folks work to accumulate power or to weaken others."

"How do you know so much about court life?"

"I don't know about court life itself, but my wizard training allows me to sense integrity. Believe me, there is none in this court, except for the queen. The ministers? Not a shred. And then there are the princesses."

Knuben frowned. "They're harmless. I should know. I grew up with them. I'm like the big brother they never had."

"How old were you when you left?"

Knuben thought for a moment. "Thirteen."

"So you haven't seen them for ten years. Girls can do a lot of growing and changing in ten years."

Knuben jumped up and paced around the bench. After two laps, he stopped and said, "They are different now. Back then, they were all skinny, brainless and they never stopped giggling. Now they've changed. Aileen is still brainless. All she thinks about is dresses and ball dances. Bridget is convinced she'll be the next queen, so she's trying to learn everything she can about diplomacy and leadership. I think she'd be a good queen. Christel is only interested in science. I think she knows more mathematiks then me."

"They are alike in one way," Ragazza said in a sad voice.

"Other than being beautiful?"

"Yes. All three are after you."

Knuben started. "I don't believe it. We're all good friends. That's all."

"Oh, Knuben. You're in danger as long as you stay in this wicked place. Let's get back on the *Rosebud* and sail away from here. Please?"

"I can't leave. I came here to help Sheena. Besides, I can't not attend the anniversary ball. That would be rude."

A cold spike of fear pierced Ragazza's heart.

# # #

After dinner that evening, the princesses lounged in their sitting room. The large room was common to all their bed-rooms. Mirrors covered much of the wall space: big ones, small ones, round ones, curved ones. In Christel's sitting area, a bookcase held dozens of scientific and philosophical tracts. Bridget's area had a globe showing the location of countries and bodies of water. Aileen had a small table covered with sketches of gowns for different occasions in-cluding balls, weddings, funerals and victory celebrations.

All three were annoyed at the queen because she had re-fused to give them money for new ball gowns. The old gowns they had picked out to wear were draped on hangers in each bedroom where seamstresses had worked all day to freshen them up and make small changes.

"My," Aileen said, "Knuben grew even more handthome during hith adventure. It mutht be the thea air."

"He'll make a wonderful consort for the next queen," Bridget said. "I look forward to having him by my side."

Aileen placed her hands on her hips and glared at her sister.

"Don't get your hopes up, you two." Christel put down a scroll on the natural properties of different woods. "I'm the only one who can interest a man with his training."

"We may have to work out a tharing procedure to keep the peace between uth." Aileen rolled up a dress design and tapped it against her lips. "For inthtance, when we are out-of-thorts each month."

"If either of you even look at my husband when I'm queen," Bridget's eyes flashed dangerously, "I'll exile you to the western boundary. You can watch the yuks make border raids."

"You always were a selfish bitch," Christel replied.

"Leth face factth, ladieth," Aileen said. "There are three of uth and one of him. If we do thith wrong, we may thcare him away. That thkinny elf witch will thcoop him up and we'll lothe out."

Bridget stamped her foot. "What does he see in that drab?"

"Perhaps she is artistic," Christel said.

"Perhaps she enspelled him," Bridget replied. "Let's accuse her witchcraft and get Mama to throw her out of the country."

"Do you seriously think Knuben will talk to any of us after that?" Christel raised a eyebrow.

"Well, we need a plan to theparate the two of them," Aileen said, "then my natural beauty will win him to my thide."

"Until he realizes your tiny mind is only concerned about dress fashions." Bridget sniggered.

"Your mania to rule the world will certainly chase him away from you," Christel said.

"Ath if a virile man would be attracted to a girl whose nothe ith alwayth buried in a thcroll," Aileen said.

"Wait!" Bridget snapped her fingers. "I have a plan." She looked at her sisters and burst out laughing.

"Thith better be good." Aileen crossed her arms and waited.

Christel drummed her finger tips on the scroll.

"What if?" Bridget held up one finger and paced the room. "What if, we have a contest to see who gets and keeps Knuben? We must first all swear an oath that the losers will renounce all further efforts to woo him. Otherwise, we will destroy each other and lose him to the witch."

"I suppose," Christel replied, "it's better if one of us gets him rather than all three lose him."

"Enough already," Aileen waved a hand to extract more information. "Tell uth the plan."

Bridget grinned and looked at her sisters. "The first one to get him into her bed, keeps him."

Aileen's and Christel's jaws dropped open.

"That's right, ladies," Bridget continued, "The first one to lose her virginity -- to Knuben -- marries him."

"Bed him and wed him," Aileen said. "I like it. I'll win thith contetht eathily."

"That's what you think, eldest sister," Bridget scoffed. "You're already past your prime, while I am in full blossom and Christel, of course, is still a child."

"This child," Christel laughed, "has weapons that far surpass anything you two have."

"Oh, pleathe," Aileen made a face at Christel. "What are you babbling about?"

"I have bigger boobs than both of you. And we all know that big boobs drive men crazy."

Aileen and Bridget glared at her, doubt painted on their faces.

#

In her private quarters, Sheena examined the new white gown she would wear tomorrow night. She ran a finger down the shiny material and thought of Knuben. After losing the tax money, he hadn't offered excuses. He went out and replaced the taxes with treasure worth more than the taxes. That showed great determination. Perhaps it also showed a large amount of luck, but it really didn't matter how he accomplished it. The fact that he had returned with the treasure also spoke volumes about his honesty. It was so refreshing to deal with someone who didn't offer false justifications like her ministers. She had inherited the entire lot of them from her mother. Back then they were younger and more flexible. Now they were all ancient and clung to power with a tenacity that denied their age-weakened physical abilities. When not throwing out excuses they offered procrastination, never solutions. She was sick of listening to the pack of old males. Maybe, she should appoint Knuben to the council. He could be a minister without portfolio. That would shake up the others. It might even motivate them to make a decision or two. Probably that was expecting too much.

She walked over to a window and admired the silvery half-moon. Maybe, she should marry Knuben. As royal consort, he would be head of the council. She wasn't so old that she couldn't keep him happy in the bedroom.

She would have to think about what to do with him. He was too valuable to let him leave her service. For once, she had a pleasant problem to ponder.

# # #

A reception line snaked along a corridor leading to the entrance foyer of the ballroom.

Ragazza stood in line between Enric and Knuben. She didn't want to be here; she wanted to stay in her room or go back to the *Rosebud*. Enric convinced her that leaving would be an insult to the queen. Her silver hair had been washed and curled but it looked nothing like the coiffures on the other women standing in line. Her sky-blue robe had been cleaned and ironed, but it still looked drab compared to the gaudy dresses in the corridor. Because of her dark mood, her foresight wasn't working properly and all she could glean was a dark cloud. Not a good omen. She worried about Knuben. Could he handle the intrigues and plotting that would take place tonight? She had her doubts.

Enric preened while the line lurched forward. He loved the way the women glared at him with mixtures of hatred and envy because of his green taffeta caftan and the pearl choker. His sandaled feet showed off his be-ringed toes. His arms carried so many gold bracelets he clanked like a knight in armor when he shifted the leather sack hanging from one shoulder.

Knuben wore a white linen shirt and tan breeches. Sheena had rewarded him with a hundred silver pennies and he used much of it to buy new clothes. In his jubilant spirit, he didn't notice Ragazza's depressed mood. He was confident that Sheena would offer him a court position that would enhance his career. He had to make sure he deported himself properly at the ball in order not to jeopardize her opinion of him.

The line crept ahead and eventually they stood in front of the queen. Ragazza curtsied and the two males bowed. Sheena looked radiant in the white satin gown cut daringly low for a widowed woman. Her short blonde hair had several jeweled pins in it. She smiled at Enric and Ragazza, but addressed Knuben, her green eyes twinkling. "I would like the pleasure of a dance this evening."

"At your service." Knuben blushed. Sheena was a beautiful woman and she carried herself as if she knew it.

"Have you two met my daughters?" she asked Ragazza and Enric. "Knuben knows them well. This is my eldest, Aileen, followed by Bridget and my youngest Christel."

Ragazza glanced at them and sucked in her breath because of the ravenous looks they cast on Knuben. Again, the thought of predators filled her mind.

Knuben was struck dumb by the princesses, their gowns and their astonishing beauty. Between the time he had arrived back in court and left on the Bermid mission, he hadn't seen much of them. Only two brief lunches when they had worn their peasant outfits.

He bowed to Aileen who wore her blond hair in an intricate braid that hung down her back. Her pink dress was cut low, showing much of her bosom and it had a side slit almost as high as her waist. Aileen shifted her weight slightly and the dress opened to expose one leg to mid-thigh.

Knuben gulped and moved in front of Bridget. Her light brown hair was arranged in an elaborate bun at the back of her neck. He jerked his eyes away from the top of her dress. It was cut so low it made him uncomfortable. Her blue gown was so tight he couldn't imagine how she got into it. Or how she could move about the hall.

Christel gave him a radiant smile. The shortest of the sisters, her dark brown hair was piled on top of her head in a bouffant. Her green gown displayed even more flesh than her sisters'. He bowed low to get her bosom out of his sight and found himself staring into her naked navel. Her dress was cut away between just below her breasts and just above her groin, leaving only a few inches of skimpy material in strategic places.

Ragazza pulled Knuben's arm and dragged him away from the acres of exposed creamy-white skin. He looked around. The ball took place in a cavernous hall. Against the wall opposite the entrance, a large table held refreshments and sweetmeats. To the right of the table, glass doors led to the gardens. The two short sides of the room held fireplaces large enough to roast a boar. Near the garden doors were dozens of small round tables and chairs. In a corner to the right, an orchestra tuned their instruments.

Enric steered them to the refreshment table and its lake-sized punch bowl. He opened his leather sack and took out a wooden box. The attendant behind the table raised an eyebrow. "Pipeweed," Enric said. "High quality, long leaf."

"Very good, sir." The attendant looked impressed.

"Will you put it at the end of the table where it will be easier to find?" Enric asked.

The attendant took the box and walked toward the end.

When the man turned his back, Enric took out a bottle of yukeste, pulled the cork with his teeth and poured it into the punch. He kicked the bottle under the table. He took out a small pouch, went to the closest fireplace and threw more pipeweed into the roaring fire. Immediately, the fire blazed and a dense white cloud of incense-like smoke flowed out of the fireplace. "Hah!" Enric exclaimed. "This is one party that won't turn dull."

Knuben noticed the ministers sitting at a table. Females sat with them and none of them smiled or looked like they were enjoying themselves.

After the last guests came through the reception line, the orchestra struck up a tune. Sheena spotted Knuben and beckoned to him. With a beet-red face, he walked to her. She held out her arms and said, "I want my first dance to be with my newest hero." They circled the dance floor to the applause of the guests.

The princesses left the reception line and rushed to the punch bowl, enraged that their mother had cut in on their prey. They grabbed cups of punch and gulped them down.

Bridget fanned a hand in front of her open mouth. "That's good punch," she croaked.

"What are we going to do if Mama won't leave Knuben alone?" Christel asked.

"We'll have to dithract her," Aileen said. "Thet fire to a table cloth maybe."

They had another cup of punch and watched the queen flirt with Knuben.

"This is embarrassing," Bridget said. "Mama is too old to be doing this."

The music ended and Knuben bowed to the queen. She threw him a smile over her bare shoulder as she walked away.

"At latht," Aileen said. "I'm the oldeth, it'th only fitting that I go firtht."

"Over my dead body," Christel snarled.

"This requires negotiation," Bridget said. "Form a circle."

They started a complicated ritual of repeatedly and rapidly throwing out various quantities of fingers accompanied by curses and foot-stamps.

A young nobleman approached them. "Are you ladith deciding who geth to dance with me firth?"

"Get lost, fool," Bridget snapped. "We don't have time for you fops."

The other two scowled at him and he fled from their presence.

When it was over, Bridget had won first crack at Knuben, followed by Aileen and then Christel.

Knuben and Ragazza stood together out of the way of the dancers and watched the other guests. Warned by Enric, they took small sips of punch. Ragazza saw the tight circle of princesses and suppressed an urge to conjure up a local area of low pressure that would develop into a cyclonic depression reeking havoc with their hair and clothes.

A few minutes later, Bridget startled both of them by grabbing Knuben's arm. She said in a loud voice, "Got you!" She dragged him onto the dance floor. Along the way, she leaned her body into his. Knuben broke out in sweat. Once in each others' arms, she said, "I will be the next queen, you know. Aileen is too scatterbrained to be the queen and Christel doesn't care about it. As the queen, I will need a strong consort to help me rule. It's never too early for my consort-elect and I to start working together." She graced Knuben with a beatific smile. "After all, look how old Mama is." She threw out her chest as she breathed deeply. "I'm going into the garden to get some fresh air. Why don't you join me in a few minutes? We can go to my room by a back way. No one will see us. We can . . . talk about our future." She slunk toward the glass doors.

Knuben regretted having his breeches cut so tight.

Before he could return to Ragazza, Aileen seized his hands and led him back onto the dance floor. He concentrated on staring at her forehead, but his peripheral vision still caught the inviting hollow between her breasts. She pulled him closer. More sweat broke out on his forehead.

"I want to thee the world," she said. "I want to meet people and thee the lateth fathionth in big citith like Dun Hythe." She smiled. "Of courth, a women can't travel alone. The mutht have a chaperon to protect her. Thomeone like you."

The music ended and Aileen released him. "I think I'll get thome freth air. Why don't you join me in a few minuteth. We can go to my room and you can tell me all about your travelth."

The musicians dropped their instruments and raided the punch bowl.

"I. . . I'll be there in a few minutes." Knuben watched the sway of her hips as she sauntered away. He turned toward the punch bowl, but the musicians beat him there and he had to wait until they tossed down several cups of punch.

Enric sat at a table launching his new business venture. The table was surrounded by women who pushed and shoved to get closer to him. One by one, they described the dress of their dreams including the cut, the fabric and the color. He made notes on a scroll for his wife. He promised to have the dresses custom-made in Zears and brought back to the court. After listening to the description, Enric stood up with a string in his hand. It had knots every inch along its length. Using the string he measured the woman's body: her height, hips, waist and bust. For that last, he stood on a chair and fumbled the string forcing him to redo the measurements a number of times. The measurement process was accompanied by much giggling and tittering by everybody.

Knuben got a punch and looked around for Ragazza. He saw her sitting alone at a table. She looked unhappy. He smiled at her, but she turned her head away. He puzzled over her actions, but couldn't figure out what the problem was.

While he thought about Ragazza, Christel pounced on him from behind. She grabbed his arm and spun him around sloshing his punch on the floor. "At last, my family has left you alone." She bestowed a dazzling smile on him. "I need more punch. Come with me." She placed her arm in his and they strolled to the punch bowl. Along the way, he noticed that folks moved out of the way for the princess. He fetched two cups of punch. While they sipped them, she leaned her body against him and he became too aware of her magnificent figure.

She said, "Have you read the latest treatise from Halgar the Calculator? It's about a mathematical concept using vectors."

Knuben took another sip to hide his astonishment. Vectors were an obscure and advanced branch of mathematiks. He would love to read the work. "No" he managed to croak.

"Why don't we go into the garden. I know a back way to get to my room. Nosey folks won't see us." She looked at him over the rim of the cup. He noticed her eyes were slightly unfocused. "You can examine the treatise . . . along with anything else that . . . umm, interests you." She batted her eyes. "I'll go to the garden. Get two more punches and meet me." She staggered away, bouncing off several other guests.

The orchestra went back to work, but with a subtle change. Not all the musicians played the same notes at the same time. Some of them lagged a few beats behind others. It gave the music a hollow sound like an echo in a barrel.

Sheena, trailed by a bevy of court flunkies, crossed the room toward him. Almost like magic, a path through the crowded dance floor opened up for her. She gave him a smile and waved a hand. The flunkies disappeared, leaving them alone. "This is the strangest ball I've ever attended," she said. "Everyone is acting goofy." She pointed to some dancers, who, under the influence of pipeweed and yukeste, leaned on each other to remain upright. "I want to talk to you about a serious problem I have. I need intelligent advice to run Sulvaria properly. Right now, I don't get it from my cabinet ministers." She linked her arm in Knuben's and he became aware -- more than he wanted to -- of her expensive and exotic perfume. "Let us stroll in the gardens."

Outside in the refreshingly cool night air, Sheena led him toward a bench. Before they reached it, they heard Aileen yell, "What are you doing here, bitch?" followed by the sound of a slap.

"You'll pay for that," Bridget snarled.

"Let go of my hair," Aileen yelped.

Sheena tightened her grip on his arm.

"Stop it," Christel yelled. "Both of you leave immediately."

"Not a chance," Aileen said in a sobbing voice. "Go inthide, the two of you."

"Don't tell me what to do," Bridget and Christel said in unison.

"It seems the gardens are in use." Sheena sighed. "We better leave before this gets even more embarrassing." Once inside, she continued, "Seek me out when the ball ends. I want to discuss some issues with you. We'll talk in my chambers. Alone." She waved a hand and her flunkies reappeared.

Knuben's mind had turned to mush, overloaded with incipient lust. After four beautiful women made offers to him, he had trouble doing ordinary things like breathing and walking straight. Wearing a lubricous smile, he sought Ragazza. He needed her levelheaded companionship to regain his equilibrium. While the princesses suggested a tryst, Sheena had issued a command. He thought about the potential consequences of meeting her in private and his breeches grew tight. Again.

He found Ragazza sitting by herself. She gave him a look of hatred which he missed. "Enjoying yourself?" He smiled at her.

Ragazza jumped up. "Leave me alone, you sex-fiend. Go back to your brazen hussies." She slapped his face and ran out of the hall.

A stunned Knuben watched her disappear. All thoughts of lusty, royal women fled from his mind. Ragazza's departure left his mouth tasting of bile. He morosely wandered over to the punch bowl.

After four cups of punch, he staggered to his room, all thoughts of the queen's order forgotten.

PART FOUR

Knuben's head throbbed. He looked at the plate of eggs, cheese and bread sitting on the table in front of him and almost got sick again. It was the morning after the anniversary ball and, while he had much to regret about last night, at the moment, he mostly regretted the yukeste. The last coherent thing he remembered about the ball was the look of anguish on Ragazza's face an instant before she slapped him and fled the hall. He needed to find a way to talk to her, to reassure her and comfort her.

He looked at Enric. The dwarf was disgusting. He shoveled food into his mouth with both hands. Enric swallowed and said, "Don't fret, laddie." He stuffed cheese into his mouth. Between chews, he added, "Females are inexplicable." Chew. "She'll get over it." Chew. "Probably." Chew. "Someday." Chew. "Eventually." Ragazza had spoken to Enric last night before she left the castle and returned to the ship.

"But . . . she was so angry."

"Aye. Females don't like others cuttin' in on their males. And the males always get blamed for the actions of the other females. Those princesses are somethin' else. I thought one of 'em was gonna drag you off the dance floor. Then Ragazza would have somethin' to be mad at."

Besides Ragazza, Knuben was sure the princesses weren't talking to him.

A courtier approached the table and said, "The Queen orders both of you to attend her immediately. She is in the council chambers." He spun on his heel and left.

Knuben recalled the queen last night and groaned. Another female that must be angry with him.

# # #

Sheena sat in the council chambers awaiting Knuben and Enric. The stained-glass windows allowed in muted light from the overcast sky. From her place at the head of the large table she watched her four ministers squirm as they attempted to decipher the meaning of the emergency meeting and her silence. She guessed what useless advice they would offer after she explained the new crisis. Dubois, the court administrator will undoubtedly object to guests at the meeting. Macleod, the Treasurer, will demand an increase in taxes on the workers. Groner will need months to recruit and train more troops before anything else can be done while Bidwell will want to ponder the situation until it goes away.

Her guests arrived and she waved them to empty chairs near the other end of the table. "Now that we are all here, we can begin."

"Majesty! I must protest." Pierre Dubois stood and waved a hand in the direction of the visitors. "Our council sessions have always been closed to outsiders. We shouldn't allow these two here." The half-pint bobbed his head and sat down.

"I asked them to attend. They have experiences that can be vital to our response to a new crisis." She stood and thumped a knuckle on the table. "Last night, after the ball, I received a message with the most distressing news. I wished I had someone to discuss the situation with." She glared at Knuben.

Knuben looked at his feet and wiped his nose with a sleeve.

"Several days ago, Egor invaded Bermid and now besieges the city."

The ministers groaned aloud.

"No matter how strong the city's walls are, it must fall eventually," she continued. "Our purpose here is to determine how we can relieve the siege."

"Her majesty is correct," General Claus Groner, the army minister, said. "We must hasten to relieve Bermid. But before we can do that, we must increase the size of the army. It will take some time to recruit and train them. Meanwhile, we can appoint a committee of officers to examine the best way to relieve the island and give us their recommendations." The dwarf looked around the table for a consensus.

"Hear, hear," Commodore Bidwell responded. "Due to the urgency, I recommend this committee make its conclusions known within two months. During that time, I will ponder the best way to transport the army to Bermid."

"Two months, you say." The elfin treasury minister, Angus MacLeod, looked shocked. "That is hardly time to gather all the facts let alone interview folks familiar with the geography and tides and whatnot. Besides, it will take longer than that to collect the tax increases we must levy to pay for the additional troops. I think three months will be a more realistic interval."

"Good point," Bidwell said. "Perhaps three months will be better."

Sheena smiled to herself. The council was in great form today. Her ministers advocated doing nothing and they wanted it done slowly. "What do our guests say?"

"The way to break a siege is to attack the besiegers," Knuben replied.

"You have experience in sieges?" General Groner sneered.

"He has more battle experience that you have," Sheena replied. "If I recall correctly, you've never been in a battle."

"I was in a siege with the Duke of Venta's army," Knuben said.

"How do we break this siege, Knuben?" Sheena asked

Knuben cleared his throat before speaking. "To begin with, we need information on how many pirates are at Bermid." He stroked his chin. "Do we know if Egor's entire fleet is there?"

"The messenger said the harbor was full of pirate ships. He said he counted sixty of them."

"Each corsair can carry around thirty-five." Enric stuck out his tongue while he calculated. "That means Egor has over two thousand pirates on Bermid."

Knuben pulled a face while he absorbed the facts. After a moment or two, he smiled. "Your Majesty, this means you face a unique opportunity."

Enric grinned at Knuben and said to the queen. "The laddie is right as rain. With Egor's entire fleet inna harbor and all his crews on land, you can crush him in one blow. If you act quickly and decisively."

"Nonsense!" General Groner said in a loud voice. "We must assess the situation and devise a strategy."

"Exactly," MacLeod said. "We can't just run off without a plan. We'll get everyone killed."

"Silence!" Sheena stood and glared at the ministers. "I don't want to hear another interruption until my guests finish speaking." She looked at Enric and Knuben. "Please explain. I'm most interested in what you are thinking."

"The biggest problem with fighting Egor," Enric said, "is that his fleet is never in one place. It's scattered all over the Sea of Gundarland, so it has to be dealt with piecemeal and that gives Egor time to replace his losses. But now he's made a mistake. All his ships and crews are together and tied down inna siege. This maybe the only time he'll give you such an opportunity."

Sheena stared at a stained-glass window while she reviewed Enric's analysis. She liked what she heard. The problem with his solution was the necessary resources. Did she have enough to carry out the plan? "And how would we take advantage of this opportunity?"

"How many ships do you have and how many troops can they carry?" Knuben asked her.

Sheena looked at the commodore. "Well?"

Bidwell looked nervous and cleared his throat several times before answering. "We have only five ships after this young man lost one of them. They can each carry perhaps forty troops along with the crew."

"The *Rosebud* can carry another hundred," Enric said. "So let's make it a total of three hundred solders. Is that enough, Knuben?"

"No, but Bermid isn't that far away, so let's say we crowd fifty soldiers on each of the Queen's ships, and put another twenty-five on the *Rosebud*. Now we have three-hun-dred-seventy-five troops." Knuben paused and looked at Sheena. "How many soldiers are inside Bermid?

"Answer him," Sheena told General Groner.

"If memory serves, there are a dozen mounted knights and an elfin archer unit of fifty longbows. Then there is the local militia."

Knuben jumped up in excitement and paced the room. "So, if we land almost four hundred soldiers outside Bermid, Egor will be forced to break off the siege and gather his pir-ates in one place to fight a battle with us, but they're spread out all around the city. Many of them won't make it back in time to get into the fight. Once they form up to fight the sol-diers, the forces inside Bermid can launch an attack and hammer Egor in the rear. Even though the relieving force will be outnumbered, the pirates can be smashed between the two attacks."

"While the land battle is going on, the fleet can destroy Egor's corsairs." Enric grinned. "I'd love to see that."

"Ahh," Knuben said. "That means Egor will have to send some of his pirates to defend his boats and try to get them out of the harbor. That leaves even less to fight the Queen's soldiers."

"These two are insane." Bidwell's face contorted with anger. "They'll get our entire military wiped out. Don't listen to them, Majesty."

Sheena ignored the commodore. "When could this attack force leave?"

"Depends," Knuben said. "How long will it take to assemble the ships and troops?"

"The ships are in port," Sheena replied. "They're always in port. There should be more than four hundred soldiers in Cintri. All they ever do is march in parades. A sea voyage will do them good."

"Majesty," General Groner wailed. "I can't defend the palace if you strip it of troops and send me to Bermid."

"The fleet has to be made ready for a long sea voyage," Bidwell said in a quavering voice. "It'll be some time before I can leave."

"The voyage is only a week," Enric snapped. "The ships don't have to be in great shape."

Sheena tapped her fingers on the table top for a few seconds. Finally she said, "Enric, I appoint you admiral of the fleet. Knuben, you are now the general in charge of relieving Bermid. I order both of you to break the siege and destroy all of Egor's pirate army and his fleet. You will leave as soon as the soldiers and necessary supplies can be loaded on the ships, but in no case will that be later then the second day from now." She pointed a finger at each minister in turn. "If any of you place obstacles in the way of this mission, I'll have you arrested for aiding the enemy and I'll charge you with treason." To Enric and Knuben, she added, "You both report directly to me. I want a report on progress in the morning and evening. Give me the names of anyone who stands in your way. This meeting is adjourned."

She walked out of the chamber with a smile on her face. Finally, a council meeting that accomplished something. The looks on the faces of her ministers were priceless. Groner and Bidwell actually looked relieved that they didn't have to go to Bermid.

She'd remember this meeting for as long as she lived.

# # #

Egor sat under an awning on the stern of his flagship. The corsair, tied up to one of the great wharfs in Bermid harbor, rocked on a gentle surf. Palm trees swayed in the hot breeze and sweat rolled down his bare upper torso. Bermid's weather was as much a bother as the city's twenty-foot walls and its archers.

So far, all he had accomplished was to inconvenience and annoy the citizen's of Bermid. He had too few pirates to make a frontal assault of the walls or to completely seal off the city. Food was now a problem. His original plan called for the conquered city to feed his crews. That didn't happen and the crops wouldn't be ready for harvesting for another six or eight weeks. The farmers had driven all their cattle into the hills where his pirates had trouble finding them. The food situation forced him to send a dozen corsairs back to his stronghold for supplies.

He had dispatched another dozen to Yukland to recruit more brigands. A few hundred additional swords could turn the tide and allow him to capture the city.

He bunched his hands into fists. So much depended on Bermid. He needed the revenues from the city to build a force big enough to invade Sulvaria. If he showed weakness here, recruits would be reluctant to join him. That concern reminded him of Enric and he smiled thinking of the tortures awaiting that dwarf.

He forced his thoughts away from Enric and back to the siege. As soon as the reinforcements showed up, he would conquer the city.

# # #

Knuben watched the troops assemble in an empty dockside warehouse. Each unit found a space and settled down to wait until they embarked on the ships. He worried about these soldiers. He knew the battle wouldn't be anything like he described it to Sheena. No battle ever unfolded the way it was planned. Some unsuspected element would throw everything out of kilter. Right now, Knuben didn't like the possible odds. He didn't have enough troops to set up a strong shield wall and, if Egor amassed enough sailors at a single point, he could burst through the shield wall with disastrous results for Sheena's army.

He needed something to equalize the odds. He needed a land version of his barrel dropper.

"The last time I was here," Enric said, interrupting Knuben's concentration, "this place was stuffed with cargo waiting for a ship."

Knuben looked around at the vast warehouse. The only light came from the open doors on front and back and windows in the upper part of the walls. "We need torches in here so the troops can see to their weapons and gear."

"Let's see if the stevedores have any." Enric indicated a group of dockworkers idling in one corner. They walked over and explained their need.

"Look over there," a grizzled worker replied. "That stuff'll make good torches."

"What stuff?" Knuben gave the worker a quizzical look. "The place is empty."

"Not quite. See those dozen barrels over there?" He pointed to a skid of large barrels against a wall.

"So?" Enric said. "What's in 'em?"

"Lamp oil. Very flammable. Don't know why they're still here. I guess the owner thinks they shipped out on one of the last boats to leave here."

Knuben experienced a tingling sensation in his brain. He took a deep breath. An idea struggled to get born. At last it blossomed and he laughed out loud. He had his new weapon. "I want three barrels loaded on the *Rosebud*." Actually, he wanted all twelve, but since his troops would have to carry them to the battle, he settled for three.

"Can't do that. You have to buy 'em from the owner first."

"I'm taking them by the authority given me by the queen."

The old worker looked dubious.

"If the owner has a problem, tell him to take it up with the queen." Knuben smiled at the worker. "You won't be blamed for the missing barrels. Now get the dockworkers to take three of them to the ship."

# # #

The *Rosebud* led the squadron of six ships as they breasted the three-foot swells and turned west. In the distance, off the starboard side, a smudge indicated the coast of Sulvaria.

Knuben stood on the quarterdeck, one hand pressing on his stomach to try to keep it under control. He inhaled the sea air. After four days, his enthusiasm for the mission still ran high, despite his seasickness. He led a force of three-hundred and seventy soldiers. It consisted of fifty elfin long-bows, one-hundred-fifty dwarf axes and a hundred-seventy swordsmen. Many of the troops seemed to have dubious military talents. Except for a handful of mercenaries in the ranks, none of them had seen combat. He suspected General Groner had hidden his best troops and officers where Knuben couldn't find them. Crammed below in the *Rosebud's* hold, one-hundred-twenty-five troops sweltered and threw up on each other. The contingent consisted of twenty-five archers, fifty swordsmen and fifty ax warriors.

Over time, Sheena's military had become quite comfortable, and enjoyed their safe and easy lives in Cintri. None of them were happy about the mission. The ships' captains despised Enric as much as the soldiers' officers resented Knuben.

The *Rosebud* heeled to port as Ragazza altered the wind direction. Knuben barely managed to keep from rushing to the rail. Life at sea was quite different without Ragazza's seasickness spells. He couldn't fathom how anyone could want to be sailors. Besides being sick all the time, he found the living conditions below deck appalling.

Enric climbed the stairs to the quarterdeck and looked at the five ships sailing in a line behind the *Rosebud*. "Now comes the hard part," Enric said. "Once we turn west, we'll be sailin' into the wind. Ragazza will have her work cut out castin' weather spells for all six ships."

The way Enric had explained it, it took a week to sail from Cintri to Bermid because of the wind conditions. Ragazza's weather magic would reduce the journey by a day, so they still had three days sailing before they attacked Egor and his pirates.

Ragazza came on deck from her cabin and approached Enric while ignoring Knuben. "A small craft approaches. From its course, it may have come from Bermid."

"Hmm." Enric stroked the stubble on his cheek. "We better check it out. With luck, we'll get news about the siege."

Ragazza adjusted the wind direction and left the quarter-deck.

"She's stubborn," Enric said shaking his head. "That's for sure. I keep tellin' her it ain't your fault the princesses threw themselves at you. But it doesn't do any good."

"I've been so miserable. The worst part is seeing her every day, being close and not being able to talk to her."

"She's as miserable you are," Enric said as he checked the ships behind him. "I don't understand why people do that to themselves."

Within an hour, they spotted a small ketch sailing east with two sailors in it. The ketch veered toward them when it spotted the Sulvarian flag flying at the *Rosebud's* masthead. After the ketch tied up alongside, the two sailors climbed aboard. Ardnt led them to Enric's cabin to meet with the captain, Ragazza and Knuben.

"We was sent by Bermid's mayor to ask the queen for help." The speaker was the older of the two, a human. "The mayor sent out other messengers by different routes. We left from the eastern end of the island. Ain't no pirates there. We're mighty glad to see you."

"What's the situation in Bermid?" Enric asked.

"The city has wells, so water ain't a problem. Food's gettin' scarce. So far the pirate scum ain't come close to gettin' over the walls. But if help don't get there soon, they won't have to climb the walls. The food'll run out."

"We'll be there in a few days," Enric said.

"The mayor thinks Egor has sent for reinforcements 'cause a coupla dozen pirate ships left the harbor and ain't come back when we left."

"We intend to put paid alongside Egor's name." Knuben said.

"It's time for you to continue on to the queen," Enric said. "Make sure you tell her that you met us."

After the two seamen left, Enric rubbed his hands together and cackled. "All those pirates ships leavin' the harbor means you'll have to fight a smaller number of pirates."

# # #

Knuben stood on the main deck watching some of the *Rosebud's* contingent of troops work out when they weren't draped over the railings puking. Dwarf ax warriors faced other dwarfs and engaged in mock combat. Swordsmen did the same while a squad of elfin archers did stretching exercises. A subaltern and a sergeant called out orders and cursed at ineffectual maneuvers and the seasick soldiers.

Some of the *Rosebud's* sailors imitated the soldiers and dueled with their knitting needles.

Ragazza and Enric conferred on the quarterdeck. The sight of the wind blowing through her silver hair made his chest constrict. She looked so sad. How was he supposed to make up with her when she ignored his presence? Any message she had for him, she delivered though Enric or Ardnt. While it was true he had been interested in the princesses and the queen -- lusted might be a more accurate description than interested -- he realized the royals were a diversion, nothing more. Ragazza was the one he wanted to spend time with; the one he wanted to explore the world with; the one he wanted to grow old with. So how was he supposed to tell her that?   The more he pondered that problem, the more his stomach clenched into a knot, and not from seasickness.

"Knuben!" Enric yelled and waved a hand for him to come to the quarterdeck.

While Knuben climbed the stairs, Enric said, "Good news." He grinned and slapped a hand on the wheel housing.

"What?" Knuben looked at Ragazza who turned away.

"A dozen ships over the horizon sailin' towards Bermid," Enric replied. "Have to be corsairs. Probably the reinforcements we heard about."

"We'll soon see what these troops are good for," Knuben said. "This will be a great time to give the soldiers a taste of combat." He hoped the officers on the other ships remembered his orders about what to do in this situation.

"Once we sight 'em," Enric said, "I'll order the fleet into an echelon formation and we'll sail straight through them."

"Well done, Ragazza." Knuben attempted to get her to acknowledge his presence. "I don't know what we'd do without your skills."

Ragazza ignored the words, walked to the far rail and stared out to sea.

# # #

An hour later, Knuben saw the corsairs appear on the horizon off the port side, heading northwest. Enric studied the enemy fleet through his eye glass. "I don't think they're reinforcements. I count only about thirty crew on each one. That's two shifts of rowers. And they're all low in the water. They must be carryin' supplies. Hmm." He scratched his stubble. "Egor must be havin' a hard time feedin' his pirates." He snapped the glass closed and turned to his signal dwarf. "Hoist the flags for echelon formation. Ragazza, give us a wind to intercept the buggers."

She sketched runes with both hands and the wind veered to the southwest and increased in velocity.

"Ardnt! Set the topsails!" Enric ordered.

"I'll get my troops ready." Knuben's plan called for the soldiers to do all the fighting without using the water barrels.

He called his officer and sergeant and the three of them sat down by the mainmast. "Just to be sure you understand the plan, I'll go over it again," Knuben said. "Assign twenty-five swordsmen to one side of the ship and a like number of dwarf axes to the other. Have them sit in the middle of the deck so the pirates can't see them. Once the pirates start to board the *Rosebud*, I'll give the signal and the troops will stand to defend the ship. I want no shirking. The troops need as much combat experience as they can get before we land in Bermid and this is a great opportunity."

"The soldiers will do their duty," the subaltern said in a quavering voice. Knuben estimated his age at seventeen. His noble family had bought his commission thinking it would be a non-perilous sinecure.

The sergeant nodded. Knuben wasn't concerned about him. He was one of the few mercenaries with battle experience. Knuben worried about the army officers on the other ships. General Groner's officers unanimously disliked the idea of fighting anywhere, but especially on a ship.

# # #

Ragazza held onto a backstay and watched the corsairs grow larger. She could hear Knuben and his soldiers preparing for battle. Since the Queen's ball, her life had been miserable. Again, loneliness stalked her. Knuben, the only male she ever felt affection for, had betrayed her that night. And now the two of them were trapped together on the small world of the *Rosebud*. Often, when the shared the quarterdeck or a mess table in Enric's cabin, she verged on forgiving him, but her resolve always stiffened at the last moment. Deep inside her heart, she regretted those moments of steely firmness, but her mind declared the wisdom of her decision. He would only betray her trust again as soon as he returned to court.

No, she reassured herself, better to suffer a little now rather than suffer a lot later on.

# # #

The corsairs turned to fight once they realized they couldn't outrun the fleet because of their heavy cargoes. Once they turned, four of them steered toward the *Rosebud* and pairs of pirate boats made for other ships.

"They spotted the *Rosebud* and they wanna capture us for Egor," Enric called to Knuben as he stood by the main mast watching the pirates approach. "We get to fight four of the buggers."

Knuben shifted his grip on the shield handle. His hands were sweaty from anticipation of battle. Even though he didn't plan to get into the fight, he carried his sword and shield to set an example for his troops.

A corsair bumped into the starboard side, followed by a similar bump on the port side.

"Steady now," Knuben said.

Grappling hooks sailed over the rails and bit into the wood.

Knuben nodded to the subaltern.

"Stand!" the officer called out in a quavering voice.

With groans and cracking knee joints, the soldiers climbed to their feet.

Knuben waited until a pirate hand grasped the rail. "Go get them."

A third corsair bumped into the port side.

The starboard squad stepped to the rails and began stabbing at the pirates. The attackers screamed and cursed when they saw the soldiers standing shoulder-to-shoulder and lining the rail for the entire length of the main deck. A few soldiers threw up on the climbing pirates. In short order, the pirates on the ropes had been cut down, leaving only a small contingent in the corsairs. The boat on the starboard side cut loose and rowed away with only half the oars in use.

Knuben stuck two fingers in his mouth and whistled a piercing signal. A dozen archers filed on deck. Knuben pointed to the starboard side where the swordsmen heckled and jeered the pirates. The archers forced their way to the rail, shoving the swordsmen out of their way. They launched a flight of arrows at the escaping ship and cut down most of the rowers. After a second flight, the corsair turned on the waves, out of control.

On the port side, the dwarfs hacked at the climbing pirates. The deck was slippery with blood and body parts. Knuben peeked over the port rail at the pirates.   The first corsair was filled with the wreckage of bodies. The second tethered outboard the first, but its crew resisted getting into the fight, and an officer screamed horrible curses at them.

Knuben looked over at the other ships in the fleet and saw similar scenes of carnage. He frowned as he realized he was missing a corsair. Four of them had sailed for the *Rosebud*, but only three had grappled onto the ship. He walked to the starboard rail and took a look. He glimpsed the end of a steering oar before it disappeared behind the *Rosebud*. The hair on his neck stood on end. The fourth corsair was attacking from the unguarded rear!

Knuben looked at the quarterdeck. There, Enric watched the slaughter while Ragazza handled the ship's wheel. Neither one knew about the corsair. He raced along the deck and took the stairs two at a time. He reached it in time to see a squad of pirate bowmen lining up the two figures on the quarterdeck.

Knuben seized Enric's arm and threw him down behind the stern rail. "What are you doin'?" the dwarf roared. Enric grabbed Ragazza around the waist and forced her to the deck. He covered her body with his and held up his shield to protect them both.

"Get off me, you id --"

Three arrows slammed into the shield, interrupting Ragazza's curse. More arrows thudded into the deck.

Enric peeked over the rail, saw the archers returning to their oars, stood and yelled, "Ardnt! Get a crew on these blasted cannons. All they planned to do was take one shot with the arrows."

"I love you, you know," Knuben whispered in Ragazza's ear. "This is the first time I've had a chance to talk to you since the ball. That wasn't my fault. I can't control what the princesses did." He climbed to his feet and held out a hand for her. She took it and he pulled her to her feet. She didn't let go of his hand.

When she saw a still-quivering arrow in the center of the ship's wheel, she turned ashen. After a few seconds, she gave Knuben a smile and said, "Thank you."

Ardnt arrived with a slow match in his hand. "Guns are already loaded, Captain." He aimed the cannon at the corsair, now turning away, and lit the fuse. A cloud of smoke and a ear-shattering bang erupted on the deck. The grape shot decapitated an innocent wave near the pirate ship.

"Bloody useless piles of metal, that's what they are." Enric banged his fists on the railing while Ardnt ignored him and aimed the second cannon. This time, the grape shot wreaked havoc on the corsair, turning it into a bloody mess and holing it in a number of places. Water rushed in and within a minute the corsair wallowed helplessly.

Enric gave Ardnt an incredulous look.

Knuben, encouraged by the hand-holding, released his hand and placed an arm around Ragazza's waist. She leaned into him and Knuben's happiness threatened to burst his heart.

"Sir," the subaltern called out.

Knuben turned to the officer. He held a bloody sword in his hand and had a lopsided grin on his face.

"The pirates have been defeated."

"Well done. All the soldiers handled themselves well. Give them my congratulations."

# # #

Sheena and her daughters ate supper together in the queen's private chambers. Servants placed bowls of hot soup on a long table already loaded with a roast, breads and vegetables. All four wore private clothing: loose sweaters and long skirts.

"When will we hear about Bermid, Mama?" Bridget speared a slice of beef.

"Soon, I hope. If all went well on the voyage, they should reach Bermid tomorrow."

"Oh, I hope he saves the city." Christel ripped a chunk of bread apart and popped it into her mouth. "And I hope he isn't wounded or killed."

"If he beatth the pirateth, Mama," Aileen said, "he'll have to be rewarded."

"Besides a reward," Sheena waved her fork, "I have to figure a way to keep him in Sulvaria. He's far too valuable to lose. I need young aggressive minds like his to offset those old ninnies on the council."

"He'll make a wonderful consort for the next queen," Bridget grinned at her sisters.

Sheena studied her daughters for a moment before replying. "He'll make a wonderful consort for the present queen."

"What!" Aileen gasped.

"How disgusting," Bridget hissed.

Christel coughed up the chunk of bread and it flew across the table. An expressionless servant whisked it out of sight.

"Really, Mama," Aileen said in a voice tinged with outrage. "You're old enough to be hith mother."

"And still young enough to please him." She grinned playfully at her daughters. "I can leave him to the one who inherits the throne. I'll have him fully trained in government by then."

Sheena enjoyed the horrified expressions on her daughters' faces. She had no intention of marrying Knuben. He could never remain faithful to her. No matter how hard or how much he resisted, he'd end up in bed with at least one of her daughters and, possibly, with all three before too long. All of this was conjecture of course. For all she knew, Knuben would sail off with the elf, Ragazza.

The fleet anchored in a small cove to land the army, a project that would take some time because of the few small boats available. Each ship in the fleet had sent its two skiffs to unload the *Rosebud*. The other ships would land their troops in turn. The cove was located five miles to the east of Bermid and screened from the city by woods. A spit of land jutted into the sea to hide the ships from Bermid's port.

Out to sea, the horizon glowed with golden-orange light presaging dawn. For now, the shore was blanketed with darkness.

Knuben stepped ashore with the first boatload of troops. He ordered six swordsmen into the woods to form a defensive screen. Slowly, the number of soldiers on the beach increased. They donned their armor once they landed. Knuben organized the units in marching order and talked to the officers who he hadn't seen since they left Cintri. All of them were glad to be ashore, but were horrified at the idea of going into battle.

He waited until the last of the troops reached the beach before ordering, "Form up!" He supervised the movement of the three oil barrels. Each was suspended by a a net borrowed from the *Rosebud* and carried by six swordsmen. "You'll get relieved after fifteen minutes," he told them. "That way, you won't get worn out."

He pointed to the lead unit and said, "Move out."

In the cove, Enric and the fleet pulled up anchors and sailed off to attack the harbor.

"Sir," Knuben's subaltern said as they moved inland. "Are we really outnumbered by the pirates?" The young man fiddled with his sword hilt.

"We are, if you count all the pirates that landed at Bermid, but we won't be fighting all of them. Many of the pirates will be on the other side of the city and won't get back in time to join the fight." He patted the officer on the back. "Besides, Egor lost over three hundred pirates when we sank his corsairs a few days back, so things aren't as a bad as they sound."

Knuben kept looking at the flank guards marching parallel to the army a hundred yards into the woods. Their orders were not to engage the pirates if they saw any, but to hurry back and report the sighting. His biggest fear was getting ambushed on the road when his soldiers were strung out. He'd feel a lot better once they came out of the woods and could form up in a battle line.

He noted the toll the march took on the troops. The stress of the voyage, the heat, the bugs and the exertion of marching with weapons and armor all wore them down. They all looked exhausted.

A scout ran back to the formation and Knuben called a halt. The troops collapsed to the ground.

"Sir," the scout said. "The woods end about a quarter mile ahead."

"Good. What can you see from up there?"

"The city. Between the city and the woods is nothin' but open space. A few hills, but they ain't very high."

"Thank you." He looked at the sky. It was approaching midmorning. He had time to kill before Enric could reach the harbor. "We'll rest for a half-hour and then resume our march."

#

Ragazza stood by the stern rail and watched Knuben march into the woods while the *Rosebud* headed out to sea and into its own battle. She worried about the man she loved and she didn't need her wizardly powers to foretell today was the worst day in her life. Her female intuition told that.

Knuben could be killed, wounded or captured before long. If he survived, but lost the battle, he would be disgraced, his career ruined. Who could tell how that would affect him? Certainly, his spirt would be crushed. Could she nurse and guide him back to normality? Would he even want her around as a reminder of the past?

She considered the alternative to defeat to be an even worse scenario. By winning a victory, Knuben would be the hero of Sulvaria and she would lose him as surely as if he was killed. The queen would reward him a court position at the very least. Ragazza couldn't live in Cintri or any other place on land. She loved the sea and the *Rosebud* was her home. If she couldn't spend her life at sea, she'd wither away, spiritually and physically. Knuben's future, on the other hand, was on land. As the victor at Bermid, he would be hailed as a great soldier and would have a bright future ahead of him leading an army somewhere, if not in Sulvaria. He would be as lost at sea as she would be lost on land.

She sighed. The only male she had ever loved would be lost to her in a few hours.

# # #

Knuben stopped his troops a half-mile from the city walls to build his defensive position. He didn't think the soldiers could march further. Most of them had been seasick for the entire voyage and the march in the heat had exhausted them. He chose a small hill to use for his battle line and let the troops rest. The site meant the enemy would expend a lot of energy getting here. The water's edge would anchor his left flank, so Egor's pirates would have a hard time outflanking him on that side.

He walked over to the soldiers with the oil barrels. "Pick them up and I'll show you where to place them." The men groaned in protest, but lifted the three heavy barrels. Fifty feet in front of the hill, Knuben marked a place in the sandy ground with his heel. "This one will be in front of the center of our line," he said. He walked to where his right flank would be and placed the second barrel there. The third went halfway between the first and the water's edge.

"These things gonna do any good?" the soldier asked.

"They'll make a nice welcome present for the pirates." Knuben grinned.

When he saw some pirates assemble and start toward the hill, he called the officers to gather around him. "Form your men into a shield wall," he told the officers of the ax warriors and the swordsmen. "Alternate axes and swords. I want a hundred troops in the front line and I want two lines behind the first." Combat classes taught that a shield wall ought to be at least seven or eight lines deep, but he didn't have enough soldiers to do that.

The officers responded without enthusiasm. None of them had ever blooded a sword and they were worried more about saving their lives than they were about defeating the pirates. Fortunately, the morale of the troops was higher than the officers. They had fought the pirates at sea and they looked forward to another victory today. The soldiers banged their weapons on their shields, producing a hideous din.

To the officer in charge of the elfin archers, he said, "Form up over there and get a fire going." Knuben pointed to a small knob of ground behind the right flank. "Your job is to protect the right flank of the shield wall. Don't let the pirates get around the edge or we're all in big trouble because we only have a small reserve force."

"We'll pop anyone who tries to get around the flank," the elf officer replied.

At least this one knows his job, Knuben thought. "From your position you can fire over the heads of our troops and reduce of number of pirates who attack the wall."

The officer saluted and ran off.

Knuben beckoned to the subaltern who had been left out of the shield wall along with twenty-five of his swordsmen. "I want you and your soldiers on that hill over there with the archers."

The officer gulped and managed to croak,"Yes sir."

"You have two tasks. The first is to protect the archers from an attack. The second is act as my reserve force. If the shield wall starts to cave in anywhere, you have to rush up and fill the gap."

The subaltern turned ashen.

"I have confidence in you. You did well onboard the *Rosebud* when we fought off the corsairs. I know you can do this." Knuben gave the lad a slap on the arm. "To your post."

The subaltern saluted and ran off to fetch his soldiers.

Knuben had nothing to do now except wait for the pirates. Already a hundred or so had assembled near the boats and many more were running from positions near the walls. He hoped Enric didn't run into any trouble. His army would have a tough time holding out if Enric didn't relieve some of the pressure.

# # #

Egor lounged under the awning on his flagship. Besieging a city had to be the dullest activity in the world. It was also the most frustrating. Until his reinforcements arrived, there was little he could do. He had grown to hate Bermid and everyone behind the walls. They made a mockery of his grand plan to conquer Sulvaria. How could he expect to conquer a province when a small city defied him?

The bodies hanging from the walls taunted him with his latest failure. Three pirates had scaled the walls last night seeking someone to betray the city and open the gates in return for a mountain of gold. His pirates had been hung at dawn this morning.

His supply problems were troublesome. The supply ships should have returned by now with supplies. Where were they? In desperation, he had sent some of his corsairs beyond the bay to catch fish to feed his sailors.

An elf ran up the wharf toward his ship, a look of dismay on the pirate's face. Egor knew he faced another problem. The elf boarded the ship and hurried to the stern. "Admiral! There's an army over there." The elf pointed to the east. "It came outta the woods."

Egor jumped up. He looked in the direction indicated but couldn't see anything because of the warehouses and port facilities.   He leaped onto the wharf and ran to the end. From there, he saw soldiers lining up in a shield wall. Why did the enemy have barrels in front of the line? He held up hand to block the sun while he studied the enemy position. There wasn't a lot of them. Unless more were still in the woods. If that was the entire force, he could overwhelm them. But at what cost? After a battle, he wouldn't have enough pirates to continue the siege. On the other hand, the morale of the folks behind the walls would be crushed by a defeat of their relieving army.

First things first, he thought. Those troops were a threat and he had to destroy them. After that, he could deal with Bermid. He grabbed the elf's shoulder. "See dose guys workin' onna boats? Tell dem to form a line." Egor pointed to a punishment gang of twenty-five scraping barnacles from the hulls of beached corsairs.

To another pirate, he said, "Go to da city. Get da crews. Dey gotta get back here quick." He shoved the pirate. "Go!"

The Bermid walls were a half-mile away and he needed time to assemble an attack force. In the meantime, the work crew would have to slow the enemy down. Egor examined the enemy again. They hadn't moved. Perfect. If they stayed in place, he would have time to organize a response that would defeat them. Whoever was in charge over there was obviously an idiot. He should have attacked while he had the element of surprise.

The work crew assembled near Egor. They laughed and shoved each other, glad to be away from their barnacle scraping.   "Getta inna line and stop horsin' around. We gotta destroy dat army. If dey start movin' forward, you gotta keep them busy and slow dem down. When da crews get back from da walls, we'll attack dem."

Egor looked to Bermid. Already, a few dozen pirates jogged toward the beach. He grinned, no longer bored. He flexed his wrists and unsheathed his sword.

# # #

Knuben watched the enemy mass near his shield wall, but out of arrow range. The original small force of pirates had steadily grown and now outnumbered his forces. Still more pirates streamed in from the city. A lump grew in his gut. Today wasn't going to be quite as easy as he told Sheena it would be. He called to the archer officer, "I want a ranging arrow."

The officer replied by launching an arrow on a high, arcing flight. It landed a dozen paces in front of the pirate formation. Knuben nodded. Now he knew when the pirates would be in range of the longbows.

The pirates unleashed an attack and surged forward a few minutes later.

Knuben pointed to the archers and the officer gave an order.

Three fire arrows flew toward the oil barrels leaving a trail of black smoke. Two hit their targets and the barrels lit up in flames. The third arrow missed the middle barrel. Seconds later, another fire arrow punctured the barrel. Burning oil spread out on the ground from all three barrels. The flames confused the pirates. Their charge petered out before reaching the burning obstacle. While they watched, the barrels exploded sending waves of oil in all directions. A dozen pirates were drenched by flaming oil and ran screaming into the water. The others milled around looking for a path to the shield wall. Several narrow paths lead through the flaming obstacle and the braver pirates tiptoed through.

The archers sent flight after flight of arrows into the bunched-up pirates. A corsair captain recognized the danger. "Move! Get past the flames and you'll be too close for the archers to shoot at you. Jump over the fire. Get to the shield wall."

While he shoved pirates forward, the flames subsided as the fuel burned up.

Knuben admired the effect his obstacle had. It slowed down the pirates and allowed the archers to take a toll. The pirate charge was ragged and uneven, consequently, the enemy couldn't concentrate a strong force against one section of the shield wall. Not yet anyway.

"Steady now!" Knuben shouted as he paced behind his troops. "Get ready for the impact. Brace yourselves." He clapped officers on the shoulders. "Don't give ground. Hold fast."

The pirates plowed into Knuben's line. Shields, swords and axes clashed together. Curses and screams filled the air.

The archers stopped firing now that the main mob of pirates were up against the shield wall. They limited their arrows to the reinforcements still coming into the battle and to anyone who tried to move around the right flank.

Knuben's strategy of alternating dwarfs and the much taller swordsmen payed off. The shorter dwarfs held their shields over their heads for protection and used their axes on the lower limbs of the pirates. The swordsmen meanwhile acted defensively protecting themselves and their dwarf partner to their right. They let the dwarfs do most of the damage. The pirate numbers continued to grow in the center and the shield wall curved inward.

After a few minutes of battle, the wall thinned down in many places. Knuben beckoned for the subaltern to bring the reserves. The archers would have to protect themselves.

Knuben recognized the reality of the battle. In another minute or two, he expected the shield wall to collapse. Once that happened the pirates would slaughter his retreating soldiers. He and the subaltern would have to slow the pirates down to give a few soldiers the time to escape. He foresaw his death on this battlefield. So be it. He had lost the battle so it was only fair that he gave his life to help some of the troops escape. He wished he had time to take a drink of water to moisten his sand-dry throat.

A trumpet blast came from Bermid. The city gates opened and a dozen mounted knights in full armor charged through and turned toward the battle line. Armed citizens on foot poured out of the city. The pressure on the shield wall lessened as the pirates in the rear fell back to face the new threat. Groups of pirate stragglers bunched up to fight the knights who ignored them and continued to race toward Knuben's forces. Their lances came down and a few pirates screamed and ran from the battle.

A new cry went up from some of the pirates. "Our ships. They're burning our ships!" They pointed to the harbor where dense black smoke rose to the sky.

"Attack!" Knuben roared. He jumped into the shield wall and hacked at a pirate. His opponent screamed and disappeared underfoot. "Push them back!" he called out. "Push!"

#

Enric stood on the quarterdeck in his battle gear, a padded doublet and red kilt. His battle ax rested on his shoulder and his two throwing axes were tucked into his belt. A few feet away, Ragazza wove weather spells to keep the *Rosebud* and the other ships on a steady course into Bermid harbor. She blew a strand of hair out of her face and paused to check on the gusting winds. A crosscurrent pushed the bow of the ship to port. A quick rune corrected the ship's course.

Enric grabbed a backstay and climbed on the rail to get a better view of the harbor. His heart skipped a beat when he saw the beach lined with corsairs. Only a handful anchored in the shallows near the shore. Just what he hoped for! Egor's fleet sat waiting for a disaster to happen.

He studied the wharves as they came closer and spotted Egor's ship docked at a wharf and flying his black battle ensign. "Ragazza! Take us to the wharves." He pointed to the far side of the harbor.

She nodded and cast a weather spell that affected only the *Rosebud*.

Enric gestured to the closest ship, indicating it shouldn't follow the *Rosebud* as it came around. He jumped off the rail and yelled, "Ardnt! Detail ten men to come with you and me." Enric jigged around the quarterdeck and grinned at Ragazza.

In a few minutes, the *Rosebud* slid up against the wharf and the crew lashed it to the stanchions. Enric and Ardnt jumped to the wharf before the ship completely stopped. Across the dock, Egor's corsair had two yuks guarding it.

Both looked ready to dive overboard as more dwarfs left the ship and gathered near Ardnt.

Enric strolled up to the yuks. "Nice day for a fight, ain't it?"

An arrow fired from the *Rosebud* grazed a yuk's arm. He roared in pain and charged Enric while waving a scimitar over his head. Enric shifted his battle ax to his other shoulder, grabbed a throwing ax and heaved it at the yuk. It plunked into his chest and he crashed to the dock. The second guard took a swim.

Enric retrieved his ax, walked up to the edge of the dock and peeked into the corsair. As he expected, a number of ironbound locked chests were stowed near the awning in the rear. "Get those chests brought aboard the *Rosebud*. I do believe it is Egor's treasure hoard."

He looked at his fleet. They had spread out and dropped sails and anchors. Fire arrows arched out from each ship. Already, several corsairs burned and black smoke rose up from the tar-laced caulking.

Enric waited until a detail of dwarfs started moving the chests before saying to Ardnt, "Let's see how Knuben's doin'."

Egor stationed himself halfway between Bermid and the battle line. To his astonishment, he recognized the knight leading the fight. How did that puppy, Knobbins or whatever his name was, survive in the open boat?

A group of thirty pirates ran up to him. He grabbed the shoulder of the one in charge. "Outflank da shield wall and roll it up."

He watched the group move forward and was shocked by how easily the archers devastated them. Only two pirates survived and they moved behind their mates attacking the shield wall.

Egor scowled. If he couldn't outflank them, he'd have to overwhelm one part of the shield wall.

More pirates came up for orders. "Get behind da ones inna middle and push as hard as ya can." The more troops he placed in the middle, the sooner the shield wall would cave in at that spot.

He sent still another batch to the middle and waited to see the results.

A piercing trumpet blast startled him. He turned to see the city gates open and a squadron of armored knights charge out and veer toward the battle line. Behind the knights came scores of militia armed with swords, axes, pitchforks and clubs.

Egor gulped. He didn't want to get caught by an angry mob of Bermid citizens. Another gang of twenty pirates came up to him. "Teach dat rabble how pirates fight." He pointed to the militia, but the look on the faces of his pirates alarmed him. They ignored him and stared at the beach with their mouths opened.

Egor turned his head and cursed. Some of his corsairs burned. Five ships filled the center of the harbor, shooting fire arrows into the crowded beach. His panic gave way to seething anger when he saw the *Rosebud* docked near his flagship. He looked back at the battle. The knights, with their lances and swords, ravaged the rear lines. His pirates would break in a few more heartbeats. After that, the battle would become a rout. His dream of conquering Sulvaria had collapsed. He would never get out of the harbor.

He made a decision. Enric had to pay for this.

# # #

Enric spotted Egor directing traffic and jogged toward him. His breathing came fast and hard. It had been only a matter of time before the two of them met for the last time. He was glad the meeting occurred when Egor didn't have the upper hand. The yuk was excitable and that made him doubly dangerous, but it could also be a fatal flaw.

"Egor!" he yelled. "Over here." Enric waved his ax in the air. "I got your treasure chests. Wanna try to take 'em back?"

Ardnt positioned himself next to Enric.

"This is between Egor and me, old friend. Stand aside, but lend me your shield."

Enric watched the enraged yuk charge across the open ground. Enric planted his legs in anticipation of the colli-sion. Egor didn't slow down when he got close. He swung his massive sword with all his momentum behind the strike. Enric raised his ax and blocked the strike, which could have decapitated him. Egor maneuvered his sword underneath the ax and wedged it between the blade and the haft. He jerked it backward and Enric barely kept his balance. Enric twisted the ax, trying to free it. It remained stuck and Egor jerked it a second time. When the pirate tried a third time, Enric let go of the handle. Egor stumbled backward. Enric rushed forward and struck Egor in the face with the shield. He stepped back a pace and drew a throwing ax. When Egor tried an off-balance swing with his sword, Enric moved forward again and used the small ax to chop through the yuk's sword hand. Hand and sword flew to the side. A look of disbelief came over Egor's face. Enric smashed him again with the shield, after getting a foot behind the yuk's leg.

Egor crashed to the ground on his back.

Enric picked up the battle ax and threatened the pirate. "Yield."

"Never," Egor snarled. "Kill me or shut up."

Enric shrugged, reversed the ax and clobbered the yuk in the top of his head with the blunt end of the weapon. Turning to Ardnt, he handed back the shield. "Have this scum tied up and put on the *Rosebud*. And get someone to stop the bleeding. I want him to make it back to Cintri. He'll be a present to the queen."

Enric walked over to the battle line, now a mass of confusion with no fighting. Most of the pirates were on the run with the knights and the militia in pursuit.

Knuben directed his soldiers in aiding to the wounded. He gave Enric a weary smile. "Took your time, didn't you?"

"Didn't want to mess up your show. Do you have a lot of dead?"

"Fifteen. And another sixty wounded. Ten of those serious."

"I'll have sailors come ashore to help carry the wounded to Bermid." Enric gave orders to Arndt who trotted off to the *Rosebud*. "They'll have doctors in the town. And they'll be a lot more comfortable in Bermid than on a ship."

"Did you destroy all the corsairs?"

"Not quite, but I bet the missing ones go to Egor's stronghold on Ancora."

Knuben stroked his chin. "I think we should stop there on our way back and burn the rest of the fleet and the stronghold. The queen did order us to destroy all of Egor's army and fleet."

PART FIVE

Sheena's excitement at the return of Knuben and Enric made her as giddy as a schoolgirl. The pirates had been destroyed, trade could begin again and customs revenue once more would flow into the treasury.

The throne room was crowded with spectators including her daughters. Knuben and Enric wore their battle gear and looked ferocious. Knuben had a hauberk and an empty scabbard. The dwarf dressed in a padded doublet, a kilt and sea boots. From the looks that passed between the two warriors and the ministers, she was glad the guards had relieved her new heroes of weapons.

She stared at the huge yuk and his leg chains. The bandaged, missing hand did nothing to lessen the sense of danger that emanated from him. His black, beady eyes glowed with hatred. "So this is Egor?" She leaned forward on her throne.

"He's my gift to you, Majesty," Enric said. "I kept him alive so you could decide his fate."

Sheena gave the dwarf a dazzling smile. "Did any pirates survive?"

"About two hundred, Majesty," Knuben replied. "They're now chained in pairs and working in the gold mines."

"Throw this one in a cell until he can be transported to an army camp where he can work on latrine duty for the rest of his life."

She waited until guards removed the pirate admiral. "I'm intrigued by these chests." She pointed to the eight chests in font of her throne.

"They all came from Egor's flagship," Knuben said.

"There wasn't any loot at Ancora?" Sheena wondered why Ragazza wasn't at court. And why did Knuben look so sad on this wonderful day. Those mysteries would have to be explored further.

"None," Knuben replied. "All we found on Ancora was the rest of the corsairs."

"Do you plan to open the chests sometime today?" Sheena almost giggled aloud.

Enric lifted the lid on one of them. "All eight are filled just like this one." Made of stout oak, the chests had a pair of black iron bands to strengthen the wood. The heavy hasps had been gouged out to force open the chests.

All who could see the contents gasped in amazement and whispered to others further back in the crowd.

"Majesty," MacLeod, the treasurer, said, "we must decide how to apportion the loot. I suggest half go to you, a quarter to your council and the remainder to be split however these two decide."

"We worked out a different split." Knuben eyed the treasurer with distrust and anger. "After we fought the battle at Bermid."

"And how did you split it up?" Sheena asked. Today was getting better than ever. She anticipated the council wouldn't like Knuben's answer.

"You get a fourth," Knuben replied. "The officers in the expedition share a fourth and troops, both army and navy, split the other half."

"That's preposterous!" Commodore Bidwell, red in the face, shouted. "The Council will decide the share out. You overstepped your authority."

Sheena looked at Knuben and Enric with a half-smile that seemed to say, "Your move."

Enric moved. He jumped on the table and grabbed Bidwell's club of hair with his left hand. The commodore, twice the size of the dwarf, was too surprised to react as Enric twisted his grip to expose Bidwell's throat. With his right hand, he pulled a dagger from his boot and placed the edge against the commodore's throat. "You did naught to earn a share." He glared at the others. "None of you did. We won the battle despite the four of you."

The audience audibly gasped.

"Enough, Enric. This is a throne room and weapons are not allowed in here." Despite the tone of voice, Sheena seemed pleased with the outburst.

"My apologies, Majesty. I forgot to give the blade to the guards." Enric released the minister and jumped off the table.

"I agree with your split of the loot," Sheena said. "The council deserves nothing. If it were up to them, we'd still be holding meetings to decide what to do. I'm pleased that the bulk of the treasure goes to the ones who fought the pirates."

"Majesty," Dubois, the court advisor, pleaded. "It is unseemly not to award a portion of the loot to the council. Remember, we serve without pay."

"The council's advice is worth exactly what I pay for it." Sheena stood. "This audience is over. I wish to speak to Knuben and Enric in private. Come this way."

The audience cheered and clapped for Knuben and Enric.

Sheena bubbled over with joy. Her two heroes had saved Sulvaria and the public knew it. So did the noble families who also now realized the ministers had done nothing during the crisis. She finally had an opportunity to break their control and she planned to exploit it.

From now on, ruling Sulvaria would be much easier and much more enjoyable. And her successor would have a smoother transition.

# # #

The three princesses watched as Knuben and Enric presented the pirate admiral and the treasure chests to their mother. They could hardly contain their excitement.

"My," Aileen whispered, "being a hero certainly fitth Knuben."

"I wonder where the elf witch is?" Bridget said. "Maybe she and Knuben have split up."

"Look at Mama," Christel said. "She's so excited, she's bubbling over."

"That's because she's now rich," Bridget said. "And the pirate problem has been fixed."

Sheena, followed by Knuben and Enric, left the throne room.

"Quick," Bridget said. "Back to our rooms. We have to talk."

\# \# \#

Ragazza leaned against the main mast and watched the crew celebrate the end of the voyage and their victory over the pirates. They were all about to get rich from their share out of the loot. Three sailors provided the music with a fiddle, a mouth organ and a drum. Others danced, drank yukeste or gambled away their anticipated share of the loot.

She was back to her usual state of loneliness. Knuben was with the queen who would give him a great reward. She doubted if she would ever see him again. It took her quite a while to convince him that they could never stay together. They were too different. She was a sea-creature. She couldn't bear the thought of living on land, even if Knuben was with her. Knuben was a land-creature. He got seasick walking up the plank to the *Rosebud* and he hated the living conditions on ships. He would never agree to spend his life at sea, even if it meant being with her. The best they could ever hope for was a life apart with an occasional, and quite random, visit. Those visits would be years apart. It wasn't nearly good enough. It required too much sacrifice for both of them. There was always the chance, however slim, that she would meet another male someday. Knuben was now free to make a marriage that would enhance his career.

She shivered despite the heat of the day. Ending her affair with Knuben was even harder than leaving her family rather than marry the old male.

Her life was now fixed, at least for the next few years. She would remain aboard the *Rosebud* as the navigator and weather witch. That life had two compensations. One was the crew who was her new family. The other advantage, she lived at sea. She thought the tradeoff was worth it, but she could never be sure if she was correct.

With all her loot, she could buy a ship and be her own captain. She made a face. That would mean leaving the *Rosebud* and the crew. Better to stay here.

She sighed. So be it.

#

Upon leaving the throne room, Knuben wiped his hands on his hauberk and winced as they grated against the metal links. In his peripheral vision, he saw the princesses watching him, but he didn't acknowledge their presence by keeping his eyes straight ahead.

He couldn't keep his hands still as he and the queen entered a chamber adjacent to the throne room while Enric awaited his turn outside.

Sheena sat at a small table and beckoned to Knuben to join her. Because of his armor, he remained standing while wondering how to wipe off his sweaty palms. He placed his hands behind his back so Sheena couldn't see them.

"So, where is Ragazza?" she asked.

Knuben felt his face heat up. "She . . . she wanted to remain on the *Rosebud*."

"Are you two still a couple?"

"No." Knuben shook his head. "We could never live together without destroying each other."

"I don't understand that."

"Well, you see, Majesty, she loves the sea. I get seasick in port and I hate the cramped quarters onboard a ship. So, I can't live at sea and she won't live on land. We still love each other, but we're better off apart."

Sheena tapped a fingernail on the table. "I don't agree. When two people love each other, compromises have to be made by both." When Knuben didn't respond, she continued, "I still have need of your services."

"I'd rather not be at court, Majesty." He didn't think he'd be able to cope with the queen's daughters.

"As it happens, I have a position that will require you to stay away from Cintri most of the time. You will be the army general in charge of Bermid and the western frontier. That frontier is a four day ride from Cintri. I suggest you set up headquarters at a halfway point because you'll have to attend a monthly council meeting."

Knuben had trouble absorbing the news. He tried to speak a few times but nothing came out. He swallowed twice while he grappled with a concern.   "What about . . . Groner? He's the minister of the army, so do I report to him?"

"No. I'm abolishing the post of army minister. Groner will be in charge of the army in Cintri and you will have the rest of the country. You will report to me and will be Groner's equal in the council meetings. Do you accept?"

Knuben had other questions he wanted to ask, but the Queen's dazzling smile made him forget his concerns. He gulped then grinned for the first time that day. "I accept."

"Fine. Let's get Enric in here." She clapped her hands and a servant appeared, startling Knuben who thought he was alone with the queen.

The servant fetched Enric. The dwarf stood alongside his friend.

Sheena said, "I've been casting about on how I could reward you for your great service to me and my country."

"I gotta pile of loot, Majesty. I rewarded myself."

"And you earned that reward. I have need of officers like you and Knuben. I need officers who can think on their feet and who carry out plans with boldness and competency. Knuben has agreed to become a general in my army. I want you to become the admiral of my fleet."

"Me?" The dwarf looked poleaxed. "An admiral? But I'm just a trader."

"Accept my offer and you'll be a lot more than a trader." Sheena smiled at Enric. "You'll have to attend council meetings once a month and you'll have a voice equal to the other ministers. Now, I believe you are married and have dwarflings?"

Enric stared, still too stunned to answer.

"If you accept my offer and bring your family to live in Cintri, I'll find an estate for them to live in. It'll be a gift from me."

Enric pulled a face. After a pause, he said, "I still gotta make one more trip inna *Rosebud*. I got all those gown orders from your anniversary ball and I gotta get 'em sewn up." He scratched his nose. "I can pack up the family and bring them back at the same time." He stood and paced the room. "But," he held up a fist with one finger extended, "but, what am I gonna do with the old *Rosebud*? I won't have time to go tradin' if I'm an admiral."

"Sell the ship to Ragazza," Knuben said. "She'd make a great captain."

"Good idea, laddie. All right, that's taken care of. But what about that tub of lard you call a commodore. I ain't takin' orders from him."

"Commodore Bidwell," Sheena giggled out loud, "will get a new position. He'll be in charge of training recruits and building new ships."

"You're gonna build more ships?" Enric said in surprise.

"No." She guffawed. "And Bidwell will be in charge of not building them."

"You got yourself a new admiral."

# # #

Knubin left the queen's presence in a state of euphoria. He reentered the throne room on his way out of the palace. Deep in thought over his astonishing change in fortune, he ignored Enric who walked at his side.

He was a general! In charge of a large swath of Sulvaria! Sheena had given him, an unknown quantity, a chance to demonstrate his mettle and he repaid her beyond his and her expectations.

Away from the court, he would have time to write papers on his two new weapons; one for sea battles and one for land battles. Combine with the Bermid victory, his school would have to promote him from warrior-tinker to knight-mechanic, the next step on the career path to hero-inventor.

A sudden idea flooded his brain and he stopped walking. His command included Bermid. He'd make his headquarters on the coast across from the island. Between trading voyages, Ragazza could ferry him back and forth between the mainland and the island. They could be together a few weeks a year. He grabbed Enric's arm. "Quick! We have to go to the harbor. I need to talk to Ragazza."

# # #

The three princesses, breathing hard from the effort of running up the stairs, fell into chairs in their sitting room.

"I'll wager that Mama will give Knuben a high position in the government," Bridget said. "Mama can't afford to lose someone as talented as he is."

"Tho, you're thaying Knuben will be around for a while," Aileen said.

"Possibly, he'll be here permanently," Christel added. "How exciting!"

"I mutht get Mama to cough up treathure for a new wardrobe," Aileen said. "I don't want Knuben to thee me in my old ragth."

"We can't go running off without a plan." Bridget pounded the arms of her chair. "Is our deal still on? Whoever first beds Knuben gets to keep him?"

Aileen and Christel nodded agreement.

"One of us will catch him." Bridget chuckled. "It's only a matter of time."

THE MERCHANT OF VENISON

In response to Bassanio's urgent plea, Antonio hurried along the still-dark streets of Dun Hythe to the home of his friend. Since Bassanio rarely awoke before noon, the reason for the early morning meeting must be extraordinary.

He turned off the cobblestone main road and walked the unpaved side streets towards the city walls where Bassanio's house stood by itself. After his experiments had destroyed his last three homes, two by fire and one by explosion, the city leaders demanded that Bassanio live in isolation from nearby houses.

In front of the house, he paused to straighten his brown jerkin and to adjust his rust-colored cloak before he knocked on the front door. Bassanio's pale face and red-rimmed eyes alarmed him. He wore a yellow dressing gown pocked with burn holes and old, fluffy slippers with bunny faces sewed into them. An elf, Bassanio towered over Antonio's dwarfish figure, but he stooped as if suffering from exhaustion. His long, light brown hair, now disheveled, partially concealed his face. Considered the most handsome male in Dun Hythe, he looked far from his best this morning. "Good! You're here," he said. "Come in." His breath reeked of stale wine.

Antonio entered the front room of the house and was greeted by the acrid stink of burnt chemicals. He noticed that more ceiling beams had been charcoaled since his last visit. Bassanio's lab was in the back of the house, but he frequently performed experiments wherever he happened to be.

"Are you all right?" Antonio asked. "You look like a zombie." He tugged his short, brown beard in distress.

"I was up late." Bassanio plowed a hand through his hair. "Working on a plan to ensure my fortune. I need your help."

"Tell me," Antonio said. Bassanio was his best friend and had been ever since they met in the Academy for Agriculture, Business and Science. He majored in business while Bassanio took science.

"It has to do with Portia." Bassanio sat down at a low table, picked up a scalpel and chopped into small bits a brown weedy material known as pipeweed, a mild hallucinogenic. "I need money to get her hand in marriage."

Antonio's heart skipped a beat at the mention of her name. "I thought you two were in love. You need to woo her some more?"

"Portia loves me and has agreed to marry me whenever her father gives permission. I need a loan so I can woo the old geezer. He suspects I'm irresponsible."

"He suspects? The man must be a lack-wit." Antonio smiled. "Everyone in town *knows* you're irresponsible."

"Very funny." Bassanio made a face while he massaged his forehead with one hand and continued cutting the pipeweed with the other.

"You must have drunk a lot of wine last night developing this plan."

"Wine loosens the brain cells and encourages innovative thinking." He scraped a pile of small brown bits into a straight line. "So, can you lend me three thousand silver pennies?"

"What? It'll take me years to sell that much venison. I'll have to take out a loan. Why so much?"

"You know Portia's old man is filthy rich. It'll take lots of money to impress him. I can pay you back right after we marry. That'll be in three months at the longest." He took a thin glass tube out of his pocket and lined it up with the brown bits.

"What are you doing?"

"Smoking pipeweed can ease the effects of a hangover, but that is inefficient. First, you have to find a pipe and then you need to light it and it takes time for the smoke to have an impact. I'm investigating a new approach. One that will accelerate the effects."

Antonio made a face and shook his head. Bassanio never stopped his experiments into new ways to get high or to mitigate the aftereffects of the high. Someday, one of his experiments would kill him. His eyebrows still hadn't completely grown back since one recent experiment ended in spectacular fashion and involved every fireman in the city.

Bassanio put an end of the tube in one nostril, stopped the other nostril with a finger pressed to the outside. He inhaled the chopped pipeweed. He gagged and dropped the tube. His eyes opened wide and his face turned red. After a few unsuccessful tries, he sneezed so violently that he and the chair tumbled backwards and crashed to the floor. After righting the chair, he sat down again, coughing and wiping his running nose.

"I guess," Antonio said, "there's a reason they call it pipeweed and not snortweed."

Bassanio groaned. "Once I marry Portia, I'll hire an assistant to do this part of the experiments." After another coughing and sneezing fit, he said, "So what about the money? I can't get a loan, but I'm sure you can."

"I hate going to a money lender, but I'll have to. Are you sure you can pay me back in three months?"

"Not a problem." Bassanio waved a hand dismissively. "I'll pay you back long before then."

# # #

Antonio walked back to his butcher shop wondering how to persuade a money lender to advance the money. He also worried about the interest rate. The bigger the loan, the higher the interest rate charged. He knew all the money lenders in town, having used a few of them for business loans from time to time. Finally, he decided he would have to approach Shylock. He was the wealthiest lender in Dun Hythe and the only one who could handle a loan this large. He shuddered at the thought of dealing with him. A bastard half-breed known as a dwelf, Shylock was a spiteful figure on the streets of the city. Dwelfs were cursed with all the bad features of elves and dwarfs and blessed with none of the good ones. Shylock was a social outcast and despised. He reciprocated the hatred.

Despite his trepidation at approaching Shylock, he owed a debt of honor to Bassanio. His friend had lent him a large sum of money to start his meat business and now it was time to do the same for him. Of course, that loan had occurred when Bassanio was rich from the inheritance left by his parents -- long since wasted.

Then there was Portia. Antonio had been in love with her ever since Bassanio introduced the two of them. She was elegant, beautiful, intelligent and educated. Of course, as an elf maiden, she was beyond his reach since mixed marriages were illegal. Nevertheless, he'd do anything to make her happy, and if she wanted to marry Bassanio, he, Antonio, would do whatever he could to make it happen, even taking out a risky loan.

He turned his mind back to the loan and the best way to approach Shylock who was as ruthless as a predatory animal. He dreaded the interview. Perhaps, he should have talked Bassanio into a smaller loan.

# # #

Antonio entered the market square in a state of trepidation. Vendors' booths lined the outside and middle of the square. The aromas of cooking chicken and vegetables blended into a low-hanging cloud that sharpened everyone's appetites. Shylock's money-lending station consisted of a small booth in a rear corner. Crowds milled about the square and filled the air with sounds of haggling. He nodded to a few acquaintances, but didn't stop to talk. He approached Shylock's booth and was relieved to see no one near it.

Shylock sat behind a table in the booth. Typical of all dwelfs, he had a wide-shouldered, slim-hipped physique that looked out of balance. He wore a black and blood-red silk doublet, brown breeches and had a small black cap on the top of his bald pate. A fringe of black hair flecked with silver ringed his head while a short, well-trimmed beard framed his face. Shylock's most startling feature was his eyes. They were as dark as the night sky and as devoid of life. He saw Antonio, stood up and grimaced in place of a smile.

"I am Antonio, a merchant," he said.

"I know who you are. You are the merchant of venison. Have you come to apologize for your despicable actions last week?"

"Huh?" Shylock's statement puzzled him. "What did I do?"

"Why, you spat at me."

Antonio didn't like the way the meeting had started. He had to put Shylock in a less hostile mood because angry money lenders charged higher interest rates. "If I spat in your presence," he prevaricated, "I aimed at the ground, not at you. If you mistook my actions, I am sorry for that."

Shylock stroked his beard and stared at Antonio. "I fear I must accept your denial, even thought it is contrary to what my eyes beheld." He sat down. "If not to apologize, then you are here to discuss business." He pointed to a chair in the booth. "Be seated."

"I need a loan," Antonio began after he seated himself on a chair that was much lower than Shylock's.

"Hmmm. How much and for how long?"

"Three thousand silver pennies for three months."

"That is a king's ransom." Shylock raised an eyebrow. "Why would an honest merchant like yourself need such a large sum? Hmmm?" From his higher perch, Shylock locked his eyes on Antonio's.

"It is for personal reasons which I can not disclose."

"Mayhap, you plan to woo a rich lady? May I know her name?"

"My reasons will remain secret." Antonio hadn't expected the money lender to probe for the reason for the loan.

"All right. What collateral do you propose?"

"My butcher shop."

"I know it. I deem its worth at five hundred pennies, leaving twenty-five hundred unsecured. A most dangerous type of loan."

"What interest rate will you charge?" Shylock's eyes never left his face while they talked. It was as if his eyes searched for a lie. Antonio squirmed under their glare. He leaned forward anticipating the answer.

Shylock didn't reply right away. He finally pulled his eyes off Antonio and examined the crowd outside the booth. "You have acquired an excellent reputation among the lenders of Dun Hythe. You have repaid several business loans on time."

"How do you know that?"

"It is my business to know such things. I'd like to have you as my friend. One finds so few upright citizens in this money-grubbing city. Therefore, I propose the following. I will lend you the funds and I will charge no interest to demonstrate my friendship."

Antonio rocked back in his chair, stunned by the offer. Shylock had a reputation as a shrewd and vicious business-dwelf. Surely, his friendship couldn't be that valuable to Shylock.

"In place of the interest," Shylock chuckled, "we can place a humorous penalty in the loan."

"What does that mean?" The offer surprised Antonio; Shylock wasn't known to have a sense of humor. A joke struck Antonio as uncharacteristic.

"Why, just this. If you default on the loan, I collect a pound of your flesh. Isn't that a delicious condition?"

Antonio suddenly recalled how irresponsible his friend was. Of all the things in the world, Bassanio was least concerned about money. He had run through his large inheritance the way a wet dog sheds water. On the other hand, Portia's fortune was immense. Once Bassanio and she married, they could easily repay the loan.

Antonio nodded to the money lender. "All right." He smiled, but his stomach felt queasy.

# # #

Antonio stopped carving a deer haunch when he saw Bassanio and Portia, hand in hand, strolling down the street towards his butcher shop. Despite his new outfit consisting of a white cambric tunic, dark blue wool braies, claret hose and tooled leather boots, Bassanio looked wan and exhausted. Even his hair looked tired. Portia, a tall, willowy elf maiden with azure eyes and red and green striped, shoulder-length hair, looked fetching in a blue silk kirtle. A white lace cap dazzled folks with the reflection from the midday sun. Both drew appreciative looks from the crowds that milled about the streets on this mild spring day.

Antonio wiped the blood from his hands with a rag while he admired Portia. If only Dun Hythe didn't prohibit mixed marriages, he would give his friend some competition for her hand.

"Hail Antonio, my old friend." Bassanio groaned and placed a hand to his forehead.

Antonio noted that whatever expensive scent Bassanio used, it attracted flies. Squadrons of them swarmed around his head. He kissed Portia's hand, lingering as long as he dared.

"I make progress with the old miser," Bassanio continued.

"Hah!" Portia slapped Bassanio's arm, not too gently. "I'm the one making progress. I persuaded my father to finally let you enter the house."

"This past month the man has taken to me like a long-lost son."

Antonio said to Bassanio, "You look like you had a fight with demons."

"It's just my new experiment. I seek to improve wine by removing the water from it."

"Why would you want to do that?" Antonio frowned, trying to think of a reason for Bassanio's project.

"Water dilutes the power of the wine. By removing the water, I strengthen it."

"You can do that?" Antonio asked.

"Of course, he can." Portia looked at Bassanio with an expression that made Antonio's heart ache.

"I have discovered that the alcohol in the wine boils at a lower temperature than the water. I collect the wine's alcohol after it steams away, thus separating the two."

"So you have succeeded."

"Aye. I have separated the two. Alas, the result tastes worse than the dregs in a cheap bottle of ordinary table wine. Mayhap, my process leaves behind the flavor of the wine."

"When will the marriage take place?" Antonio asked.
"Time is not endless. Already, Shylock has meandered past

my shop with a smirk on his ugly mug. Every time he does so I lose my appetite."

"With my new clothes," Bassanio ran a hand over his finery, "her father thinks me a wealthy nobleman. I gifted him with a box of pipeweed cigars and two cases of fine wine, one red and the other white."

"And tonight, we are taking him out to eat in one of the finest inns in Dun Hythe," Portia said. "The Blood and Guts."

"Please hold the marriage soon." Antonio's voice cracked. "The penalty on the loan is severe." Antonio shuddered at a mental image of himself hanging from a butcher's hook while the dwelf carved him up.

"Not to worry." Bassanio waved a hand as the couple ambled up the street.

# # #

Antonio knocked on Bassanio's door and pushed it open without waiting for his friend to respond. Bassanio sat in a chair holding a glass of water against his forehead, his legs splayed out in front of him and his dressing gown loosened. One wall of the front room now held a table with kegs of ale, whiskey and wine. Antonio ignored the kegs and approached Bassanio. "Well? When's the wedding? I haven't heard from you in a week. The loan is due in five days."

Bassanio flapped a hand and winced in pain. "Soon."

"Soon isn't good enough. You aren't the one losing a pound of flesh."

"What nonsense. Shylock will never hold you to the contract. It's too grisly. Even for a dwelf."

"When are you getting married?"

"Portia's old man is a cunning rascal." Bassanio rubbed the glass of water across his brow. "Someone told him about the fires and the explosion I caused. He decided it was too dangerous for his daughter to live in my house. Just when he was on the verge of giving his permission."

"So you're not to marry her?" Antonio grabbed a table to steady himself. "What am I going to do? I'll lose my shop. And quite possibly end up dead."

"Don't fret. I'll marry Portia in the end. I promised her father that I wouldn't perform any experiments while Portia was in the house. That didn't satisfy him. Finally, I promised to build a laboratory in a separate building a distance from our house."

"So you will marry before the loan is due." Antonio exhaled loudly.

"Umm, soon after." Bassanio groaned as he stood up. "When the loan is due, go to Shylock and tell him you need an extension and agree to any monetary penalty he wants. He'll get his three thousand pennies and more within a few days of the due date."

"I'm not going by myself. You're coming with me." Antonio looked at the kegs. "What are they for? Are they the reason you look so bad?"

"Aye. My new experiment causes me anguish."

"What are you trying to accomplish besides your early death?"

"I want to develop an elixir that will combine the potency of all three in a single drink. An instant drunk, in other words."

"Are you mad? Folks go to taverns to socialize. They drink. They sing. They flirt. They gossip. They gamble. They don't want to get oblivious with one drink."

"Bah! They aren't the customers for my elixir. I'm after the males who spend the night at home alone. It'll make their loneliness disappear. Until the morning anyway. And then there is the surgical market."

"What surgical market?"

"Surgery is a painful ordeal performed by butchers. No offense. If the surgeon gives the patient a draft or two of my elixir, the patient will soon be comatose and the surgeon can do his bloody work without worrying about the patient. I have harnessed my vast experience on getting high with my scientific mind. My name will be enshrined with the greatest medical practitioners."

"So you've developed it already?"

"Not quite. I don't have the proper formula. Every combination I've tried tastes like frog piddle and doesn't have a very powerful effect. I need more experiments."

"Make sure you're in decent condition when we meet with Shylock."

# # #

Bassanio showed up at Antonio's shop just after the churches rang the noon bells. Together they pushed through the crowded streets toward the market square and Shylock's booth. Antonio's mind was filled with dire thoughts. If Shylock didn't extend the loan, he could end up maimed or dead.

"Are you listening to me?" Bassanio asked.

"Sorry, what did you say?"

"Portia made me stop my elixir experiments until after the wedding."

"And when is the wedding?" Not that it mattered, Antonio thought. Whenever it occurred, it was too late.

"Tomorrow." Bassanio looked around the street. "Since I didn't do any experimentation last night, the world looks different today. The air is clearer. Flowers look more vivid. Birdsong doesn't pound in my head. Folks look friendlier."

"It must because your mind and body aren't warped by the strange concoctions you drink."

"No doubt, but I can't take too much more of these unfiltered sensations. My senses are being overwhelmed. Especially by the swill and night soil in the streets."

They turned into the market square and Antonio paused to collect himself and to take a deep breath.

"Remember," Bassanio said. "Let me do the talking. I understand dwelfs."

Shylock saw them and smirked. He stood up and awaited them. "Excellent. You arrive on time with my money."

"Actually," Bassanio replied, "Antonio needs a few days extension on the loan."

"An extension, you say!" Shylock dashed his hat on the table. "The contract terms are clear. The loan is to be repaid this instant, not on some morrow."

"Be not difficult. It matters not a whit if you get the money today or a few days into the future. You still get the money."

"The penalty for default is severe. A pound of flesh is what the contract states and that is precisely what I'll get unless you repay me immediately."

Blood rushed to Antonio's head and his peripheral vision narrowed.

"You dwelf dog!" Bassanio roared. "How dare you threaten my friend with your hideous torture."

Shylock snapped his fingers to wake up his servant. "Lancelot. Fetch a constable. These contract breakers will soon get violent."

Lancelot, an old and partially crippled dwelf, lurched his way out of the booth and disappeared into the crowd.

"All right," Bassanio, said in a quieter voice. "We'll give you a bonus for your troubles. All you dwelfs love money more than life. Extend the contract and you'll make more money."

"I want Antonio's pound of flesh, not your money." Shylock stared boldly at Bassanio as if challenging him.

"Why?" cried a trembling Antonio.

"Because it says so in the contract. The terms of the contract must be satisfied. It is the first law of money-lending."

Lancelot returned with a member of the Troll Patrol. The troll wore only tan breeches, chewed on a twig and looked disinterested in the proceedings.

"Officer," Shylock said. "This dwarf borrowed a huge sum from me and the repayment is due today. He doesn't have the money. Arrest him and throw him in jail until the penalty clauses of the contract can be enforced."

"Come along, sir. Ya look like ya got some money. I think us can fix ya up with a nice room instead of a jail cell.

Dey pretty nasty, ya know. And yer gonna wanna have yer meals brought in. Jail grub ain't too good."

"I'll cover his fees," Bassanio said to the troll. "Make sure he gets the best room and the best meals." He turned to Shylock and pleaded, "I'll give you double the amount of the loan."

"Take him away, officer." Shylock stood with arms crossed and a pleased expression on his face.

The troll grabbed Antonio's arm and marched him toward the center of town where the municipal building and the jail stood.

Antonio glanced around. This might be the last time he would ever see the streets and the folks.

# # #

Bassanio and Portia, still in their wedding clothes, visited the depressed Antonio. Bassanio wore the suit he had bought with the loan. Portia looked beautiful in a brocaded satin purple gown with matching shoes. The groom acted subdued while the bride radiated energy and happiness. Portia looked around the room. "How drab." It contained a bed, a table and a chair. A window high in the wall let in a measure of light. "Staying here is a penalty in itself."

Behind the married couple, three servants carried trays of food and drink.

"We stayed awhile with other guests," she said, "then came here to share our happiness with you. Without your help, my father never would have permitted me to wed Bassanio."

"I wish I could say I'm glad, but my imminent demise
has me a bit distracted." On the other hand, he had never
seen Portia happier or more radiant. His only regret about
the loan was that he might not see her again.

"Bosh!" Portia gave Antonio a radiant smile. "I have a
cousin who is skilled at law. He is from out of town, but is
in the area. I contacted him and he will be in court on the
morrow to defend you."

"A cousin?" Bassanio looked puzzled. "Why wasn't he
at the wedding?"

"A business engagement, but he is free tomorrow." She
took Antonio by the hand. "Everything will be all right. Tomorrow, you will be freed from the awful penalty demanded
by that dwelf."

Antonio knew Portia tried to cheer him up, but it didn't
work. He didn't think an unknown cousin would save him.

"I'd defend you myself," she gave him another smile, "if
the city allowed females to be lawyers."

# # #

Antonio sat in the prisoner's chair. He needed a bath and
clean clothes, but, he mused, that was the least of his problems. Much to his surprise, he accepted his fate. Bassanio
had helped him out with a loan and he had reciprocated. Unfortunately, his loan ended badly. Nevertheless, the loan directly resulted in Portia's happiness. He consoled himself
with the knowledge that he was responsible for that. For
him, that was the true meaning of friendship. If he had to die
because of his actions, he'd die picturing Portia in her bridal
gown.

A stir in the rear of the crowded courtroom caught his attention. Shylock and Lancelot entered the room. The servant carried a knife and a scale. Antonio sobbed out loud when Shylock took off his cloak to reveal a butcher's apron worn over his tunic. He smirked at Antonio.

Bassanio, sitting directly behind his friend, reached forward and squeezed his shoulder with a hand.

With an effort, Antonio composed himself and said, "Where's Portia?"

Bassanio shrugged. "She said she'd be here."

Another stir from the crowd. A tall, slender elf male strode down the aisle and stopped in front of him.

"Antonio, I am Balthasar, your attorney. I am Portia's cousin. Don't worry. I'll get you out of this trouble." Balthasar wore the usual black attorney's robes and a shoulder-length white wig. He looked behind Antonio. "You must be Bassanio. I am sorry I missed your wedding." He sat down on the bench alongside Antonio.

Antonio felt a deep sense of gratitude to Portia for getting him an attorney, even if it probably didn't matter. He peeked out of the corner of his eye at Balthasar. The resemblance to Portia was remarkable. They could be brother and sister.

The bailiff called out in a loud voice, "All rise."

The door to the judge's chamber opened and the judge, dressed in a carmine, fur-collared robe, hobbled into the courtroom.

"Judge the Duke will preside at this proceeding," the bailiff shouted.

Judge the Duke, a tall, gaunt, seventy-year-old human, climbed to his bench and sat down with an audible groan. A dusty, ragged peruke sat crookedly on his head. A few be-draggled whiskers tried to come together on his chin to form a beard, but without much success. He was descended from the dukes who once ruled the city, but a revolution had replaced them with elected mayors. The ousted noble families were granted sinecures such as trial judges and allowed to keep their titles.

Judge the Duke found his gavel and banged it vigorously on the desktop. The effort left him panting for breath. After a few gulps of air, he said, "This court is in session. What is the matter before it?"

"I am Shylock the moneylender." He jumped up and faced the judge. "The defendant failed to live up to the terms of the contract for a large loan."

The crowd hissed at the dwelf.

"Stop whispering and speak up." The judge eyed Shylock. "Or are you trying to hide some facts?"

Shylock repeated himself, yelling this time.

"A serious matter." The judge pulled a face. "Contracts are sacred. Everyone knows that."

"I am Balthasar the attorney for the defendant. I will demonstrate that the contract is not valid."

Judge the Duke squinted at Balthasar. "I don't recognize you."

"I am from out of town. While passing through this area, I heard about the trial. I volunteered my services to defend Antonio."

Antonio leaned back and whispered to Bassanio, "Is that Portia in disguise?"

"Don't be ridiculous." Bassanio dismissed the idea with a flap of his hand.

Judge the Duke cocked his head and listened for a moment to the quiet courtroom. "Order!" He seized his gavel and banged it three times. "Order in my court or I'll have you all thrown out." He peered around the room. "That's better." He pointed to Shylock. "Present your case."

Shylock paced to the center of the room and addressed the judge. "This cretin begged me to lend him three thousand silver pennies."

"That's a lot of money," the judge said sympathetically as he counted on his fingers. "That's three hundred gold pennies. A small fortune."

"We agreed to a novel penalty for nonpayment. Antonio has to forfeit a pound of flesh if he didn't repay the loan in the stipulated time."

The crowd stirred in excitement at this unusual development.

"A pound of flesh you say? You dwelfs are whimsical. Abhorrent, but whimsical."

"On the day the loan was due, Antonio and his friend Bassanio came to me and demanded an extension. When I refused, they became angry and insulted me."

The judge lifted his peruke to scratch his bald head while he scowled at Antonio.

Balthasar interrupted. "Isn't it true that Bassanio offered to repay double the loan for a few days extension?"

"Double?" Judge the Duke looked shocked. "What say you?" he asked Shylock.

"Perhaps they did, but only after I called for a constable. They were trying to prevent Antonio's arrest."

"I want to hear a reason for the bizarre penalty," Balthasar said.

"It's my money." Shylock gave Balthasar an angry look. "I can lend it for whatever interest or penalty I chose."

"So why enforce a penalty that very well may kill Antonio?" Balthasar asked.

"I can give no reason other than my hatred and loathing of all dwarfs and elves. Antonio and his kind think they can insult me because I'm a dwelf." He shook his fist at Antonio. "I regret I can't extract a similar penalty from Bassanio. I know Antonio borrowed the money to give to his friend."

The crowd gasped at this revelation.

Judge the Duke hammered his gavel. "There will be a ten minute recess." He painfully stepped down from the bench and out the door.

"Balthasar," Bassanio called in low voice. When the attorney approached him, he continued. "Shylock's servant sitting over there is the one who called on Portia's father just before the old man found out about my experiments."

"So?"

"Don't you see. Shylock found out Antonio gave me the money and he tried to make sure the loan couldn't be repaid in time."

Balthasar pondered the news.

Antonio wiped sweat from his brow. His stomach felt like he had swallowed a rock.

Judge the Duke returned. "Let us continue."

"I move that the trial be ended and that I be allowed to collect my loan penalty," Shylock said.

The judge ignored Shylock and said to the bailiff, "Fetch me a glass of water."

"I have evidence," Balthasar said, "that Shylock deliberately tried to prevent the loan from being repaid on time."

The crowd stirred in anticipation.

"That's preposterous," Shylock replied. "What evidence?"

The bailiff returned with a stemmed glass filled with water. Judge the Duke sniffed the water. "What is the provenance of this . . . water?" he asked the bailiff.

"I procured it from your favorite watering hole."

"An excellent vintage . . . for water." He banged his gavel. "Are we done yet?"

"Does the defense deny the debt is in default?" Shylock asked.

The judge used his gavel again to get Shylock's attention. "You like 'D' words, do you? Listen to this. You dastardly dwelfs are devious and duplicitous." He sipped his water.

"The defense does delay a decisive denial or a definite declaration." Shylock crossed his arms and stared at the judge.

"If I may disrupt this discourse," Balthasar said. "I demand the dismissal of the debt document from the docket." He made a rude gesture at Shylock when the judge wasn't looking.

The crowd applauded Balthasar's declaiming.

"Damn these D-declensions! I will declare my decision on the deposition." Judge the Duke hammered the gavel. "As much as I hate the penalty in this loan, I see no reason not to allow it. We will proceed after another ten minute recess."

"Why another recess?" Shylock asked as he picked up the knife.

"I'm old. I have to pee a lot. Be right back." The judge left the courtroom.

Antonio broke into loud sobs.

Shylock waited until the judge returned then advanced on Antonio with the knife and the scales.

The crowd leaned forward in anticipation of a bloody entertainment.

"I don't see a physician here to bind the wounds," Balthasar said.

"What do I care about Antonio's wounds? I only care about getting my pound of flesh." Shylock asked Antonio, "Do you prefer I take it from your stomach or back?"

Antonio interrupted his sobbing to say, "My back." He rubbed a sleeve over his tearing eyes.

"Remove your jerkin."

The crowd stirred.

"Exercise care, dwelf." Balthasar said. "Your contract stipulates only flesh, so shed no blood."

Shylock started. "How can I take flesh without shedding blood? The contract implies there will be blood shed."

"Judge the Duke. I ask for your help. Instruct Shylock of the penalty for shedding a citizen's blood."

The judge looked like he had been slapped. He chewed on a few strands of his wig. Finally, he said, "It's bad. That's all I'll say about it."

"You jackals! You seek to cheat a poor dwelf of his revenge. I won't have it."

The judge banged his gavel again and smashed his water glass. Shards flew throughout the courtroom. "Now look what you made me do, you treacherous cur!" He pointed the gavel, dripping with liquid, at Shylock. "No blood. Is that clear? If you can't take your flesh without shedding blood, your contract is voided. The case is over." The judge stood up and hobbled out of the court while mumbling, "I need more water."

Shylock threw his scales into the wall and fled the courtroom muttering imprecations.

The crowd booed Shylock for being a sore loser.

Antonio stopped sobbing and held on to the bench to remain standing on his quivering legs. "Thank you," he said to Balthasar. "You saved my life. How can I repay you? Need any venison steaks? How about a quail or two?"

"I also thank you," said Bassanio.

"Do you love your wife very much?" Balthasar asked Bassanio.

"Indeed."

"Would you recognize her even if she was in disguise?"

"Of course I would." Bassanio bobbed his head.

Balthasar lifted the wig from his head. "Hah!" Portia exclaimed. "You didn't recognize me."

"I knew it was you," Bassanio hugged her, "but I didn't want to give it away to Shylock or the judge." He looked at Antonio over her shoulder and rolled his eyes.

"I'll take you up on the offer of venison steaks," she said to Antonio. "Bring them over to the house and I'll cook dinner for the three of us."

THE INTER-RACIAL MUSICAL PLAY-OFFS

Bertha sat at her desk in the Dun Hythe police building on a Friday morning. She frowned while observing the white begonia plant in front of her. If her spell worked properly, the petals would change color in the presence of sorcery. She had concocted the spell to help her detect magical skulduggery, but the plant hadn't been put to a test yet.

"Hey, Bertha." Sergeant Nark from the Troll Patrol stood in the doorway to her office. Wide-shouldered with yellowish skin, he had his stripes tattooed on his biceps. Nark wore the Patrol's dress uniform: dark brown pants made from linen. Stains from the troll's last few meals covered the front of his pants.

He pushed a middle-aged man into the room. The balding stranger looked . . . dusty, as if he had spent the night sleeping in the woods. The man also had quite a few bug bites on his face, hands and scalp. Bertha stood up, noticing the contrast between herself and the stranger: tall versus short, slender versus chubby.

"Dis is dat Andante guy," Nark said.

"Maestro Andante?" Bertha's eyebrows rose while she pushed a strand of brown hair away from her forehead. Andante's name was the center of gossip about tomorrow's Play-offs because of his sudden disappearance.

"Dat's him," Nark said. He turned to Andante and added, "Dis is Officer Bertha. She's de forensic wizard."

"What's that mean?" Andante scratched a bug bite.

"It means, Maestro, that I investigate crimes that employ magic. I assume Nark brought you here because of magical chicanery?"

"Yesterday, as I rehearsed the Dun Hythe Symphonic Marching Band, I became dizzy. Then everything turned black. When my sight cleared I found myself far away . . . on the Trade Road . . . near milestone fifteen . . . with my entire band."

"Oh dear," Bertha said. Andante described the typical symptoms of a transport spell, illegal in Dun Hythe because the transportee frequently landed in the wrong place or the wrong position, causing damages and injuries.

"Not only that, we landed in the middle of a scrum between yuk marauders and a troop of Road Rangers."

"It's a wonder you weren't killed." Bertha's mind raced through a list of spell casters with the power to transport a small group of people. She came up empty.

"I rallied my forces. After we put our instruments on the side of the road for safety, we charged the yuk positions. The cowards soon fled, but the Road Rangers acted as if we had ruined their afternoon's entertainment."

"You charged them?" Bertha's mind was agog; yuks were renowned for their ferocity.

"Of course. Our priceless instruments could be damaged by the riffraff. What else could we do?"

"Weren't you afraid?" Bertha found it inconceivable the mild-looking man possessed such raw courage. Perhaps it was derangement, not courage.

"Madam, musicians understand true terror. It is knowing the next number in the program is a classical piece when the audience is filled with low-lifers. Have you ever been hit in the head with a cucumber? It hurts. Even if it is a rotten one."

Bertha put that aside and asked, "Where were you when this happened?"

"In a warehouse we use for rehearsals."

"Exactly how many were transported?"

"Let me see." Andante counted on his fingers. "Thirty-six."

"Stars above!" Bertha was agog. No wizard had that kind of power. "How did you get back?"

"After we routed the yuks, we walked until we came to a roadside camp where wagons pull up for the night. We slept on the ground and, in the morning, we had to give an impromptu concert before the retarded wagon crews would give us food. Then we walked back to Dun Hythe because the wagons were all full. My musicians are exhausted, sunburned, bug-bitten and sweaty. Ugh!"

"Take me to the rehearsal area so I can look for evidence." Bertha grabbed the flower pot, stuffed it into her shoulder bag with the white petals peeping out. Perhaps she could find a test for her begonia spell at the warehouse.

"Meet ya dere," Nark said. "Wanna check on sumthin'."

# # #

Bertha wandered around the empty warehouse seeking clues about the spell casters. When she had entered the rehearsal room, different petals of the begonia plant turned red, green, yellow and brown. She made a face at the plant. The colors indicated four different styles of magic. Obviously the spell didn't work properly and needed more work. She dropped the flower pot on a table.

Looking up at the ceiling beams, she noticed a subtle design burned into a few of them. She fetched a chair to get a closer look.

Fifteen minutes later, she scribbled notes in her parchment pad while she shook her head in amazement; the flower worked better than she could have imagined!

"Well?" Andante asked. "Have you discovered anything?"

"Four wizards participated in your transportation. Three are elven wizards and the fourth isn't an elf."

"How can you tell all that from looking at the beams?"

"Each wizard casts spells differently and each leaves a distinctive magical signature. Signatures from elven wizards tend to be very neat and precise. There are three separate signatures like that on the beams. The fourth signature is irregular, sloppy even."

Bertha looked around as a few people wandered in to the room.

"We have a rehearsal session," Andante said. "We have much work to do before tomorrow and we're dreadfully behind because of the unscheduled trip."

Nark sauntered in. "Gotta possible motive," he told Bertha. "And suspects."

"You do?"

"Talked to de bookies. Four guys put down bets onna elf band at five-to-one odds."

"And?" Bertha frowned.

"Each bet was fifty silver pennies." Nark chuckled.

"That's a lot of money." It would take her more than four years as a forensic wizard to earn that much. "But, so what?"

"Three of de guys were elves and wore wizards' robes. De last one looked like Cenwig. An hour later, dis guy," Nark pointed to Andante, "gets magicked outta the city."

Bertha's mouth dropped open. Cenwig was the Grand Wizard, the head of the Wizards Guild and a familiar sight in town.

"How dastardly," Andante said. "Attempting to fix a competition by eliminating the favorite."

"You're favored to win the competition?" Unsorted bits of information swamped Bertha's mind. Could Andante be the victim of greedy wizards?

"We're listed at even odds," Andante replied. "After all, I have assembled the best musicians. They come from all over Gundarland to play in my orchestra. Our only real competition is the elves."

"Dese wizards gonna make a lot of money if de elves win," Nark said. "Dey win two-hundred-fifty pennies each. Da silver kind."

Bertha walked away from Nark and Andante while she processed information that didn't add up. Why go to the trouble of transporting Andante if he could return the next day in time for the competition? That bordered on stupidity. He should have been dumped much further away. Or transported today instead of yesterday. She looked at the gathering musicians and pulled a face. There was something about them that hinted at an answer. But what?

A local vendor walked in carrying a tray of sticky pastries, placed it on a table and left. The musicians descended on the sweets and within minutes, the tray was empty.

Bertha snapped her fingers. Andante was dropped fifteen miles away because of a miscalculation. The wizards underestimated the collective weight of the orchestra. Every musician was overweight. Many of them were fat! The wizards should have exerted much more magical power. With the amount of money at stake, they would surely try again, this time with the proper amount of magical power. "Andante!"

"Yes?" The maestro stopped supervising the musicians in tuning their instruments.

"You must leave here immediately. The wizards will strike again. Don't rehearse until I get some magical resources."

"Are you mad? We must and we shall rehearse."

"Give me an hour. I know someone who may help."

"Not a minute more." Andante folded his arms across his chubby chest and glared at her.

"Spread out the musicians in small groups. Far apart"

# # #

Bertha left Nark with Andante and hurried to find her friend Brodwin. The fact that Cenwig was a suspect in a tawdry betting scheme disturbed her. If he was the culprit then he violated a sacred trust; the Wizards Guild dedicated itself to using magic for good purposes. His actions also jeopardized her career aspirations. In three months, she would be eligible to apply for Guild membership as an associate wizard. Membership would give her access to many experienced wizards and a library filled with spell books. It would enable to her to grow professionally. Unfortunately, Cenwig approved each application and he wouldn't approve hers if she threw him in a jail cell.

She found Brodwin sitting outside his tower sunning himself. Tall and lean with blue eyes and a long white beard, he looked ageless.

"Bertha!" Brodwin stood and bent over to kiss her on the cheek. "How nice to see you again. Why are you carrying a flower pot in your bag?"

Bertha's mouth fell open in surprise. The plant had blue petals; it had detected Brodwin's magical aura. The spell real did work. She described her flower pot spell.

"How unusual. You show great skill in your spell development. What brings you here?"

"I need your help. It appears that a group of wizards committed a magical crime."

"What?" Brodwin sat down again and gave her a studied look. "Who?"

"I suspect your Grand Wizard and three elf cronies, but I have no proof."

Brodwin's facial muscles twitched between a smile and a stern look. "Tell me everything." He leaned forward.

Bertha related the events and the results of her investigation. "So," she concluded, "we have an illegal transport spell and an attempt to fix the musical play-offs."

"I know Cenwig has financial problems," Brodwin said when she finished her tale. "He lost a large investment in a company that tried to make artificial compost. If he placed a big bet on the play-offs, then someone lent him the money.

If the elf band wins, he'll pay back the money he borrowed and still clear a lot of coins."

"It's despicable to misuse magic that way." Bertha placed a hand of Brodwin's forearm. "I'm sure they'll try again now that Andante has returned. Will you help me protect Andante?"

"Professional courtesy and Guild rules dictate that I not take on a consulting assignment that interferes with other members' plans --"

"Ohhh!" Bertha stamped her feet. "I expected better from you."

"You didn't let me finish." Brodwin chuckled. "If you request my help as your unpaid assistant rather than as a paid wizardly consultant, I will gladly comply. Besides, I want to get involved if only to embarrass Cenwig. The man is an elitist. He thinks the law is for the small people and doesn't apply to him. So, will you ask me to assist you?"

"Yes." Bertha's chances of joining the Wizards Guild dropped precipitously. So be it. She had a job to do and the job meant protecting Andante. She grabbed Brodwin's hand and pulled him towards the warehouse.

# # #

When they arrived there, Andante and Nark stood outside. The troll leaned against the wall and picked his teeth with a splinter while watching a construction crew work on a new building directly across the street.

"How is one to prepare for the competition with all the noise they're making?" Andante told Bertha. "Make these cretins stop so we can hold our final rehearsal."

"I don't have the authority to make them stop," Bertha replied. "This is Brodwin. He's a wizard and he'll help us protect your orchestra."

Andante nodded to Brodwin. "Our work goes badly. My musicians lack concentration because they're afraid they'll be harassed by another travel spell."

"They're safe with both of us to protect them," Bertha said. "Why don't you rehearse? We'll stay out here and keep watch."

Andante nodded and disappeared through the doorway while calling for his musicians to reassemble.

"To use a travel spell," Bertha said, "the perpetrators need a clear view of the warehouse." She pointed to the roof of the four-story Wizards Guild building several blocks away. "The spell traces I found here indicate the travel spells came from that general direction. Let's go inside and let Nark be our eyes. That way, the wizards won't notice we are here." She and Brodwin stepped inside the door and stood in the shadows.

Andante counted, "One . . . two . . . three." The orchestra launched into a piece and music filled the warehouse.

A few minutes later, Nark called out, "We got people onna roof. Three tall, skinny ones and Cenwig."

"Quick!" Bertha said. "Cast a ward."

Brodwin and Bertha wove their hands through the air as they mumbled spells to attach wards to the front of the warehouse. Seconds later, a loud crack drowned out the orchestra. The building rumbled and shook as if caught in an earthquake. Dust fell from the ceiling beams. The eyes of the musicians showed white and their faces turned pale. Andante stood rooted in place, his baton frozen in his hand.

Bertha's flower fluctuated through red, green, yellow and brown colors with dizzying speed.

"Whoa!" Nark said. "Dat's really strange."

Bertha and Brodwin rushed outside where a fog of rainbow colors hung over the area. Flower beds with black flowers lined the street. Bizarre paintings covered the walls of nearby buildings.

"All de workers disappeared." Nark pointed to the construction site then to the roof. "And de wizards left."

"Ahh," Brodwin said. "Our wards splintered the spell into smaller, uncontrolled spells that rebounded into the street and the work site."

"Those wizards cast a powerful spell," Bertha said. "I've never seen so much magical mayhem."

"It'll take quite a bit of time for them to regain their power," Brodwin said.

Bertha approached the work site. Several pieces of lumber smoldered, giving off a smell like a fireplace. She looked around, saw an empty bucket and told Nark, "Quick! Fill the bucket with water and douse this wood before any spell signatures are burned away." She examined a few planks that didn't smoke.

"But we saw who cast the spells," Brodwin said. "Why bother looking for signatures?"

"Because," Bertha smiled, "I want proof that the same gang cast both sets of spells.

"Ahh," Brodwin said again.

"They'll try again. I know it." Bertha set her hands on her hips and bit her lip. "How can we protect these people after they leave the rehearsal? They'll be scattered all over the city."

"Once they leave here, Cenwig won't be able to track them all down," Brodwin replied. "I think he'll only try to get Andante. I can protect him if he stays in my tower tonight."

\# \# \#

The morning of the Play-off dawned sunny and mild, ideal weather for the competition.

Bertha, Nark and Brodwin escorted Andante to the warehouse where his orchestra assembled for the march to the parade grounds. Today's competition had energized Andante. Yesterday he had acted like a fussy, insecure martinet, but today he radiated confidence and strutted around like the cock in a hen house. In a voice that brooked no nonsense, he ordered the musicians into the street and formed them into their marching array.

Four drummers, three bagpipers, a concertina player, four flutists, three fiddlers, four lutists, seven pipers, three horn players, a washboarder, three kazooists and two harmonica players formed up and stood at attention. The musicians wore gold lamé trousers, white silk shirts, blue cravats and black cutaways topped by black shakos decorated with a dyed golden feather. Their uniforms, designed by Andante, sparkled in the sunlight. Dressed in an identical uniform, Andante carried his baton tucked under an armpit.

At Andante's command, the drummers beat out a march tempo and the musicians stepped out.

"Do you think Cenwig will try anything along the route?" Bertha asked. "By now, some of their magic must have been replenished." She eyed the plant looking for any color changes.

While she looked forward to arresting the criminals and closing the case, she rued the damage to her wizardly career. She had a spent a restless night seeking a third alternative. Without success.

"No," Brodwin replied. "It's too open. My revered Grand Wiz likes to work in the shadows where he can't be seen."

"Dey gotta be gettin' nervous," Nark said. "Dey bet a lotta money."

On Dun Hythe's main street, throngs of locals and visitors lined both sides of the road and cheered the band's arrival.

Bertha and Brodwin stayed close to Andante as parade marshals bullied the competing bands into the marching order. Her eyes scanned the crowds.

"Oh, look." Bertha pointed to the knee-high gnomes in their leaf-green uniforms who led the parade. "They're so cute." Because of their small stature, they rode in a wagon while the rest of the bands walked.

After the gnomes, the gruesome yuk band slouched and scowled at the spectators. Dressed only in tan canvas pants held up by greasy ropes, the green-skinned band consisted of six drummers and a dozen singers. Trolls and yuks were distantly related, but compared to yuks, trolls were considered handsome. Compared to any other race, the trolls were considered ugly. The kilt-wearing dwarfs came next followed by a large elf band in brown breeches and doublets shot throughout with silver thread.

"The roofs," Bertha said. "I think we should keep watch just in case."

"All right. You stay on this side." Brodwin jerked a thumb towards the other side of the street. "I'll cross over and watch from there."

"And Nark can keep an eye on Andante during the parade."

# # #

At the parade grounds, the throngs of spectators cheered or booed each band as it marched onto the field and stopped near the center. Along the length of one side of the field, temporary seating had been erected for paying customers and the seats overflowed. Two other sides of the field were filled with standing, nonpaying spectators while the fourth side, opposite the stands, remained empty and was reserved for the bands. Food stalls lined the areas behind the spectators and the smell of roasting meat and nuts wafted through the air. The cries of the vendors grated on everyone's ears.

A leather-lunged herald, standing in the center of the field, introduced the entrants to the crowds and the announced the order of the performances. Andante's band, representing the host city, would play last. At the conclusion of the announcements, all the bands marched to the sideline except the yuks who would perform first.

Bertha and Brodwin walked the parade grounds. "Now what?" she asked.

"I don't think Cenwig and his friends'll be sitting in the stands," Brodwin said. "It will be too difficult to escape after they pull their mischief."

Bertha and Brodwin wandered through the crowds. She kept glancing at the flower pot as she clenched and un-clenched her fists.   She wished she could unclench her stomach the same way she did her hands. Anxiety and anti-cipation took a toll on her nerves. They finished working one end of the field. "They have to be here someplace." Bertha gnashed her teeth.

The yuk band slouched at attention, while the herald an-nounced that they would play a traditional yuk folk dance. The six drummers started banging away with no discernible rhythm or synchronization while the other musicians grunted. After a few minutes, the performance ended with a flourish of obscene gestures towards the crowds. The audi-ence responded with catcalls. The yuks stalked towards the seats, intending to crack a few heads, but were headed off by the Troll Patrol reinforced by Road Rangers.

Meanwhile, the herald took to the field to announce the score. "The judges have awarded the yuk entry minus one point for performance and plus five points for combative-ness. Their final score is plus four." The yuks ceased their threats to the crowds to exchange grins and hugs. The herald added, "This is the highest score ever recorded by a yuk entrant."

She and Brodwin circled the field without finding Cen-wig or the other wizards. Dreading the confrontation, Bertha gnawed a fingernail. If she arrested Cenwig, she destroyed any chance of joining the Wizards Guild. If she didn't arrest him, could she live with herself? She wanted to find him just to end her anxiety.

The dwarf band, all drummers and bagpipers, marched onto the center of the field, resplendent in multicolored kilts,

doublets and matching, dyed beard braids. As soon as the instruments started squealing, the experienced spectators
pulled out small pieces of cloth to stuff into their ears while
the band played an ancient dwarfish folk tune that no one
knew.

After the dwarfs finished, the herald strode to the center
of the field, made gestures as if pulling something out of his
ears. When the crowd responded by unplugging their ears,
he announced the score: "Minus two for their abysmal
sounds and plus nine for their colorful beard braids. Total
score, plus seven. The dwarf entry is now in first place."

The spectators with bets on the dwarfs cheered.

The yuks made hideous faces at the dwarf musicians.

"Wait." Bertha pointed to the plant now displaying red,
green and yellow petals. "Three of them are close."

"There they are." Brodwin pointed to the backs of three
figures dressed in black robes with cowls drawn over their
heads.

"Nark," she said. "We need some help from the Patrol."

Nark returned after several minutes with three more
trolls.

Brodwin walked over to the wizards and tapped one on
the shoulder. "Good morning, my esteemed colleagues."

The elves turned around. They didn't appear to be overjoyed to see Brodwin.

"Do you know, Bertha, Dun Hythe's talented forensic
wizard?"

"It is quite unlikely we would know a so-called wizard
who has a job." The middle elf sneered at Bertha. The other
two smirked at his jibe.

"Bertha's talents," Brodwin continued unflustered, "include an ability to interpret trace signatures made by spells. Yesterday, she examined the signatures of the illegal travel spell you and Cenwig cast at Andante. She was not surprised to find the signatures identical to a spell you cast earlier in the week."

"We don't cast illegal spells," one elf replied, but without the confidence of the first speaker.

"I have witnesses who saw you three and Cenwig cast a spell from the roof of the Wizards Guild." Bertha crossed her arms and glared at the elves. "And I know you're planning some devilment during the Play-off."

"If Cenwig doesn't win the bet," Brodwin said, "he'll blame you three and we all know how vindictive he is."

"You're all under arrest," Bertha said.

"One doesn't arrest wizards." The center wizard shrugged.

"They think they're privileged," Brodwin said, "and can ignore the laws. Just like Cenwig."

"I assure you," Bertha smiled at the elves, "I can arrest wizards and I will put you on trial for your crimes." She looked to the trolls. "Tie their hands behind their backs. Let's see if they can cast spells without using their hands."

"Who came up with the scheme?" Brodwin asked while the trolls carried out their chore.

After a brief hesitation, the elf on the right said, "It was all Cenwig's idea. He threatened to remove us from our Guild positions if we didn't help him."

"He needed money," said the one on the left.

"Who lent Cenwig the money to place the bet?" Bertha asked.

The question surprised the elves. They glanced at one another then the center one said, "It wasn't a loan. He said it had to be a gift."

"The man really is despicable, isn't he?" Bertha scowled at the elves, as if daring them to contradict her statement.

"Where is Cenwig?" Brodwin said.

"We don't know." The elves shuffled their feet. "He's here someplace."

The herald shouted to get everyone's attention. "The next performance will be by the gnomes who will play a traditional lullaby." He turned to face the middle of the field and exclaimed, "Where'd they go?"

The green clothes and matching caps that the bantam musicians wore blended in perfectly with the grass on the field rendering them almost invisible. The group played small flutes so high-pitched that most of the crowd couldn't hear them, but the dogs of Dun Hythe could. Canines all over the city howled and whined.

When the dogs stopped, the judges conferred and gave the herald the results. "The judges have awarded zero points for the performance since they couldn't hear the music. Six points have been awarded for general cuteness. The total score of the gnomes is plus six. The dwarfs remain in first place."

Bertha walked through the throngs again searching for Cenwig while Brodwin remained with the elf wizards. Unsure about Cenwig's reaction to a confrontation, she decided to take a precaution. She found a Patrol troll leaning against a tree picking his nose. She sent him to the guards at the closest city gates with orders to prevent the Grand Wizard from leaving.

"The elf band will play a medley of tunes depicting scenes from an unspoiled woodland." The herald walked to the sidelines as the elf musicians began their performance. The sounds of lutes and woodwinds filled the area. Soon, the spectators imagined they heard a breeze ruffling leaves. They heard a brook bubbling over rocks and they heard rain falling on a meadow. Before long almost everyone wiped away tears. The band ended with a few bars that reminded all of an approaching thunderstorm. The crowd applauded long and loud.

The herald marched back on the field with the judges' decision. "The elves get plus twenty-five points for their performance and minus three points for making the judges weep. The total score is plus twenty-two giving the elves first place."

The petals assumed a tan color. She continued to walk around and the plant changed to light brown. Finally it became dark brown. Cenwig had to be close. She spotted him hiding behind an old elm tree beyond the crowds. He wore a workman's garb of trews and a tunic, both gray in color and stained with paint blotches. A floppy hat kept his face in shadows. Her heart jumped when she realized his disguise meant he planned to escape by mingling with the throngs of workers. The wizard's attention was focused on Andante as he marched onto the field. Cenwig's face contorted with hatred.

Maestro Andante, head back, chest puffed out, strutted on to the field followed by the Dun Hythe Symphonic Marching Band playing a popular marching tune. His baton made a circle over his head and the band turned their instruments to the right then to the left and finally back to center before stomping their feet and halting.

The crowd ohh-ed and ahh-ed.

"The final contestant will perform," the herald announced, "the Dun Hythe Fight Song originally written for a drum and fife corps by Maestro Andante and transcribed for a full orchestra by the same Maestro Andante."

Andante raised his baton over his head. When it fell, the band broke into the opening bars of the fight song and stepped forward. After a dozen steps, the entire band pivoted to its left flank.

They crowd roared approval.

Bertha circled around and approached Cenwig from behind while the wizard focused on the marching band. She stopped a few feet behind him and cast a ward to protect herself. The ward shimmered with magical energy and felt like a glass coffin. "Cenwig! You are under arrest."

Cenwig's feet almost left the ground as he jumped in surprise. He whirled around and confronted her. He stood half a head shorter than her.

From the maniacal expression on Cenwig's face, Bertha steeled herself for an assault, either physical or magical. "You are charged with casting illegal travel spells and insider betting." She paused a beat. "We've already caught the elf members of your gang."

After every dozen steps, Andante's band pivoted into oblique turns, flanking steps, reverses and half-turns. The crowd screamed in delight.

Cenwig recovered from his shock and cast a spell at Bertha. Her ward shattered his spell, but the force of it knocked her backward and she tripped over a tree root.   Magical elements sprayed the air. Some resembled ill-formed, miniature black lightening bolts. The grass around her had turned orange, and purple roses decorated the lower limbs of the elm tree. Cenwig looked confused by the effects of his spell. Bertha jumped up and grabbed his arm. He shook her off, spun on his heel and sprinted towards the main road. She trailed after him. She knew where he headed.

With a few more maneuvers, Andante stopped his charges in their original position on the field, gave a flourish with his baton and ended the performance. He bowed three times, once towards each group of spectators.

The applause from the crowds was deafening.

The herald fetched the results from the judges and marched to the center of the field close to where Andante stood at attention. "The decision of the judges is as follows. The Dun Hythe contestants are awarded twenty-two musical points--"

The crowd roared disapproval at a score lower than the elf score.

"-- and twenty-five entertainment points giving them a total of forty-seven points. Maestro Andante and his band win the contest."

Bertha caught up with Cenwig at the city gate. When she trotted up, Cenwig threatened to change the guards into toads if they didn't let him through.

"That's enough, Cenwig. Come with me to patrol headquarters."

Cenwig gave her an oily smile. "Perhaps, my dear, we can come to an accommodation. One that lets this unfortunate incident disappear."

"I'm about to add bribery charges to your list of crimes."

"Bribery? That's such a negative word. Are you interested in joining the Wizards Guild? The membership committee takes a dim view on applications from working wizards, but I can fix that problem in a trice. Of course, I have to be free to act before I can fix it."

"Membership in the Wizards Guild? With full membership rights? Not just associate status?" Bertha smiled.

"What?" Cenwig blinked a few times and frowned for a brief second. "I suppose full membership can be arranged." He smiled again. "In fact, I know it can arranged. So, can we put this grubby process behind us and go forward as two intelligent people?"

Bertha's stomach heaved from revulsion. She wanted no part of a Guild where the Grand Wizard was so reprehensible. "Such a gracious offer. What can I say, except you're still under arrest." Bertha turned to the gate guards. "One of you help me escort the prisoner. If he looks like he is about to cast a spell, knock him unconscious." To the other guard, she said, "Unbar the gate and open it."

# # #

Bertha and Andante joined Brodwin in his tower to drink a celebratory toast. Andante was ecstatic over the results of the competition. So were his musicians who split a purse of two thousand silver pennies.

"With Cenwig disgraced and in jail, the Wizards Guild will have to hold an election to replace him." Brodwin beamed. "I've been planning to run for Grand Wizard when Cenwig retired, but he stayed in office forever, it seemed. However, that gave me time to line up the necessary votes, so I'll be the next Grand Wizard." He looked down his long nose at her. "You will apply for membership, won't you?"

Bertha choked up and replied by nodding.

"Good. Our Guild is getting stodgy and a bit complacent. We need new, young wizards. Especially ones with experience in practical magic."

TACTICAL SURPRISE

Fergus MacDwarfen ambled around his castle. Even though the sun had almost reached the midpoint of its daily journey, MacDwarfen still wore a robe and sleeping clothes, much to the chagrin of his batman. His belly length beard remained unbraided.

A carrier pigeon landed on a window sill and cooed. MacDwarfen went to it and untied the scrap of parchment on its leg. He read it, walked to a table with a chess board and moved a black knight. He studied the board, moved a white piece and wrote the move on the reverse side of the parchment. After he fastened the paper to the pigeon, he lifted up the bird and threw it in the air. So, he thought, that's it for today's activities. Ever since his wife died six months ago, he had no reason to get dressed. All he ever did was play chess with the village blacksmith at the bottom of the mountain using pigeons.

Once, not long ago, he would have been dressed and out among his soldiers before dawn. That was when he commanded the army for the Council of Seven Provinces. The Council ruled a large portion of central Gundarland and it passed a law forcing him to retire when he reached the age of seventy. That was the good reason. The real reason the Council got rid of him was to get a replacement who wasn't as outspoken and who was more conventional. The Council refused to believe his argument that conventional minded generals unnecessarily killed large numbers of troops while unconventional tactics saved lives.

"Sir?" His batman, a former sergeant, entered the room carrying a set of formal clothes.

MacDwarfen raised an eyebrow.

"Riders are coming from the village, sir. I think they represent the Council. It is time to get dressed."

"All right, but first I want to see who it is." He led the way to the battlements in the front of the castle. From there, they could see down the steep road to the village. On the road, a squadron of riders labored to climb the mountain. In front of the column, an officer carried an upright lance with the pennant of the Council flapping in the breeze.

"Show them to the main room," MacDwarfen told the batman. "I'll meet them there after I get dressed."

When MacDwarfen entered the room, Colonel Ricci, an elf, stood and saluted. All the visitors wore the Council uniform, black tunics with silver epaulets and trim and black pants. MacDwarfen, wearing a kilt, doublet and boots over knee-high wool socks smiled at his old friend, ignored the salute and punched him lightly in the arm. "How are you and your family, Colonel?"

"We are all fine, sir."

Behind Ricci a gaggle of unknown captains and lieutenants stood at attention. MacDwarfen pegged them all as staffers and disregarded them. "What brings you all the way to Castle MacDwarfen? It isn't exactly on a main road."

"Council business." Ricci gave MacDwarfen a grin that lit up the elf's face. "They want you back."

MacDwarfen had a coughing fit over the unexpected news. Ricci pounded him on the back. "Really?" MacDwarfen finally replied. "Whatever possessed them to do that?"

"It's a rebellion and it's serious."

"Hmm. I've heard rumors of some unrest down south, but I didn't know it was a full-blown rebellion."

"The general who replaced you lost two battles and enormous numbers of soldiers. He's been dismissed and his replacement lost a third battle. Now, the Council wants you to take over."

"Who leads the rebels?" MacDwarfen asked to cover his rising excitement. He had a chance to show the Council how bad a mistake they made when they got rid of him.

"Stilken."

MacDwarfen's mouth dropped open at the news. Stilken was an old family friend. Fighting against friends made the situation doubly tricky. "Is that the entire offer from the Council? Simply take command? I'll accept as long as the Council doesn't try to interfere."

Ricci took out two scrolls from a pouch and handed one of them to MacDwarfen. "I don't think you'll have to worry about that."

MacDwarfen read the scroll. It gave him complete and unfettered command of a new army. He noted the surprising lack of conditions in the document. He held out his hand for the second scroll. Ricci gave it to him. MacDwarfen opened it and gasped. The scroll was blank except for the signatures of all seven councilors.   "They're really serious, aren't they?"

"Desperate is more accurate, sir," Ricci replied. "They are terrified of Stilken."

"I will have to recruit some auxiliary troops and the Council will have to bear the expense."

"Agreed," Ricci said. "When can you leave to take command?"

"Within the hour." MacDwarfen's life suddenly had meaning again.

#

Three weeks later, General MacDwarfen halted his warswine, Begonia, and stood in the stirrups to take advantage of his three-foot height. Using a spy glass, he scanned the distant forest searching for signs of the rebel army. All he saw were the vivid red and gold leaves.

His last report claimed the rebel forces had increased in numbers. Stilken now had many more soldiers than he had. Not that the numbers bothered him. What mattered more than numbers was what you did with what you had. Still, the small number of his troops, many of them conscripts, along with their mediocre quality didn't leave him many options. He had to manage a battle very carefully with this lot. He needed tactical surprise to have a chance of winning. His situation was similar to a chess game in which he gave his opponent a two-piece advantage.

He sat down and adjusted his armor-plated kilt. The colors of his ancient dwarf clan -- red, black and green -- embellished the kilt, his doublet and his three beard braids.

Around him, the army set up camp for the night creating an appalling din: officers bellowed orders; equipment thudded on the ground; weapons clanged; troops cursed.

"I still don't understand why we have a bunch of chimney sweeps," Colonel Dockery, his second-in-command said. The contingent marched passed and dipped their long brushes to salute MacDwarfen.

"One never knows," MacDwarfen returned the salute and grinned at Dockery, "when one'll find a use for them."

Two hundred archers from the Wurst tribe of elves followed the chimney sweeps. Skilled sausage makers, they carried large quantities of empty casings besides their long bows and arrows.

When a loud squeal caught his attention, he stuffed a finger in each ear just as the bagpipers drew near playing some ghastly marching tune. MacDwarfen hated the bagpipe noise, but he took them along because they could cause massive confusion among the enemy forces.

"These noncombatants waste food that the real soldiers could be eating." Dockery had to shout for MacDwarfen to hear him.

"These noncombatants," MacDwarfen chuckled, "will turn the tide of battle for us.

"Your bizarre scheme will never succeed."

"It's creative, not bizarre. And it leads to tactical surprise, the key to victory."

"Dirty fighting is what most generals call it."

"Bah! Generals always claim they lost because the winning general fought dirty, or used magic, or whatever."

Dockery didn't reply leaving MacDwarfen alone with his thoughts. Somehow, he had to end the rebellion without

shaming Stilken because friendship can't survive humili-
ation. That was the difficult problem he pondered.

A hairy-footed half-pint in the camouflaged uniform of a
scout ran towards him. The scout stopped, knuckled his
forehead and stuck a stubby finger up his left nostril. MacD-
warfen waited. When the scout continued to root around, he
said, "Well?"

The scout removed his finger with an audible plop.
"Right. I found General Stilken." The half-pint initiated
mining operations in his right ear.

"Can I expect to hear this report before dark?"

"Oh, aye. Stilken is on the other side of the forest. And
comin' this way. Split the army into two groups. The
second one is marchin' in our direction further west of here."

"Any cavalry?"

"Didn't see anyone on horses except officers." The half-
pint spit to show his opinion of officers.

"Archers?"

"Only a few, but no long bows."

"Dismissed. Thank you for the information." MacD-
warfen had to admit that half-pints made the best scouts and
spies, but their real talent lay in thievery. Unfortunately,
they made terrible warriors and he had five hundred of them
in his army, more than ten percent of the total. The Council
had recruited them to build up the troop count while ignoring
their lack of fighting qualities.

A general had to be crazy to rely upon the half-pints;
their shield wall never lasted more than a few minutes before
disintegrating. Once the fleeing half-pints got into their
stride, they could outrun a wolf pack. Sometimes, they
didn't stop running until they reached the next county. Still,

if a general knew what the half-pints would do in combat, then that should be factored into the battle plan.

"This ground is too flat and too open to offer battle," he said to Dockery. "In the morning, we head south. Perhaps we can pick up some more troops and find a good place to defend." His best chance of success was to secure a strong position and let Stilken's army destroy itself attacking him. Finding the right position always proved to be the hard part.

"My men are tired of marching." Dockery led the swordsmen that made up the bulk of the army, twenty-five hundred troops lacking in battle-experience. Tall, well-built with craggy features, Dockery was a seasoned officer and an excellent warrior, but relied upon traditional tactics. "I think they'll start to desert soon. I say we make a stand here and get it over with."

"Not here." MacDwarfen shook his head. "But soon. We'll have to fight before the winter sets in." Every day seemed colder than the previous and the ground froze on some nights. He wiggled his rump and, out the corner of his eye, saw Dockery gnawing on his mustache.

# # #

For three days, the armies marched and counter marched. Stilken matched MacDwarfen's every move and foiled his attempts to isolate a part of the rebel army. MacD-warfen's troops, footsore, tired and almost out of food, couldn't stay in the field much longer.

MacDwarfen sat on Begonia eating a chunk of cheese for breakfast. Around him, the army broke camp and ate on the march. The terrain puzzled him; something about the hills and streams looked familiar. He stroked his beard-braids and scrutinized the land some more. After a minute, he snapped his fingers. He was on the edge of an area that he had hunted in many times. He recalled a steep, grassy knoll with a large lake behind it, an ideal place for his battle. A nearby village could provide him with a few specialized troops; just what he needed to back up the half-pints.

"We go east," he said to Dockery. "There's a good piece of ground about three miles away. We'll have time to prepare our defenses before Stilken shows up."

MacDwarfen rode ahead with six half-pint scouts and reached the hill before the sun topped the trees. He found it as good as he remembered. Forests anchored the flanks and the enemy shield wall would have to advance uphill.

He rode to the top and scanned the terrain with an experienced eye. He overlaid a mental image of a chessboard on the battleground and positioned his troops on it. Except for the ones that wouldn't be on the board at the start of the battle. Next, he looked at his battle line through Stilken's eyes and modified his mental dispositions.

"Orders, sir?" The half-pint sergeant made a gesture that vaguely resembled a salute.

"Have your men scout the forests. I want to know how thick they are and whether the enemy could send a large force to outflank us."

He grinned as the sergeant ran off. The lake should persuade the half-pints to stick around for a while since few of them could swim. He mused some more about his plan to put the half-pint force on his flank. No enemy general could see them and resist an attempt to smash the half-pints and turn MacDwarfen's flank.

He was still grinning when Dockery joined him.

"I'm going to visit a nearby village to see if I can enlist some warriors."

"Farmers?" Dockery frowned. "They won't do us much good."

"This village doesn't farm. Put the elves to work catching fish and gutting them. I want a lot of guts mellowing in the sun."

Dockery gasped. "But . . . Chivalry demands that we adhere to traditions."

"Tradition is for losers."

# # #

MacDwarfen awoke at dawn and dressed. He faced the day with conflicting emotions; exhilaration at the start of battle and dread at the end of the rebellion. In a few hours, the Council wouldn't need him anymore and it would probably fob him off with a sinecure and hand over the army to another conventional general. Of course, he still had the blank scroll, but he didn't want to use it to keep his command.

Outside his tent, officers hurried the soldiers to form up. The shouted commands, the tramping feet, the squeaking leather, the clank of metal, all fed his enthusiasm to get on with the business of the day. Let the future take care of itself. He reviewed, for the last time, his mental chessboard now filled with living pieces. His job was to keep as many pieces alive as possible.

When he emerged from the tent the sun, barely above the horizon, shown through the almost leafless trees and cast long, thin shadows. A brisk breeze blew in from the lake; ideal conditions for one of his tactical surprises.

Across the field, Stilken's army deployed behind a line of troops to screen against a sudden attack. A few minutes later, a sheaf of battle flags emerged from the woods. Stilken, taller and thinner than most dwarfs, rode a small pony in the midst of the flags. Even from afar it was hard not to notice her regal bearing.

MacDwarfen raised his spyglass. His hand trembled slightly at seeing Stilken again. They hadn't met since the funeral of her husband, the Duke, who was executed for treason. The Duchess wore a silver breast plate and green trews. Her cape displayed the green, yellow and blue of her clan colors. She had pulled her dark hair in a ponytail over her left ear, in the fashion of ancient dwarf warriors. Unlike most female dwarfs, the Duchess was clean-shaven. MacDwarfen recalled the smell of her exotic after-shave lotion and it sent his blood boiling. She looked in his direction for a moment and then stuck out her tongue. What a female! Brains, beauty and wit. Fighting her was such a waste!

MacDwarfen snapped his attention away from Stilken and asked Dockery about the disposition of their troops.

"All the troops are in the positions, as you ordered last night."

"Excellent." He scanned the backs of his troops. In the center stood the main shield wall: twenty-five hundred swordsmen, five deep and packed shoulder-to-shoulder. Opposite them, companies of Yuks formed for an attack. The fearsome, green-skinned Yuks were such a formidable foe that his shield wall would soon need relief. No matter what he did, he couldn't prevent a lot of killing from occurring in the shield walls.

On his left flank, he had four hundred doughty dwarf warriors armed with nose plugs and axes. His Wurst elves hid in the forest beyond the dwarfs. He turned to the right and couldn't keep a smile off his face. From the looks of the half-pints, one would never suspect they were about to enter battle. They lounged around eating sandwiches, playing cards and bartering stolen goods.

His new allies from the village sat on top of the hill directly behind the half-pints. He hoped the half-pints remembered their instructions. Forgetting them would be fatal to the little buggers. Once the allies charged, there would be no way to stop them.

Out of sight on the reverse slope of the knoll, his additional secret weapons awaited orders.

A horn blast signaled Stilken's attack. Enemy troops swarmed towards his positions.

"Uh-oh." Dockery pointed to the right flank. "We have a problem."

MacDwarfen bit his lip. Wolverines, hidden until now, trotted out of a clump of trees in front of the half-pints. Hundreds of them with gnome riders. The half-pint front would crumble immediately against such a charge.

On the left, a thousand dwelf swordsmen advanced towards his lines. Thin elfin faces and bulbous dwarfish noses disclosed their mixed blood.

A glance over the field told him that Stilken wanted a quick victory. All her soldiers swarmed into the battle, leaving only a small force in reserve.

The two armies collided with a cacophony of sound, none of it pleasant. The screaming Yuks pushed uphill against his shield wall of swordsmen who leaned on the Yuks while slashing at their heads and roaring back. On the right, the half-pints screeched and broke before the growling wolverines could reach them. They started to the rear just as an officer released the allies: ten warriors from a village of rock-folk. Three feet in diameter, the silent rock-warriors slowly gathered momentum, increasing the rhythmic thumping of their movement. The half-pints saw the boulders rolling downhill and split into two groups. One ran to safety behind the shield wall and formed up to protect the flank. The second scampered into the forest. The densely packed wolverines dashed through the empty space left by the half-pint retreat and straight into the path of the rock-warriors. Their growls turned to howls of terror.

From his command post, MacDwarfen could feel tremors caused by the charge of the rock-warriors. The wolverine formations broke apart and scattered. His dwarf cavalry, mounted on war swine, charged from the trees and attacked the wolverines. The half-pints, ferocious when they smelled easy loot, charged back into the fray. They jumped on the wolverines' backs and slashed at the cinch straps. Saddles, gnomes and half-pints tumbled to the ground where other half-pints pounced to strip the gnomes of armor and to empty the saddle bags.

Meanwhile, the dwarf ax-men faced the dwelf onslaught. From the trees on the left flank, the elves emerged and hurled sausages at the dwelfs. The casings ripped apart on contact and showered the dwelfs with rotted fish guts. The stricken dwelfs gagged and retched. More sausages flew

through the air and more dwelfs fell to the ground incapacit-
ated by wet or dry heaves.

MacDwarfen judged the shield wall fracas in the center
had gone on long enough. He wet his finger, held in the air
and smiled. The stiff breeze continued to blow in from the
lake. It would protect his own swordsmen from the devasta-
tion he was about to unleash. He turned and pointed to the
captain of the chimney sweeps. "Break the Yuks."

The chimney sweeps marched over the crest of the hill
with brush-tipped ten-foot poles balanced on their right
shoulders and buckets of soot in the left hands. The detach-
ment spread out behind the last rank of swordsmen and
dipped the brushes into the soot buckets. They hoisted the
poles over the heads of the swordsmen until they reached the
Yuk lines then gave the poles a vigorous shake. The Yuks reacted to the soot with coughs and sneezes. Many stopped attacking to rub their eyes. The sweeps withdrew their brushes
and reloaded twice more. After the third soot volley, the Yuk
lines fell apart and Dockery's swordsmen pushed the enemy
down the slope.

MacDwarfen gave an order and stopped the advance at
the base of the hill. The swordsmen retreated to their original position to await another onslaught by the Yuks who re-
grouped under Stilken's tongue lashing and marched back
into battle. MacDwarfen waited until the Yuks got closer.
Again he turned to his hidden forces. "Household dwarfs!
Form a spearhead array and attack!"

The fifty dwarfs arranged themselves into a triangular
formation. With their shields locked into an overlapping,
turtle-like shell, they roared down the hill. Junior officers
moved a number of swordsmen out of the line to make an

opening for the dwarfs. The dwarfs barely slowed down as it carved a gap through the Yuk lines.

A whiff of fish guts brought MacDwarfen's attention back to the sausage makers who continued to throw casings at the dwelf warriors. Many dwelfs writhed on the ground. Still more tried to advance, slipped on the fish guts and fell into the disgusting mass. The ax-men, breathing through their mouths, used the blunt ends of their weapons to knock them unconscious.

On the right, his swine cavalry and the rock-warriors fought the wolverines while the half-pints took an early lunch break.

Time to finish up, MacDwarfen decided, while the bloodshed was still minimal. He sighed at the imminent end of his command and signaled the bagpipers. While they marched into position, he stuffed pieces of cloth into his ears.

The twenty-five pipers squealed a well-known tune always played at victory parades. They strutted behind the line of swordsmen and MacDwarfen noted their astonishing effect on the faces of the foe. Hearing a victory march, each enemy solider believed the battle had been lost in another sector of the field and each of them tried to disengage before he became surrounded. First, the wolverines fled to the woods. Most of the gnome riders were on foot scurrying after their mounts. Any dwelf capable of retreating did so. The yuks simply backed down the hill to disengage from the swordsmen then turned and ran. Stiken's staff officers spurred their mounts and rode away before the bulk of the army blocked their way.

Within the space of five minutes, Stilken sat alone on the battlefield.

MacDwarfen turned to Dockery. "Send a company of soldiers to escort the Duchess to me. Then chase this rabble out of the Seven Provinces."

# # #

MacDwarfen sat on a camp chair and watched Duchess Stilken ride up. To a commanding general, only one situation was worse than watching your army flee a battle; that was watching your army get annihilated. At least Stilken was spared the guilt pangs that always followed a wholesale slaughter of one's troops. It wasn't much, but perhaps the two of them could maintain their long friendship.

Stilken's hair wasn't as carefully arranged as before and a layer of dust covered her cloak and face.

"Sit down," he said after she dismounted. "Would you care for wine?"

She frowned then nodded. "I'm afraid I'm ignorant of the protocol of defeat."

A half-pint servant bought two goblets of wine.

"Many of my peers insist on executing a captured general immediately. Others turn the general over to the government for execution. In any event, losing a battle and getting captured isn't a good career move."

Stilken turned pale under her layer of dust and gulped her wine. "The other generals were so predictable" she said. "I forgot how unconventional you always fought. I guess the easy victories made me overconfident. At least many of my soldiers survived. Unless you plan to pursue them and kill them."

"I gave orders to chase them out of the province, that's all." He shifted his weight in the chair. "To business." MacDwarfen cleared his throat. "My orders were to break your army -- which I have done — and end the rebellion."

"You can kill me, but I won't renounce the rebellion. Not until my husband's confiscated estates are returned to me. I'll die first."

MacDwarfen started. "Is that what the rebellion is about? The Duke's estates?"

Stilken nodded.

MacDwarfen stroked his beard-braids and stared into the distance. "I wrote to the Council advising it not to confiscate the lands. I had a feeling nothing good would come of it."

"You always were one of the more perceptive people I've ever met. The Duke and I considered you a valuable friend."

"Do you play chess?"

Stilken started and blinked at the change in topic. She nodded. "I always beat the Duke when we played."

"So did I. And now, it's time to end the rebellion." He took a gulp of wine.

Stilken's eyes widen and her complexion turned pale.

"No, Duchess," MacDwarfen chuckled. "I'm not going to execute you."

Stilken eyed him warily.

"I'll arrange for the return of your estates if you give me your word to end the rebellion."

"You have that much power?"

"I have a blank scroll from the Council. They'll honor whatever I write on it."

Stilken tapped a purple nail on the arm of the camp chair. "Why am I receiving this charity?"

"Friendship is a precious commodity. I won't squander it needlessly." He grinned at her. "It's not charity. The estates come with conditions."

Stilken stared at him with a look of disdain.

"You and I will hold a chess tournament at my castle. One game a day."

"So, I'm to be your prisoner."

"Never! You'll be an honored guest free to come and go as you choose."

She tapped her finger some more. "How many games in this tournament?"

"Let's say one . . . or two hundred."

"I'll agree to five hundred games. Half in your castle, half in mine."

"Let us not quibble, Duchess. A thousand games. We alternate castles every hundred games."

"Done." Stilken gave MacDwarfen a ravishing smile.

MacDwarfen decided he didn't need to keep his command. He now had something to occupy his time and energy.

AUTHOR'S NOTES:

Ralf and Rolf will return in other stories. I like them too much to ignore them.

Brodwin and Burga will also show up in future stories.

As for Knuben and the princesses, I'm not sure if they're done or not.

You can learn more about my books at my website: http://strangeworldsonline.com

You can follow my antics, rants and occasional snippets of wisdom on my blog: http://hank-quense.com/wp